M
THE DRAYCOTT MURDER MYSTERY

MARY 'MOLLY' THYNNE was born in 1881, a member of the aristocracy, and related, on her mother's side, to the painter James McNeil Whistler. She grew up in Kensington and at a young age met literary figures like Rudyard Kipling and Henry James.

Her first novel, *An Uncertain Glory*, was published in 1914, but she did not turn to crime fiction until *The Draycott Murder Mystery*, the first of six golden age mysteries she wrote and published in as many years, between 1928 and 1933. The last three of these featured Dr. Constantine, chess master and amateur sleuth *par excellence*.

Molly Thynne never married. She enjoyed travelling abroad, but spent most of her life in the village of Bovey Tracey, Devon, where she was finally laid to rest in 1950.

BY MOLLY THYNNE

The Draycott Murder Mystery

The Murder on the Enriqueta

The Case of Sir Adam Braid

The Crime at the 'Noah's Ark': A Christmas Mystery

Death in the Dentist's Chair

He Dies and Makes no Sign

MOLLY THYNNE

THE DRAYCOTT MURDER MYSTERY

With an introduction by
Curtis Evans

DEAN STREET PRESS

INTRODUCTION

ALTHOUGH British Golden Age detective novels are known for their depictions of between-the-wars aristocratic life, few British mystery writers of the era could have claimed (had they been so inclined) aristocratic lineage. There is no doubt, however, about the gilded ancestry of Mary "Molly" Harriet Thynne (1881-1950), author of a half-dozen detective novels published between 1928 and 1933. Through her father Molly Thynne was descended from a panoply of titled ancestors, including Thomas Thynne, 2nd Marquess of Bath; William Bagot, 1st Baron Bagot; George Villiers, 4th Earl of Jersey; and William Bentinck, 2nd Duke of Portland. In 1923, five years before Molly Thynne published her first detective novel, the future crime writer's lovely second cousin (once removed), Lady Mary Thynne, a daughter of the fifth Marquess of Bath and habitué of society pages in both the United Kingdom and the United States, served as one of the bridesmaids at the wedding of the Duke of York and his bride (the future King George VI and Queen Elizabeth). Longleat, the grand ancestral estate of the marquesses of Bath, remains under the ownership of the Thynne family today, although the estate has long been open to the public, complete with its famed safari park, which likely was the inspiration for the setting of *A Pride of Heroes* (1969) (in the US, *The Old English Peep-Show*), an acclaimed, whimsical detective novel by the late British author Peter Dickinson.

Molly Thynne's matrilineal descent is of note as well, for through her mother, Anne "Annie" Harriet Haden, she possessed blood ties to the English etcher Sir Francis Seymour Haden (1818-1910), her maternal grandfather, and the American artist James McNeill Whistler (1834-1903), a great-uncle, who is still renowned today for his enduringly evocative *Arrangement in Grey and Black no. 1* (aka "Whistler's Mother"). As a child Annie Haden, fourteen years younger than her brilliant Uncle James, was the subject of some of the artist's earliest etchings. Whistler's relationship with the Hadens later ruptured when his brother-in-law Seymour Haden became critical of what he deemed the younger artist's dissolute lifestyle. (Among other things Whistler had taken an artists' model as his mistress.) The conflict between the two men culminated in

Whistler knocking Haden through a plate glass window during an altercation in Paris, after which the two men never spoke to one another again.

Molly Thynne grew up in privileged circumstances in Kensington, London, where her father, Charles Edward Thynne, a grandson of the second Marquess of Bath, held the position of Assistant Solicitor to His Majesty's Customs. According to the 1901 English census the needs of the Thynne family of four--consisting of Molly, her parents and her younger brother, Roger--were attended to by a staff of five domestics: a cook, parlourmaid, housemaid, under-housemaid and lady's maid. As an adolescent Molly spent much of her time visiting her Grandfather Haden's workroom, where she met a menagerie of artistic and literary lions, including authors Rudyard Kipling and Henry James.

Molly Thynne--the current Marquess has dropped the "e" from the surname to emphasize that it is pronounced "thin"--exhibited literary leanings of her own, publishing journal articles in her twenties and a novel, *The Uncertain Glory* (1914), when she was 33. *Glory*, described in one notice as concerning the "vicissitudes and love affairs of a young artist" in London and Munich, clearly must have drawn on Molly's family background, though one reviewer reassured potentially censorious middle-class readers that the author had "not over-accentuated Bohemian atmosphere" and in fact had "very cleverly diverted" sympathy away from "the brilliant-hued coquette who holds the stage at the commencement" of the novel toward "the plain-featured girl of noble character."

Despite good reviews for *The Uncertain Glory*, Molly Thynne appears not to have published another novel until she commenced her brief crime fiction career fourteen years later in 1928. Then for a short time she followed in the footsteps of such earlier heralded British women crime writers as Agatha Christie, Dorothy L. Sayers, Margaret Cole, Annie Haynes (also reprinted by Dean Street Press), Anthony Gilbert and A. Fielding. Between 1928 and 1933 there appeared from Thynne's hand six detective novels: *The Red Dwarf* (1928: in the US, *The Draycott Murder Mystery*), *The Murder on the "Enriqueta"* (1929: in the US, *The Strangler*), *The Case of Sir Adam Braid* (1930), *The Crime at the "Noah's Ark"* (1931), *Murder in the Dentist's Chair* (1932: in the US, *Murder in the Dentist Chair*) and *He Dies and Makes No Sign* (1933).

Three of Thynne's half-dozen mystery novels were published in the United States as well as in the United Kingdom, but none of them were reprinted in paperback in either country and the books rapidly fell out of public memory after Thynne ceased writing detective fiction in 1933, despite the fact that a 1930 notice speculated that "[Molly Thynne] is perhaps the best woman-writer of detective stories we know." The highly discerning author and crime fiction reviewer Charles Williams, a friend of C.S. Lewis and J.R.R. Tolkien and editor of Oxford University Press, also held Thynne in high regard, opining that Dr. Constantine, the "chess-playing amateur detective" in the author's *Murder in the Dentist's Chair*, "deserves to be known with the Frenches and the Fortunes" (this a reference to the series detectives of two of the then most highly-esteemed British mystery writers, Freeman Wills Crofts and H.C. Bailey). For its part the magazine *Punch* drolly cast its praise for Thynne's *The Murder on the "Enriqueta"* in poetic form.

> *The Murder on the "Enriqueta"* is a recent thriller by
>   Miss Molly Thynne,
> A book I don't advise you, if you're busy, to begin.
> It opens very nicely with a strangling on a liner
> Of a shady sort of passenger, an out-bound
>   Argentiner.
> And, unless I'm much mistaken, you will find
>   yourself unwilling
> To lay aside a yarn so crammed with situations
>   thrilling.
> (To say nothing of a villain with a gruesome taste
>   in killing.)

There are seven more lines, but readers will get the amusing gist of the piece from the quoted excerpt. More prosaic yet no less praiseful was a review of *Enriqueta* in *The Outlook*, an American journal, which promised "excitement for the reader in this very well written detective story ... with an unusual twist to the plot which adds to the thrills."

Despite such praise, the independently wealthy Molly Thynne in 1933 published her last known detective novel (the third of three consecutive novels concerning the cases of Dr. Constantine) and appears thereupon to have retired from authorship. Having proudly dubbed herself a "spinster" in print as early as 1905, when she was but 24, Thynne never married. When not traveling in Europe (she seems to have particularly enjoyed Rome, where her brother for two decades after the First World War served as Secretary of His Majesty's Legation to the Holy See), Thynne resided at Crewys House, located in the small Devon town of Bovey Tracey, the so-called "Gateway to the Moor." She passed away in 1950 at the age of 68 and was laid to rest after services at Bovey Tracey's Catholic Church of the Holy Spirit. Now, over sixty-five years later, Molly Thynne's literary legacy happily can be enjoyed by a new generation of vintage mystery fans.

Curtis Evans

CHAPTER I

THE WIND SWEPT down the crooked main street of the little village of Keys with a shriek that made those fortunate inhabitants who had nothing to tempt them from their warm firesides draw their chairs closer and speculate as to the number of trees that would be found blown down on the morrow.

All through the month of March it had rained, almost without ceasing, and now, in the fourth week, the north of England had been visited by an icy gale which had already lasted two days and showed no signs of abating. The lanes, that for weeks had been knee-deep in mud, had dried with almost miraculous swiftness and the more frugal of the cottagers had gleaned a fine store of wood from the branches with which they were strewn. To-night they were thankful to sit indoors and enjoy the fruits of their industry.

The gale swept on its devastating way across the open meadow-land that surrounded Keys, increasing every moment in violence and causing the timbers of the small farmhouse which stood at the end of a blind lane about a mile from the village to creak and groan under its terrific onslaught.

The front door of the house stood open and, with each gust of wind, it swung with a heavy thud against the inside wall of the dark passage, but no one came to close it and there was no light at any of the windows of the apparently deserted house.

Once the gale dropped for a moment and the monotonous barking of a dog in a distant farmhouse could be heard; beyond this there was no sound but the renewed, long-drawn howl of the wind, the protesting creak of the trees as the heavy branches were swept across each other, and the dull thud of the swinging door.

The sun had set and it was already dark when the first sound of footsteps was heard in the lane. The walker approached quickly, with an odd, shuffling tread that became almost noiseless as he neared the house. Arrived at the gate which led into the little front garden, he paused for a moment, then, without opening it, slid away like a shadow in the direction of the barn that stood on the other side of the farmyard. Whatever his business may have been there he made no sound, and for nearly an hour after he had passed the farmhouse stood silent and deserted and the open door continued to swing monotonously on its hinges.

Then a second shadow loomed out of the darkness of the lane. This time there was the click of the latch as the newcomer opened the gate and went quickly up the path to the front door. Here he paused with a sharp exclamation of surprise, then passed on into the hallway beyond. There was the scratch and flare of a match, followed by a steadier glow as he lit an oil-lamp that stood by the door. Carrying the lamp, he went first to the front door and examined the latch to see that it was undamaged before closing it. Then he passed on into the little kitchen at the back of the house, placed the lamp on the table, and was about to put a light to the fire when he discovered that his matches had run out. He had used the last one to light the lamp.

With an exclamation of annoyance he picked up the lamp once more and made his way to the sitting-room, one of the two rooms that lay right and left of the front door. He moved quickly, his mind intent on the food and warmth he needed badly, for he had walked a long way in the bitter wind and was feeling both hungry and tired. Dazzled by the glare of the lamp in his eyes, he was already well inside the door of the sitting-room when he saw the thing that pulled him up with a jerk as sharp as though some one had laid a detaining hand on his shoulder.

He stood arrested, holding the lamp at such an angle that it smoked violently. But the black fumes drifted past his nose unheeded.

For the room which he had thought untenanted save for himself held yet another occupant.

Seated at the writing-table facing the door, her arms outflung across it and her head pillowed on the open blotter between them, was a woman.

From where he stood he could see only the top of her head, a tangle of fair curls that gleamed yellow as spun gold in the lamp-light, and the rich fur collar of the coat in which she was wrapped. He could see her hands, too, and the sparkle of her rings. There was something about those hands, with their strangely crisped fingers, as though they had been arrested in the very act of closing, that somehow gave the lie to the woman's attitude of sleep.

But it was not her hands or the beauty of her hair that held the eyes of the man at the door. They were glued to the open blotter and the stain which had spread across it, a stain which had already stiffened the fair curls that lay so still upon the once white paper into hard little rings and which was even now fading from its first bright scarlet into a dull rust.

He stood motionless, oblivious of the acrid odour of the smoking lamp, then, with an effort, pulled himself together and crossed the room. Placing the light on the mantelpiece, he bent over the woman and laid his hand gently on hers; but he knew, even before he touched her, that she was beyond all human aid. Raising the thick fair hair at the side of her head he revealed a wound in the temple from which the blood had already ceased to flow.

As he straightened himself after his brief examination, his eyes went instinctively to the window; but he was not quick enough.

Had he been a second earlier he would have seen the white face of a man, pressed against the glass outside, taking in every detail of the room and its grim occupant. As he was in the very act of raising his head the watcher ducked below the sill of the window and when, a few minutes later, he ran out of the front door, after a hurried search through the house, there was no one either in the barn or any of the outhouses.

The unseen watcher at the window had vanished like a shadow into the darkness of the night.

CHAPTER II

POLICE CONSTABLE George Gunnet bent down with a grunt of satisfaction and slowly unlaced his second boot. He was not a quick mover at the best of times and the pleasant kitchen, with its glowing fire and appetizing aroma of toasted cheese, was conducive to drowsiness. He had just come in from his last round and, to one fresh from the wild night outside, the kitchen was a haven of peace and comfort. His tunic hung over the back of a chair and he sat, very much at ease, in his shirt-sleeves, waiting for Mrs. Gunnet to finish her bustling preparations for the supper he felt he had more than earned.

"Nobody been, I suppose?" he asked, according to custom, as he filled his pipe.

"Who should have been?" his wife countered tartly. Mrs. Gunnet had once, some twenty years ago, been in service in Glasgow and, as she often said, never could get used to a dead-alive little place like Keys. "Nothing ever happens here, as I'm aware of." Gunnet stretched his legs luxuriously towards the warm glow of the fire.

"There's quite enough happening for me, if it's all the same to you," he said comfortably. "There's a big elm down in Fanning's meadow and there'll be more before morning if this goes on. All I could do to stand up against the wind at the Four Corners and it fair blew me home. Oye, shut the door, can't you?" He made a grab at the newspaper as, in the path of the wind, it leaped from the table and scudded across the room into a corner. It was followed by a half-empty packet of tobacco which was too late to save.

"Here, will you shut that door!" he shouted, his head half under the table. Then, emerging and catching sight of the visitor: "Beg your pardon, Mr. Leslie; I didn't see as it was you. What with that outer door opening straight onto this room like, the wind comes in something cruel."

But Mrs. Gunnet's sharp eyes had already detected something unusual in the caller's bearing.

"There's nothing wrong, is there, sir?" she broke in. "Was you coming after George?"

The newcomer nodded. He was panting with the haste in which he had come and his face had a queer, grey look underneath the natural tan of an open-air man. When he spoke it was in a hard, dry voice, carefully devoid of all emotion, as if he were afraid that, at any moment, it might get beyond his control.

"I say, Gunnet, I want you up at the farm. Something's happened."

He stopped, apparently not wishing to go further before Mrs. Gunnet, who was gazing at him, her round eyes wide with curiosity.

Gunnet got slowly to his feet.

"Anything wrong, Mr. Leslie?" he asked. "It's a wild night, for certain, but if I'm really needed ..."

Leslie gave a high-pitched laugh that ended in a crow. It was evident that he was keeping himself in hand with difficulty.

"Needed, man!" He pulled himself up once more. "I'm sorry, Gunnet, but I'm afraid I shall have to haul you away from your supper. I won't keep him longer than I can help, Mrs. Gunnet," he went on as his eye fell on the meal she had been just about to dish up.

Gunnet heaved himself reluctantly into his tunic and buttoned it, his eyes on the troubled face of his visitor.

"Look here, sir," he said weightily. "I'd better know what it's all about. You can talk in front of the missus, here. She knows when to keep a still tongue in her head."

Leslie gripped the back of the chair behind which he was standing. His throat seemed to have grown suddenly dry.

"There's a woman up at the farm, in my sitting-room," he said, his voice unnaturally quiet. "And she's dead."

Gunnet stared at him for a moment in silence, then, with an assumption of officialdom that contrasted almost comically with his usual bluff good-humour, pulled out his notebook.

"A woman? Who is she?"

"I don't know. Never seen her before, to my knowledge. I found her when I got back this evening."

Gunnet unhooked his great-coat and got slowly into it.

"Better keep the rest till we get there. And don't you get talking, Mother," he added gruffly as he went out.

"There ain't nobody to talk to except the cat," retorted Mrs. Gunnet, "and she don't answer."

She had no cause, however, to complain of the village of Keys that night. Even in Glasgow she had never spent an evening more replete with variety. Gunnet's return, and almost immediate departure, an hour later, was followed by the arrival of the Sergeant and a Constable from Whitbury, the market-town to which Gunnet had telephoned. To Mrs. Gunnet was left the important task of directing them to John Leslie's farm and she would have given a great deal to have gone with them.

Gunnet opened the door to them when they arrived at the farm. John Leslie was standing just behind him and did not miss the sharp, appraising glance bestowed on himself by the Sergeant as he came in.

"Have you got the doctor?" was his first question.

"Couldn't get him, sir," Gunnet answered. "He was out when I telephoned, but I left word for him to come up the instant he returned to inspect the deceased."

Overshadowed as his spirits were by the whole unpleasant affair, Leslie could not resist an internal chuckle at this new aspect of Gunnet. The easy-going, rather garrulous villager had already draped himself in the majesty of the Law and was expressing himself accordingly.

Gunnet led the way into the sitting-room. Leslie had placed the lamp on the mantelpiece before making his hasty expedition to the police station and it still burned there, lighting up the writing-table with its tragic burden.

The Sergeant bent down and felt the cold cheek of the woman who lay across it. Then he lifted her eyelid and looked under the soft, bobbed hair that fell round her face.

"Dead, all right," he said. "She's just as you found her?"

Leslie stepped forward into the ring of light.

"I didn't touch her, except to feel her face, just as you did. I knew then that she was dead."

He could hear the scratching of the Constable's pencil as he made his notes.

"You're sure she was dead then?"

"I don't think there was the faintest doubt. If I'd had the smallest suspicion she was alive I should have tried to do something for her, but I was so sure she was dead that I went straight for Gunnet. The blood on the blotter was almost dry then."

"What time was this, Mr. Leslie?"

"Just about eight. The clock in the kitchen struck while I was in here."

The Sergeant, a tall, lean man with a shrewd, typical North-country face, scratched his chin thoughtfully.

"You live here alone, I think?" he asked.

Leslie nodded.

"Mrs. Grey, the carter's wife, does for me. She comes in the morning and leaves about two."

"So that when you are out the house is deserted?"

"Absolutely, unless Grey is about in the yard. He was up at the station fetching some stuff this evening and didn't get back till about nine. Gunnet was here then."

"Could any one get in easily?"

"Quite. There is nothing here to steal. It's only occasionally, when there's money in the house, that I lock the front door."

The Sergeant was about to speak again when Leslie interrupted him.

"I've just remembered. I forgot it till just now. The door was wide open when I came in. I've never found it like that before."

"It was unlocked when you went out?"

"Yes, but it was latched. I always shut it. It's a good latch, too."

"Were you about the premises at all this afternoon, Mr. Leslie?"

So far, except for the Constable and his busy pencil in the background, the interrogation had been more or less friendly and informal. Now there was an official ring in the Sergeant's voice that made Leslie look carefully to his answer.

"I went out about four this afternoon and did not get back till just before eight."

"You weren't near enough at any time during the evening to have heard a shot? This is a shooting case, you know."

Leslie shook his head.

"I went for a long tramp across country. Unless it was done just after four or just before eight I couldn't have heard anything."

"An unusual time at which to take a walk, Mr. Leslie."

The Sergeant's voice was noncommittal, but Leslie felt himself flush.

"I was too busy to go before and I needed exercise," he said shortly.

"You can account for your time, I suppose? I must ask you to think carefully ..."

Leslie broke in on him. His nerves had already been badly jarred by the events of the evening and the man's manner was beginning to annoy him.

"Good Heavens, man, you're not going to tell me that anything I may say may be used against me? You're welcome to what I can tell you, but it isn't much. I never saw this lady before in my life till

I came in at eight and found her in my room. How she got here I've no idea. You surely don't think I've murdered her!"

But the Sergeant refused to be drawn.

"All the same, we should like to know where you were during the evening and whether you spoke to any one who could identify you during that time."

"Who was I likely to speak to? I tell you I went on a long, cross-country tramp. I don't suppose I met a soul, certainly not any one who could identify me."

"Four hours is a long time. You were walking all the time?"

"Yes."

Leslie spoke curtly. He was tired and the whole thing was beginning to get on his nerves.

"Then, if that's all you can tell me, Mr. Leslie, I'll take a look round here. If you'll step into another room ..."

Leslie opened his mouth as though about to say something, and then, apparently, thought better of it.

"You'll find me in the kitchen if you want me," he volunteered as he went out. "There's some coffee on the stove for any one who would like it."

The Sergeant looked after him thoughtfully, then strolled to the door.

"I should be obliged if you wouldn't leave the house just at present," he called after him.

Leslie suddenly lost his temper.

"My good fellow, I'm not going to run away!" he exploded.

Once in the little kitchen he sank into a chair by the stove and ran his fingers through his hair. He was abominably tired, too tired to think properly, but it was beginning to strike him that he was in a tighter place than he had realized. He had been a fool to lose his temper like that. After all, the chap couldn't be blamed for feeling a bit suspicious.

With a long sigh, he dropped his head into his hands and tried to view the situation calmly. But the thoughts went chasing round in a futile circle in his tired brain, and at last, in despair, he gave it up and straightened himself. If only the police would hurry up and get through with the job!

He reached for the coffee-pot and poured himself out a big cup of black coffee.

"Damn!" he said with heartfelt emphasis. "Oh, damn!"

Meanwhile the Sergeant was pursuing his investigations. With the help of Gunnet and the man he had brought with him he raised the body from the table and laid it on the floor. As the head fell back against his shoulder Gunnet gave vent to an exclamation.

"It's her from Miss Allen's! Her sister, I think she is. I see her in the village this morning!"

"Miss Allen of Greycross?"

"That's right. Been here a matter of five years now. I heard tell somewhere that she was expecting her sister, and this lady come yesterday. A Mrs. Something, I think she is. The wife'd know. She's a rare one for picking up news, she is."

The Sergeant was examining the wound that was hidden under the thick, fair hair.

"It's a bullet-wound, all right, and fired at fairly close range. Any sign of a weapon anywhere?"

But there was no trace of the weapon by which the unfortunate woman had met her death. The little room seemed unnaturally tidy and normal for the scene of so grim a tragedy; an ordinary man's room, giving no sign of any struggle; the only feminine note in it being the still figure on the ground and a brocade bag which, with the ominous, suggestive stain on the blotter, supplied the only touch of colour on the dark wood of the writing-table. The Sergeant opened the bag. A small powder-puff, a cigarette-case and holder, a stick of lip-salve, a tiny gold purse with a few shillings in it, and a lace handkerchief, were all it contained. The handkerchief bore an embroidered monogram in the corner. "R. D." or "D. R." were the letters, but, as Gunnet was unable to remember the name of Miss Allen's guest, this was of little use for purposes of identification.

The contents of the bag were costly and the woman's clothes in keeping with them. She was expensively dressed in a long fur coat which fell open as they moved her and revealed a fawn-coloured georgette dress, heavily trimmed with sequins, underneath. As well as the rings on her fingers she wore a long chain of rhinestones and a gold watch-bracelet set with diamonds. Fine silk stockings and brown glace beaded shoes with very high heels covered her feet. To the soles of the shoes dried earth was clinging and a dead leaf was adhering to one of the heels.

"Doesn't look much like robbery," remarked Gunnet.

"She came here of her own accord, too, I should say. There is no sign of any struggle. Her clothes are as tidy as when she left home." The Sergeant stood looking down at the calm face upturned to his. "She was a beauty, poor thing, and no mistake," he added gently. "It must have been sudden, the end. She never knew what was coming to her. Look at her face."

It was true. Except for the smear of dried blood down one side of the cheek, and its ghastly pallor, there was nothing to suggest that she was not quietly sleeping. The still lips even held a faint smile and it was evident that death had come swiftly and mercifully.

"It looks as if the murderer must have been some one known to her, some one she would have no cause to fear," went on the Sergeant. "Either that or she thought she was alone in the house and he came on her unawares from behind. That young chap in there," he continued, indicating the direction of the passage with a jerk of his head. "He knows Miss Allen, doesn't he? I seem to remember him and her at the Point to Point together."

"Very good friends, they are," assented Gunnet. "But this lady only came yesterday, I'm thinking, and I don't remember ever to have seen her here before. Likely he doesn't know her."

He stood stolidly by the table while the Sergeant proceeded with his examination of the room; once, only, he volunteered a statement.

"He seemed proper upset when he came down to the station," he remarked thoughtfully.

The Sergeant looked round sharply.

"In what way, upset?"

Gunnet's ruddy face took on an even deeper hue in his efforts to express himself clearly.

"Startled like, as any one would be that had found a thing like this in his room. More excited than guilty, if you understand me. By the time we got back here he was acting quite natural. Lit the fire and made coffee and all while we was waiting for you. I shouldn't say he acted suspicious."

If the Sergeant held any opinion on the subject, he kept it to himself. He finished his examination of the room and moved to the door.

"Nothing here," he said. "Give me your lantern and I'll have a look outside. You stay and keep an eye on things here. Come on, Collins."

He went out, followed by the man he had brought from Whitbury, a young Constable, fresh to his job and awed into silence by the magnitude of his first case.

Meanwhile John Leslie sat huddled over the stove in the kitchen, half asleep. It seemed to him as if this pleasant country life to which he had retired so thankfully after four hideous years of warfare had suddenly merged itself into a nightmare which would never end. His one longing was for bed and sleep and yet even that seemed out of the question so long as the farm housed that tragic figure. Meanwhile there seemed nothing for it but to hang about until all this sordid official procedure was over.

He was roused by the entry of Collins.

"Sergeant Brace says would you come outside for a minute, sir," he announced.

Leslie rose wearily to his feet and followed the man. Brace stood just outside the door leading into the garden.

"We've found footsteps in the bed under the sitting-room window. Looks as if some one had stood there looking into the room. Perhaps you'd have a look at them."

He led the way to the flower-bed and turned the lantern on it. The footprints were distinctly to be seen in the soft earth. They were large and curiously undefined in outline.

"That's not a clear-cut mark like you or I would make," commented the Sergeant. "I should say they were done by some one in an uncommonly old pair of boots. There's more upper than sole to those! What sort of boots does your man wear?"

"The usual heavy labourer's boot with nails in it. Good solid sole. I'm not an adept at this sort of thing, but, if what you say is true, he did not make those marks. Neither did I, for the matter of that."

He held out his own foot for inspection.

For the first time Brace permitted himself to smile.

"I never suspected you of boots like the ones that made those prints, Mr. Leslie. But I wanted to make sure that they were not the carter's. There's been no rain for three days and those marks may have been there some time, provided the bed hasn't been raked over lately."

"As for that, I raked it over myself yesterday morning; but that doesn't tell you much, I suppose, as they might have been made any time afterwards."

In spite of his fatigue and distaste for the whole business, Leslie was beginning to grow interested.

Brace flashed his lantern on the brick path that led across the front of the house.

"Nothing there, unfortunately, but there's something I'd like to show you over here."

Leslie followed him to the barn. Here the footsteps were distinctly discernible on the earthen floor, but less clearly defined and, in some cases, blurred in a manner that suggested that the walker had crossed his own tracks. But they led quite obviously to the foot of the ladder up to the loft.

Brace went on ahead up the ladder.

"Here's something you might be able to help us with," he said as they reached the top.

He pointed to the straw in the corner.

"That's been slept on lately, and look at this."

He indicated a couple of dirty rags that looked as though they might have been used as bandages, except that they were bare of any stain.

"Probably some tramp. I've had them in here more than once in cold weather," said Leslie.

"It's a tramp, right enough. Those are the rags they mostly bind their feet up with instead of socks. They stick to them, too, as a rule. Looks as if this chap must have been disturbed and left in a hurry. It's probably his footsteps under the window. You don't recall turning a tramp out of the barn any time lately?"

Leslie shook his head.

"I don't think I ever have turned one off. I sometimes find their traces in the morning, but, even if I knew one of them was here, I should probably wink at it and let him stay. The fowls are all securely locked up and the tramps round here are a harmless lot, as a rule, so long as they don't smoke in the straw and fire the old place. It wouldn't be much loss if they did. It's not even weather-tight."

"You haven't seen one hanging round the last day or so?"

"No. They don't hang round much in the daytime, anyhow, because of the dog. They slip in at night after he's chained up."

"He's a sound sleeper, that dog!" commented Brace. "We've made noise enough and he hasn't stirred."

"He's not here. I had intended to go to London tonight, so I took him down to the Greys this morning."

"And then didn't go, after all?"

"I shouldn't be here now if I had," said Leslie wearily. "I had a wire saying I wasn't wanted, after all."

"What was the appointment, if I may ask?"

Leslie was tickled, in spite of himself. His irritation was beginning to wear off, no doubt due to the coffee which had begun to allay his fatigue.

"The appointment was at the Law Courts," he said dryly. "Not in the dock, however. Just a perfectly respectable witness for the prosecution. Case of a stolen car, to be exact. Unfortunately for me, I happened to be talking to the owner when we saw the chap actually making off with the car."

"Case of identifying the thief," remarked Brace with professional interest.

"That's the idea. Wish to goodness I'd gone now, then I should have been out of all this, but the case was postponed. You'd have accepted that alibi all right, Sergeant?"

"I'd accept any alibi you like to offer if it was authentic, Mr. Leslie," answered Brace soberly.

That the whole business was awkward Leslie had been slowly realizing ever since his first interview with the Sergeant, but there was that in Brace's voice now that, for the first time, gave him a feeling of real apprehension.

"I'd give you one like a shot if I could," he answered quickly.

Brace moved the lantern so that the light fell full on Leslie's face.

"Have you seen Miss Allen lately?" he asked suddenly.

Leslie, dazzled by the glare of the lantern and bewildered by the inconsequence of the question, hesitated.

"Miss Allen? I saw her in the village yesterday—no, the day before. Why?"

"Did she say anything about expecting a visitor?"

Leslie blinked and turned his face away from the blinding light.

"She said she was expecting her sister, a Mrs. Something-or-other. She mentioned the name, but I've forgotten it."

"You wouldn't recognize the lady if you saw her?"

"I shouldn't think so, unless she's some one I've met in some other part of the world. I've never seen her here, if that's what you mean."

"Doesn't often stay with her sister, eh?"

"I don't think so. Miss Allen didn't say much about her, but, from what she did say, I gathered that they were not very intimate. She mentioned that she'd proposed herself and seemed rather surprised at it."

He saw no reason to repeat Miss Allen's actual words. That elderly and very downright spinster had spoken with her usual incisive frankness. "What Tina's up to, I don't know and I don't want to know. Some mischief, I'll be bound, and possibly crooked mischief at that. I don't trust her. She's got some good reason for wanting to spend a week with her old sister. I told her she could stay as long as she liked, provided she didn't try to ride my horses. She's got a seat like a sack of potatoes; and as for her hands! Luckily scented cigarettes and a chair by the fire are more in her line."

The wind had dropped and, for the first time for three days, a fine rain was falling. As they left the barn they heard the sound of a car making its way up the lane.

"That'll be the doctor, I expect," said Brace, obviously relieved. "After that we shall be able to get away to our beds."

The doctor met them at the door. After a few words of explanation on both sides he hurried into the sitting-room and knelt down beside the body, drawing off his thick driving-gloves as he did so. His hands were cold and he seemed to have some difficulty in freeing them from the stiff leather. As he pulled at the gloves his quick eyes scanned the body, taking in all the details of its appearance. Leslie, who was standing immediately opposite to him, was struck with the keen alertness of his glance and revised his opinion of him then and there. Gregg had always struck him as rather a stupid person and he made a mental note of the fact that, until you have seen a man at his job, it is wiser not to pass judgment on him.

Gregg parted the hair over the side of the head as Brace had done.

"Good Lord! Shot!" he ejaculated.

Leslie noticed that the hands with which he unfastened the woman's dress to make a further examination were not quite steady, and again decided that he had never done the man justice. He was evidently genuinely moved at the sight of the pitiful figure before him.

"Can you arrive at any conclusion as to how long she's been dead?" asked Brace when he had finished his examination.

"Difficult to say with such a cursory examination, but, roughly, four or five hours would cover it."

"Not longer?"

"I don't think so. I shouldn't like to say within an hour or so. Not more than six hours, certainly."

"Would death be instantaneous?"

"Almost certainly. Shot in the temple. Who killed her?"

He swung round, still on his knees, and looked up at the Sergeant.

Brace answered with another question as sharp as his own.

"You don't admit the possibility of suicide?"

"Quite possible. For a left-handed woman. The wound's on the wrong side."

"On the wrong side for a right-handed person," commented Brace. "But we've no reason to think that she was right-handed."

Gregg rose to his feet and dusted the knees of his trousers.

"Probably was. Most women are," he said slowly.

He bent down and examined the hands carefully.

"She wrote with her right hand, anyway," he said. "Look at this."

There were faint stains, evidently of ink, on the first and second fingers of the right hand.

"One to you, Doctor," conceded Brace good-humouredly. "Apart from that, it was a good shot of yours. There's no weapon."

"Who found her?"

"Mr. Leslie here. Whoever did it seems to have got away."

Brace looked sharply at Leslie.

"A nasty jar, eh? Feel all right?"

"Quite, thanks. But it's a beastly business and I wish it had happened anywhere else."

"Ever seen the lady, Doctor?" asked Brace.

Gregg scrutinized the delicate features of the unfortunate woman.

"No friend of mine," he said curtly. "Any idea who she is?"

"Gunnet here has recognized her as a lady staying with Miss Allen, of Greycross. Thinks she's her sister."

Leslie's exclamation of horrified astonishment was drowned by Gregg.

"Good God!" he shouted. "Not Miss Allen's sister!"

"I'm afraid so, from what Gunnet says. However, we shall know soon enough."

Gregg seemed aghast at the discovery.

"Miss Allen's sister!" he repeated. "It's impossible! Why, they're as different as chalk from cheese."

"There's a difference in age, too. But Gunnet saw her in the village this morning."

Gregg picked up his coat.

"Well, it's a queer world," he said reflectively. "You'll want me, I suppose, for the inquest. Are you moving her?"

The Sergeant nodded.

"Gunnet's gone down to fetch a van from the village and we'll get her over to Whitbury to-night. I'm going on from here to see Miss Allen. It's not a job I'm hankering after, to tell you the truth."

"Want me to come along?" asked Gregg. "I might be needed, but I doubt it. She's a strong-minded woman, Miss Allen, and I shouldn't say hysterics were much in her line."

"I'd be grateful if you would, all the same. It's not a pleasant thing to have to tell a lady."

Gregg nodded.

"Righto," he said. "It's all in the day's work."

They went back to the kitchen and sat by the fire, talking desultorily while they waited for Gunnet and the van. Leslie produced drinks and did his best to join naturally in the conversation, but he was ill at ease. He found himself wondering what was passing in Gregg's mind. Was he, too, curious as to what part Leslie had played in this tragic drama? Leslie tried to visualize the whole thing from the point of view of a casual observer, and failed. Already he was too deeply entangled in this gruesome business to see it in its right proportions.

He was thankful when Gunnet arrived with the van and a stretcher to bear away the corpse. Brace and the doctor left five minutes later in Gregg's little two-seater. It seemed to Leslie that there was an unusual warmth in Gregg's voice as he bid him good night. He had never liked the doctor, but he felt grateful to him now, for his hearty handshake came hot on the heels of Brace's last words as he climbed into the car.

"I must ask you to hold yourself at the disposal of the police until further notice, Mr. Leslie."

CHAPTER III

"HOW LONG IS IT since you have seen Cynthia, Mr. Fayre?"

Lady Staveley's fine eyes were alight with amusement as she turned them on her guest. He had just alluded to Lady Cynthia Bell as "a demure little thing" and was now discussing his tea-cake with the serenity of one quite unaware that he has been guilty of an in-credible misstatement.

Allen Fayre, better known to his friends as "Hatter," a nickname he had somehow managed to collect in his unregenerate Oxford days, paused for reflection.

"Quite twelve years, I should think. She was a leggy little thing of about eight when I last set eyes on her."

Lady Staveley gave a soft gurgle of amusement.

"She's leggy still! All these modern girls are, you know, but I'm afraid you'll find that the demureness has evaporated. She's decid-edly what the children's old nurse used to call 'a cure' now."

Hatter Fayre caught the mirth in her voice and responded to it. When he smiled it was easy to see how he had come by the network of fine wrinkles at the corners of his keen grey eyes and why the old Oxford nickname had persisted through all the long years of his ex-ile in India, for a nickname, unless it is an unkind one, rarely sticks to a man who is not beloved of his friends.

"I do seem to be a bit of a back number!" he admitted ruefully. "Girls occasionally were demure, you know, in my day."

"I'm fond of Cynthia," went on his hostess thoughtfully. "But she sometimes makes me rejoice that my peck of troubles are all sons."

Fayre turned to his other neighbour.

"What do you say, Sybil? You know Lady Cynthia, don't you?"

Lady Kean, who had been listening to the discussion in silence, shot a languid glance of derision at her hostess.

"Eve's a cat," she said. "She's only trying to assert her independence. Cynthia can twist her round her little finger. She twists us all, I think, except perhaps Edward. He's untwistable."

Sir Edward Kean, catching the sound of his name, strolled towards them.

"What about Edward?" he asked, smiling down on his wife from his great height. "Something flattering, I hope."

To Fayre, deeply interested in these old friends from whom he had been separated for so long, there was nothing he had come across since his return to England more surprising or touching than Kean's attitude towards his wife. Fayre and Sybil Kean had known each other since their nursery days; had played together as children in the country and had foregathered again later in London. Kean had come into both their lives later, at a time when he was a struggling young barrister and Fayre was cramming for the Indian Civil. When Sybil Lane, as she was then, fell madly in love with her first husband, a handsome guardsman, married and was carried off by him to Malta, Fayre had a suspicion that Kean was badly hit. Certainly he had remained single and had developed a capacity for work which, according to his friends, was almost demoniacal. To Fayre, far away in India, had come, first the news of the death of Sybil's husband, killed in the first year of the War, and second the report of her marriage to Kean five years later, and now he was back in England for good, picking up old threads once more and keenly interested to see how time had dealt with the friends of his youth. For a week, now, they had been at Staveley together, and what he had seen there had both saddened and touched him.

To the outside observer it would seem that Kean had at last achieved the two great ambitions of his life. He had married the woman of his choice and a knighthood had already set the seal on his fame as the most brilliant counsel of his day. But to Fayre, who had known Sybil Kean too well in the past to be deceived by appearances, his absolute devotion to his invalid wife seemed little short of tragic in its intensity. For Sybil Kean was of the kind that does not forget. Her husband's death had come near to killing her; for weeks she lay hovering between life and death, only to emerge with her health shattered and an empty life before her. When, at last, Kean's insistence was rewarded and he persuaded her to marry him, she gave him all she had to give, a sympathy and understanding such as has fallen to the lot of few men and a rare loyalty. But her health had grown steadily worse and Fayre, on first seeing her after the lapse of years, had been appalled at the change in her.

He had often wondered, during the long hours on shipboard, how these two would run in double harness and, curiously enough, his fears had been all for Sybil. For even in his youth Kean had been hard, as hard perhaps on himself as on others, in the pursuit of his aims, a man who did not make allowances and expected none. His judgments were ruthless and pitilessly exact and he had carved his way, with neither influence nor money to help him, by sheer strength of personality and an amazing brilliance both of mind and speech. When addressing a jury he used sentiment with a skill that is only shown by those whose perceptions are never blurred by emotion and he was a cruel cross-examiner. Kean, the lawyer, had been no surprise to Fayre, who had watched him in the first stages of his career, but Kean, the husband, had come as a revelation. To Fayre, the tenderness and consideration he showed towards his wife was almost incredible, until he remembered that, even in his youth, Kean had always been a man of one idea. Then he had sacrificed everything, sleep, diversion, even food, to his work, his whole being concentrated on achieving success in the career he had chosen, and now an influence even stronger than ambition had come into his life and he had given himself up to it with that complete absorption that was so characteristic of him. And the pity of it was that all his devoted care, backed by the luxury with which he was now able to surround her, did not serve to strengthen Sybil Kean's frail hold on life.

Fayre's kindly heart was troubled as he watched these two: Sybil Kean, incredibly slender and still beautiful, in spite of her forty years, lying half buried in the cushions of a huge armchair, and Kean standing over her, his height accentuated by his habit of standing with his hands in his pockets and his shoulders hunched, dark and saturnine, his face alight with amusement at something his wife had just said.

"When do you get back, Edward?" asked Lady Staveley.

"Thursday, at latest, if you can really put up with me for a little longer. I'll try to get through to you to-morrow; I shall know better then."

"Meanwhile I shall have Sybil to myself for a couple of days. On the whole, I think I'm glad you're going, Edward!"

Kean laughed.

"Make her behave herself, and if that minx, Cynthia, arrives in the middle of the night, as she no doubt will, keep her out of Sybil's room, will you? They haven't met for at least a month and she'll want to tell her the story of her life."

"You must admit that it's a good story," murmured Lady Kean from the depths of the big chair.

"It will keep," said her husband dryly, "till breakfast to-morrow morning. I must go now, if I'm to catch the five-forty."

"What time do you get in?" asked his wife as he bent over her.

"Six-twenty to-morrow morning. A barbarous time."

"Make them give you a good breakfast before you go on to Chambers."

"You'll be all right?" Fayre heard him murmur.

"Of course. Run now, or you'll miss it. I wish it wasn't such a vile day. Listen to the wind!"

"Excellent weather for traveling. Good-by."

He was gone, and soon afterwards Lady Kean disappeared with her hostess and Fayre was taken off by Lord Staveley to the billiard-room.

After dinner that night he gravitated as usual to Sybil Kean's side. For a long time they discussed old friends and Fayre gradually became well posted in all that had happened during his absence.

"Tell me about Cynthia," he said at last. "What *is* she like now. You've all been rather mysterious about her, you know."

Sybil Kean glanced at him. There was the same spark of amusement in her eyes that he had surprised in Lady Staveley's.

"I wonder how you'll like her," she said thoughtfully. "I believe you *are* rather old-fashioned, Hatter. She's a very perfect specimen of the modern girl, plus extreme good looks and a charm that's quite her own. She manages her elders perfectly, when she takes the trouble; when she doesn't, she just goes her own way and entirely ignores us."

"She sounds a minx," remarked Fayre dryly.

"Oh, no, she isn't! Besides, there are no minxes nowadays, my dear. She's very affectionate, very loyal, and with an excellent head on her shoulders. When I say she ignores us, I simply mean that she considers her own judgment quite as good as ours and goes by it. I'm not at all sure she isn't right."

"Which means that she'll ride for a fall one of these days and get it and then her elders will have to pick her up and see to the damage."

Lady Kean's eyes were very thoughtful.

"I wonder. The new generation is better able to look after itself than any of us are willing to admit. If she does come a toss, which is more than possible, I'm inclined to think she will pick herself up and say nothing about it. She's got more grit than I ever had, Hatter."

"Nonsense!" Fayre began explosively; but she interrupted him.

"It's true," she went on, her voice half whimsical, half sad. "I never stood up to life and it broke me. If I had, I should not be the useless creature I am today. Cynthia will fight like a little tiger and come out at the end, scarred perhaps, but probably a wiser and better woman than she was before. There's something gallant about her. ..."

Her voice trailed off and he knew she was thinking of the past.

"Useless creature is grossly inaccurate," he said gruffly. "No one who has seen you with Edward could call you that."

She turned on him eagerly.

"Do you think he's happy?" she asked with an insistence that surprised him. "He gives so much and I seem to have so little to offer in return."

"You are everything to him," he answered with conviction. "I have never seen a man so changed. I believe he's younger now at heart than he was when I first knew him."

"His capacity for work is still inhuman. If he hadn't got nerves like steel he would have broken down long ago. I feel frightened about him sometimes. He's so incapable of half-measures. Sometimes I think these very strong people are really the weakest. Their hold on things is so tremendous that when they lose them ..."

She made a little gesture with her hand, a hand so frail that Fayre turned his eyes away from it quickly. His protest was as much for his own reassurance as for hers.

"I don't think Edward's of the kind to lose anything once he's got it," he asserted with a cheeriness he tried to feel. "He's a very lucky man, Sybil."

He was more moved than he cared to show, and for a time he sat smoking in silence. When he spoke, it was to lead the conversation back to its original subject.

"I'm intrigued about our friend the minx," he said. "What's she up to that she should arrive at country houses in the middle of the night?"

Lady Kean laughed.

"That's an exaggeration of Edward's. She's motoring over and dining with a Miss Allen on the way. She'll probably be here before twelve. As to what she's up to, I've got my own suspicions."

Fayre settled himself comfortably in his chair.

"This is gossip," he said fervently. "Tell me some more."

"It isn't gossip; on the contrary, it's solid fact. Cynthia is at present engaged in bringing down her mother's grey hairs with sorrow to the grave. The result is that she's having rather a thin time at home just now."

"It's a long time since I've had the pleasure of seeing Cynthia's mother," remarked Fayre thoughtfully. "But I seem to remember that I never liked her."

"She set her heart on a good match for Cynthia and of course the inevitable happened. The wretched child has engaged herself to a boy with nothing to recommend him but a fine war record and an inadequate pension. Her mother is beside herself and, in a way, I don't blame her. Cynthia might have married anybody."

"Instead of which she's marrying a nobody. And you like him."

"How on earth did you know that?" said Lady Kean, startled. "You're quite right, I do. John Leslie's a nice boy and he knows how to manage Cynthia. There's plenty of money on her side of the family and he's working hard, farming on a small scale, and, I believe, manages to make it pay. The last I heard of the affair, he had been forbidden the house."

"In spite of which, the engagement continues?"

"Of course! And I happen to know that Cynthia's people went up to London this afternoon. John Leslie's farm is halfway between Callston and Miss Allen's. All of which accounts largely for Cynthia's decision not to arrive here till late this evening. I don't know anything; this is pure conjecture."

"It seems sound reasoning. Who is this Miss Allen?"

"Mrs. Draycott's sister."

"Oh!" remarked Fayre, taking another cigarette and lighting it thoughtfully.

Lady Kean regarded him with approval.

"That was nice of you," she said. "I don't like her, either. The sister's quite different, though. She went on to stay with her yesterday. I expect Cynthia's meeting Mrs. Draycott to-night and if *she* doesn't like her she'll say so!"

Fayre meditated, enjoying his cigarette.

"No, I don't like her," he said at last. "We get women like that in India."

"We get them in England too."

Lady Kean's voice sounded suddenly flat and lifeless and Fayre, realizing suddenly how late it was, decided that she was tired and that he had better leave her to herself for a time. In any case, he had no desire to discuss Mrs. Draycott. She had been his fellow-guest at Staveley for the past week and he had been glad to see her go.

He had just risen to his feet when the door opened and Lady Cynthia came in.

She stood in the doorway, straight and slim, sheathed in vivid blue, her dark shingled hair clinging in tight waves about her beautiful little head and, at the sight of her, Fayre realized the truth of Lady Kean's description. There *was* something "gallant" about this quaint mixture of youth and self-reliance, and it appealed to him at once. That she was popular, there could be no doubt. A chorus of welcome greeted her entrance, and Lady Staveley swept to meet her and draw her up to the lire.

"Cynthia, dear, you must be frozen. Your hands are like ice. Is it bitter outside?"

The girl nodded.

"Pretty bad. The wind's dropped, though."

To Fayre, observing her with frank curiosity, her voice sounded tense and there was a glitter in her eyes and a flush just beneath them that troubled him. Was the "modern" girl, he wondered, usually as exotic as this? If so, heaven help her! He watched her as she bent over Lady Kean and was struck by the real affection and solicitude she showed in her manner.

"You look tired, child," said her hostess. "Was it very dull at Miss Allen's?"

"It wasn't dull," answered Lady Cynthia slowly. "Anything but."

She stood by the fire warming her hands in silence; then, abruptly, as if she had come to a sudden decision, she drew herself up and faced the room.

"You'll hear it to-morrow, so I may as well tell you now," she cried with a ring of defiance in her voice. "Mrs. Draycott was killed this afternoon. She was found shot in John's sitting-room at the farm."

CHAPTER IV

Sir Edward Kean's separation from his wife was to prove shorter than he had anticipated. On the local train which dawdled its lazy way to Whitbury he dozed fitfully, only to have the fumes of sleep drastically swept from his brain by the biting wind that met him as he stepped onto the platform at the Junction. The journey from Staveley was always a tedious one, with its change from the slow train to the London express at Whitbury and the long wait at Carlisle where the dining-car was picked up. This, however, was the only long stop and after a passable dinner Sir Edward was able to settle down to a long evening's work, being one of those fortunate people who can concentrate their minds as easily in a crowded train as in the seclusion of their studies.

He alighted at Euston probably having slept less than any of his fellow travellers and looking infinitely less jaded. Also he had got through all the work he had intended to do on the journey and was ready for a strenuous morning at his Chambers. His wife had been right in saying that only a man with an iron constitution could have stood the pressure under which he lived.

He drove straight to his house in Westminster, where breakfast was awaiting him and then, after a bath and change of clothes, took a taxi to his Chambers.

"Farrer, ring up Mr. Carter and tell him I should like to see him before he goes into Court," he called to his head clerk as he hurried to his room.

"You know the case is postponed, Sir Edward?" ventured the old man nervously. He had not expected Kean until late in the evening and was uncomfortably aware now that he should have wired instead of writing about the postponement of the case.

Sir Edward stopped dead, his hand on the latch of the door.

"What's that?" he said sharply. "Strickland v. Davies postponed?"

"Yes, Sir Edward. We understood that you were leaving the North this morning and that a letter would reach you if it was posted yesterday afternoon. Had we known …"

His voice trailed off into silence. In all the years he had worked for Kean he had never seen him look so angry.

"Knowing you were coming up, in any case, for the other consultation," he began again.

"My instructions were that I was to be notified immediately." Kean's voice was icy.

"I wrote, Sir Edward."

"And gave me a night's journey for nothing! Always telegraph if there is any doubt as to my movements. You knew I was coming up to-day."

"Yes, Sir Edward."

"In the future I should be grateful if you would obey my instructions. I suppose the witnesses have been notified?"

"Bentley's will have seen to that, Sir Edward."

Kean closed the painful interview abruptly by vanishing into his room.

"All because he's missed twelve hours up in the North," muttered Farrer, as he hurried thankfully out of range. "He never used to be so set on holidays. His heart's more with her Ladyship than his work, nowadays."

Sir Edward, having said his say, did not refer to the matter again, but he proved a difficult task-master all through that day. He worked ferociously and his staff found themselves hard put to it to keep the pace he had set. It was late before he left his Chambers and then it was with a sheaf of papers that kept him hard at it till the small hours, in spite of which an accumulation of work still remained which would keep him in town till late the following day. Ever since a severe heart attack had brought Lady Kean almost to death's door he had dreaded leaving her for any length of time and, on the few occasions on which any great distance lay between them, he was a difficult man to work with. He went to bed fretted and out of patience and his first act on reaching his Chambers in the morning was to ring up Staveley, ostensibly to let his hostess know when to expect him, but actually in the hope of a few words with his wife and an assurance that all was well with her.

There was the usual vexatious delay over the trunk call, but when he did get through, he was surprised to hear Lady Kean's voice at the other end. She should, by rights, have been breakfasting in her room according to her wont, and he said so.

"I might have known you'd be up to your tricks as soon as I turned my back," he told her.

"In spite of which, you were going to ask for me and drag me out of bed in your usual heartless way," she mocked.

"You could have gone back again as soon as I'd done with you. As it is, I suppose you are up and dressed and in for a strenuous day. The folly of women!"

For the first time since his arrival in London he ceased to feel at odds with the world. Even at this distance his wife's influence made itself felt and already all his annoyance had evaporated in the mere delight of listening to her voice.

"There's wisdom in my madness this morning, though," she assured him. "I guessed you'd ring up early and I wanted to catch you myself. I should have rung up yesterday if I had not known you were too busy to help. I'm worried, Edward, and I want you."

In an instant he was on the alert.

"You don't feel seedy?"

"No, no. I'm all right. It isn't that. But come back as soon as you can, my dear. That child, Cynthia, is in trouble and I want you to see her."

Kean's face darkened. As far as it was in him to take an interest in any woman besides his wife he liked Cynthia Bell, though it is doubtful whether, if it had not been for Lady Kean's fondness for the child, he would have paid any special attention to her. He did not, however, propose to have Sybil worried by the consequences of any of that young woman's mad escapades.

"What has she been up to?" he demanded sharply.

"Nothing. It's not her fault this time. But that young man of hers is in a very nasty position, from all accounts. Come back as soon as you can, dear, and see what you can do."

Kean's scowl deepened.

"Young Leslie? I'd forgotten that affair of hers. Well, what's he been doing?"

He paused for a moment as though trying to control his impatience, then:

"I won't have you worried over the affairs of a couple of children, Sybil!"

Sybil Kean laughed in spite of herself at the intense exasperation in his voice.

"My dear, it doesn't do me any harm and, anyhow, I shall worry much less if I know that you have taken a hand in things. They really do need advice, Edward."

"If you take my advice, you'll keep out of the affair. Let them settle their troubles in their own way."

"You don't even know what their troubles are! Don't be difficult, Edward!"

Lady Kean's voice was very appealing. She did not often take this line with her husband, but when she did she almost invariably got her own way.

"Well, I want you to keep out of it, whatever it is," he said curtly.

"Edward, John Leslie's mother was a great friend of mine and she was extraordinarily kind to me as a girl. I really do owe her something and I am fond of both John and Cynthia. I can't keep out of it and I am counting on you to stand by me. Be nice about it and come back as soon as you can."

"Well, you haven't told me yet what *is* the matter," he temporized.

In as few words as possible she repeated all she had been able to learn from Cynthia, supplemented by the account of Dr. Gregg, who had turned up on a professional visit to Lady Kean on the day after the girl's arrival. Kean heard her in silence and, for some moments after she had finished, made no comment. Then he gave vent to a muffled exclamation.

"What did you say?"

"I said 'The Devil!'" he replied grimly. "What on earth did the young idiot want to go roaming all over the country for at that time of night? Very well, I'll see what I can do, though I should have preferred it if you had managed to keep out of it altogether. It's bad for you and I don't like it."

"When can you come? Cynthia's aching to see you. Nobody seems to be doing anything and the inaction is hard on the child."

"I can't get away before this evening, but I'll come straight through on the night train. It means I shall have to come up again for a consultation at once. After that I shall be free for a bit."

"When were you coming if this hadn't happened?"

"I had intended to drive down the day after tomorrow. I'm going to bring the car and take you back by road when we go. It's less tiring for you than the train."

"My dear! Two night journeys and then a long motor drive!" Lady Kean's voice was full of compunction. "Don't do it," she went on. "Stick to your original plan and come down with the car the day after to-morrow. I don't suppose the extra day will really make much difference. It's only that the child's fretting."

"And so are you!" he retorted grimly. "No, I'll come to-night and see what I can do, though I don't suppose there's much. I'm inured to journeys and I can work in the train. Meanwhile, don't wear yourself to fiddle-strings. It will all come right in the end. I know you haven't much opinion of the law, but it doesn't often make mistakes. If the boy's innocent, he will come out of it, you'll see."

"Thank you, Edward. I don't believe you'll ever fail me!"

There was more in her tone than in the words and he felt amply repaid for having yielded as he hung up the receiver. But he found it difficult to fix his mind on his work that morning and he wished with all his heart that his wife had been safe in London at the time of the murder. He knew that she would not know a night's real rest so long as any friend of hers was in trouble and, in spite of his brave words on the telephone, he thought things looked awkward, to say the least of it, for John Leslie.

And once more he cursed the Fates that had decreed the post-ponement of the case of Strickland v. Davies. For Leslie had been subpoenaed as a witness and, if things had taken their normal course, would have been in London at the moment when Mrs. Draycott met with her tragic end. And if it had not been for that unfortunate blunder of old Farrer's he would have heard in time about the postponement and would have been at Staveley instead of in London when Lady Cynthia arrived with the news.

Kean was usually studiously courteous in his dealings with un-derlings, but he was positively brutal to the old head clerk when, later in the day, he had occasion to pull him up for a slight error in the wording of a letter.

CHAPTER V

AT THE BEST of times Whitbury Junction cannot be described as an attractive spot, with its three long platforms, flanked on either hand by sidings with their usual array of cattle-trucks and, apparently, derelict, third-class coaches. An uninspiring collection of faded posters, imploring the weary traveller to hasten at once to Ostend or the Cornish Riviera and a row of battered milk-cans embellish the platforms; and the porters, elderly men of pessimistic habit, take even the arrival of the London train with complete lack of enthusi-asm. At seven o'clock on a chilly March morning the Junction is at its worst, and Sir Edward Kean, alighting somewhat stiffly from his first-class carriage after a night of mingled boredom and discom-fort, eyed his surroundings with marked disapproval. The fact that he would have over an hour to wait before taking the local train to the little station of Staveley Grange did not serve to cheer him, and he was entirely unprepared for the apparition of Cynthia Bell, the last person he desired to see under the circumstances, waiting for him on the platform.

There was a hint of shyness in her greeting. Sybil Kean's distinguished husband was one of the few people of whom she stood in awe and she not only felt responsible for his presence at an unearthly hour at this dreary spot, but was quite aware that, but for his wife's persuasion, he would not have made the journey at all. It was this knowledge that had decided her to meet the train and see him first alone, in the hope of winning his sympathy and inducing him to take more than a cursory interest in John Leslie's affairs. The sight of his dark, inscrutable face and thin-lipped, relentless mouth sent her courage into her boots and she felt pitifully young and very helpless as she hurried to meet him.

"I wanted to see you and thank you, Sir Edward," she began rather breathlessly. "Sybil told me you were coming down on purpose. ..."

In spite of his annoyance Kean was touched by her distress.

"It seemed better to look into things at once," he said kindly. "Sybil said you were anxious to see me."

"I wanted to ask your advice. There's something I'm worried about and no one seems to know in the least what's going to happen or what one ought to do. It's the waiting that's so hard. It makes one imagine things. They haven't even said they suspect John yet, but they behave all the time as if they did and they've searched the farm as if they expected to find something. Meanwhile one hangs about. ..." She was getting almost incoherent and Kean could see that she was on the verge of tears and was holding them back with difficulty.

"You've let this get on your nerves," he said quietly. "I suggest that we shelve the subject altogether till you've had some breakfast. We'll go over to the station hotel and see what they can do for us, and afterwards you shall put the whole case before me and I'll give you what advice I can. There's plenty of time before my train goes and you'll take a different view of things after you've eaten something."

She gave him a swift look of gratitude and followed him without speaking. At the hotel he ordered food and, when it came, quietly but firmly insisted that she should do it justice, making an excellent breakfast the while himself and keeping the conversation rigidly to impersonal topics. It was not till the meal was over and he had handed her a cigarette and lighted one himself that he allowed her to unburden her mind.

"First of all, what did you wish to consult me about?"

His tone was curt and business-like and, fortified by the food which she had badly needed, she was able to collect her thoughts and put them more clearly into words.

She gave him a brief account of what had happened. The main facts he had already learned from the evening papers, in which Mrs. Draycott's latest photograph, over the caption of "The Murdered Woman," had confronted him. He questioned her sharply on one or two points, otherwise he let her tell the story in her own way. When she had finished he sat back in his chair, smoking thoughtfully, for a minute. Then he leaned forward, his keen eyes on hers.

"Where was Leslie while all this was happening at the farm?" he asked sharply.

Cynthia met his gaze without flinching.

"With me," she answered simply.

"Then why doesn't he say so?"

"That's what I wanted to see you about. It doesn't clear him. You see, he wasn't with me at the time they seem to think the murder actually took place. And now he doesn't want me to say anything because he's afraid it will drag me into it for nothing. I think he's wrong and he ought to tell them. Mother being so hateful about our engagement makes it all so much more difficult."

"When was he with you?"

"From five till nearly half-past. Then he did exactly what he said, took a long walk and did not get back to the farm till about eight. It was all my fault, really."

She broke off, as though she found it difficult to continue.

"You'd better tell me exactly what happened," came in Sir Edward's quiet voice.

"It's all rather complicated," she went on haltingly. "You know what Mother's been, about our engagement. Daddie likes John and he'd be all right if it wasn't for her. Lately she's been trying to get round John too, telling him that he is ruining my young life and all that sort of rot. And poor old John gets fits of the blues and then he swallows everything she says and behaves like a blithering idiot afterwards, offers to let me off the engagement and all that sort of thing. He's done it once already and we had an awful row and I wouldn't speak to him for nearly a week. On Monday the parents went up to London and, thank goodness, they're there still, or else I don't think I could bear it. John and I arranged to meet in a copse near the Home Farm at five, after they'd gone, and go for a long walk. After that I was going home to dress for Miss Allen's dinner and we'd planned that John should pick me up at her house and drive me in my car to Staveley at about eleven. You see, when the parents are at home, we never seem to get much time together and we were going to take advantage of their being away. We met at five, just as we'd arranged, but we did not go for the walk. John had met Mother somewhere the day before and she'd filled him up with the usual nonsense. He began to talk all sorts of rot about not being able to marry me for years, and all that kind of thing, and wanting to break it off. It ended in our having a fearful row, me saying he didn't care for me and all the things one says when one's in a rage, and so we parted. And I suppose the poor old thing was upset and went crashing off on this rotten walk and here we are in the soup. If only I hadn't been such an ass we should have been together and everything would have been all right."

"I don't know that you would gain anything by coming forward now," commented Kean thoughtfully.

"That's what John says and, of course, after the line Mother's taken, he doesn't want to mix me up in it. What I say is, that sane people don't go charging about the country for nearly four solid hours, unless there's something wrong with them, and of course everybody thinks John must have been up to something. If he'd tell them exactly what happened and what *was* wrong with him, there'd be some sense in the whole thing. Of course, we should both look awful fools," she finished ruefully.

"I'd better see Leslie to-morrow and then you can appear at the inquest if we think it's advisable. Tell him I'll come over to the farm in the course of the morning."

Kean rose and picked up his overcoat.

Cynthia hesitated, then took her courage in both hands.

"Sir Edward, Mr. Fayre is at the farm now with John and he wants to see you. Won't you come over with me now? I've got the car outside and I could run you over to Staveley afterwards. Sybil knows. In fact, it was her idea, so she won't be expecting you."

In her anxiety she forgot her shyness of him, clinging to his arm, her beseeching eyes fixed on his face.

"Won't you come now? Please, Sir Edward! The inquest's this afternoon and it would make all the difference if you could see John first."

Kean's face had begun to darken at her first words, but, at the mention of the inquest, it sharpened to a look almost of anxiety.

"The inquest? Already? I was afraid of that!"

"Sir Edward! They can't arrest John!"

"I don't know. It all depends on what the police have up their sleeve. I think you're right; I'd better come up to the farm now."

On their way they spoke little. Cynthia drove with all the recklessness of youth, and less than half an hour had passed before they turned into the little lane that led to the farm.

Fayre and Leslie were at the door to meet them. "It's very good of you, sir," said Leslie. "I seem to be giving you a fearful lot of trouble."

He looked worn and anxious, but his eyes met Kean's fearlessly and the lawyer, accustomed as he was to read faces, was both attracted and impressed by his manner.

He laid his hand on Leslie's shoulder.

"Come inside," he said. "And let's talk things over. So you've got a finger in this pie, Hatter? You always were an old busybody!"

There was a hint of annoyance in his voice. For one thing, he had all the professional's dislike for amateur interference, and he knew Fayre too well not to be aware that he was lamentably thorough in his methods. Also, he would be yet another link which would serve to draw Sybil still more surely into this unsavoury business.

There was a gleam of mischief in Fayre's eyes as he answered.

"Beastly nuisance, Edward, an outsider butting in! I know. I've had experience of them in the East. Don't worry; I'm only here in the capacity of family adviser. I've constituted myself a sort of adopted uncle of Cynthia's. After all, I've known her since her pigtail days."

He tucked the girl's arm under his as he spoke, with a smile so friendly and encouraging that she felt her heart lighten.

"Mr. Fayre's been most awfully decent," said Leslie impulsively. "It's made all the difference, feeling we've got him on our side. And now you've come! I *am* grateful, sir!"

"Everybody's been decent," put in Cynthia. "I can't tell you what a brick Lady Staveley was when I told them all on Monday. And Miss Allen has written to ask me to go there and see her this morning. I don't know why, unless it's just to show that she believes in John. They've always been jolly good friends, but it's pretty wonderful of her to see me at all, considering what's happened."

"It's unusual. And not in the best of taste, either, in the circumstances. Still, as you say, she may want to show herself definitely on your side. All the same, I think you'd better let me see her instead. It will be best for you to keep away until after the inquest."

"You don't think Cynthia will have to appear?" put in Leslie anxiously.

"I'm inclined to agree with her that it may put your actions in a more favourable light if she tells her story. After all, so long as your engagement holds she is involved, in any case. Her name is in the papers already and five minutes in the witness-box won't make much difference."

Cynthia shot an indignant glance at him, and Leslie's face took on an added gloom.

"I told her we'd much better consider it off, at any rate till I was clear of all this business," he said miserably. "But she won't listen to me."

Cynthia turned in desperation to Fayre.

"Uncle Fayre! You're the only one of the lot with a gleam of sense. Do stop him! If he starts this argument again, I shall go mad! We've had enough rows already about it, and I should have thought the result of the last one might have taught him a lesson! Tell him what a fool he is, Uncle Fayre! You said you agreed with me. If I argue any more about it I shall lose my temper."

She swung round on Leslie.

"Understand this! I'm not going to let this make any difference. I'm going to hang on like a leech, whatever happens! So you can't get rid of me!"

Kean's eyes met Fayre's meaningly.

"I think she's right," he said quietly, and left it at that; but the other knew what he was thinking. If Leslie were to find himself in the dock the fact that his engagement to Cynthia still held would tell in his favour.

He nodded absently. His mind was on the coming inquest. While they were talking they had drifted into the sitting-room, and he saw Kean's face harden into grim lines as he took in the scene that had staged so dramatic a drama. It struck him that the lawyer, in spite of his air of calm efficiency, was taking anything but a light view of Leslie's predicament.

The table had been cleared of all its paraphernalia. No doubt the blotter was in the hands of the police. Fayre and Cynthia sat down near the table and Kean took up his position on the hearth-rug in his favourite attitude, his hands in his pockets, his shoulders hunched almost to his ears. Leslie stood behind Cynthia, his eyes on Kean's face.

"What's this about a police search?" asked Kean abruptly.

"They went through the entire house," answered Leslie. "Goodness knows what they were looking for. They wouldn't let me go with them."

"What have you told them so far about your movements on Monday evening?"

"Simply that I went for a walk. I wanted to keep Cynthia out of it."

"You're sure you met no one who could identify you?"

"I'm afraid not. I was riled and I wanted to walk it off. I went clean across country, away from the roads. I did see a chap with a spade over his shoulder, some labourer going home, I suppose, but he was a good way off and it was getting dark. I remember him because his dog barked."

"What time?"

"Round about six, I should think. I'd been walking for about an hour."

"We might trace the fellow. In any case, I'm afraid there's nothing for it but to give a clear account of your movements, including the time you were with Cynthia. You will gain nothing by holding it back at this juncture. I'll go now and see this Miss Allen. She may possibly have something to say that throws a light on things. Is it within a walk?"

"Take the Staveley car which brought me," suggested Fayre. "It's waiting at the gate and Staveley said I was to use it as I liked."

"In that case, I suggest that we all meet for lunch at the hotel at Whitbury. We shall be on the spot, then, for the inquest. You're sure Sybil is not expecting me?"

Fayre smiled.

"This is one of her little plots. Didn't you recognize her hand behind it? She told me to say that she would expect you when she saw you."

"We meet at the hotel, then."

Fayre accompanied him down the little path to the gate, where the Staveley car stood waiting. They had almost reached the end of the path when Fayre, who had been walking with his eyes on the ground, deep in thought, bent down suddenly and picked up something from the long grass that bordered the path.

"Found anything?" asked Kean.

"An old stylographic pen," said Fayre, examining it curiously. "I remember them in my youth. 'Red Dwarfs,' I think they used to be called. I wonder how it got there."

Kean held out his hand for it.

"It's probably been there some time. We'll ask Leslie if he recognizes it. We'll stick to it, anyway. It may prove of interest."

Fayre was peering about in the grass.

"There's nothing else," he said, "except some copper-coloured spangles, three of them, here on the path. I believe the poor creature was wearing a brown-spangled dress, so, as we know she probably came up this path, that does not lead us anywhere. The pen may prove more useful."

"It has probably got there since the murder," Kean reminded him. "It's hardly likely the police would have missed it. They must have gone over this ground pretty carefully. The pressmen have been down here already, remember. One of them may have dropped it."

He slipped the pen into his pocket as he spoke.

After Kean had climbed into the car Fayre stood for a moment, his hand on the door.

"I'm not going to make a nuisance of myself, Edward," he said. "But, if there's anything I can do, you might put me onto it. I'm sorry for those children and would give a great deal to help them. Also, I'm at a loose end and I've no ties. If there's any special line

you want followed I could do it more tactfully, possibly, and unob-
trusively than one of these fellows from an agency."

Kean nodded.

"I'll remember. Don't underrate the private detective, though.
It's not such an easy job as you seem to think. Meanwhile, if you can
keep Sybil from worrying herself silly I should take it as a kindness.
I've got to go back to town to-night and I should like to leave her in
good hands. Yours are the best I know, old chap."

The car slid away, leaving Fayre, for all his even temper, a little ruffled. His offer, not a very practical one, perhaps, but none
the less heartfelt for that, had been quietly, but firmly, put aside.
The lump of sugar, skilfully administered after the pill, did not de-
ceive him and he was human enough to feel snubbed. There was
something significant, too, in the way in which Kean had quietly
pocketed his find in the garden. Evidently he had no intention of
taking his old friend into his confidence with regard to his conduct
of the case. Fayre, who had meant to ask him his intentions should
Leslie be committed for trial, decided to leave all such negotiations
to Lady Kean. They had both hoped that he might be persuaded
to undertake the defence and he felt now that she was the only
person who could be counted on to influence him, should the occasion arise. He returned to the farm in as near a bad temper as was
possible to one of his temperament and thoroughly out of patience
with the legal mind.

"If Edward takes this line, blessed if I don't do a bit of investigating on my own," he told himself doggedly. "He always was a hide-
bound beggar. Come to that, why couldn't he let Cynthia go and see
Miss Allen? She'd probably get more out of her, as woman to woman, than he will. Another of his absurd points of legal etiquette."

Meanwhile the object of his wrath was reviewing the situation
as the motor bore him swiftly on his way to Greycross. If Cynthia
had seen his face now she would have been robbed of even the faint
hope that had been kindled by his visit to the farm. But he felt no
doubt as to Leslie's innocence. His manner, all that he knew of him
in the past, the complete lack of motive, even the very weakness of
his alibi, all served to exonerate him; but, as Kean knew from long
experience, only the lack of motive would weigh with a jury. He had
guessed that part of Leslie's time on the Monday had been passed

in the company of Cynthia Bell and had counted on her to produce a sufficient alibi, expecting to be confronted with nothing more serious than the boy's chivalrous desire to shield her. He had been far more concerned than he had chosen to admit, even to Fayre, when he found that Cynthia's evidence would be worse than useless. He was so deep in thought that he was taken unawares when the motor drew up in front of Miss Allen's pleasant, picturesque old house.

A bulldog ambled out onto the drive to greet him and a couple of terriers sniffed at his legs as he waited in the comfortable drawing-room into which the maid had shown him. The pale March sunlight filtered in through the long French windows, but the blinds had been drawn in the ante-room through which he had passed and he knew that probably all the other windows of the house were shrouded. An ominous quiet seemed to brood over the whole place and he found himself moved for the first time by the realization of Mrs. Draycott's death. Until now he had been too occupied with the consequences of the murder to give much thought to the woman who had, after all, been his fellow-guest at Staveley for over a week. Now, in her sister's house, the sense of tragedy deepened and, when Miss Allen found him standing by the window, staring with sombre eyes into the sunlit garden, she was struck by the weariness of his pose and the almost haggard pallor of his face.

He, summing her up sharply in his turn, was surprised to see but little sign of the violent grief he had expected. Her plain, fresh-coloured features were grave and a little sad, but she was obviously not prostrated by the loss of her sister. She greeted him frankly and with a certain quiet dignity.

"My maid said that you wished to see me?" she said simply.

"I must apologize for intruding on you at such a time, but I have come from Lady Cynthia Bell. She tells me that you very kindly offered to see her and she asked me to express her gratitude and appreciation. I am afraid that I am responsible for her failure to take advantage of your suggestion. ... It is difficult to explain my interference without encroaching on a subject which, I am afraid, must be very painful to you."

He broke off, his face alight with a very real sympathy.

"You mean my sister's death," she said steadily. "I know your name well, Sir Edward, and if you have come on Cynthia's behalf, there is one thing I should like to make quite clear before we go any further. You have guessed, probably, why I wanted to see her and I am very glad to have the opportunity of saying as much to you as I had intended to say to her. It is simply this: I have known John Leslie for some time and I'm not a bad judge of character. I am absolutely convinced that he had nothing to do with my poor sister's death and, what's more, am practically certain that he had never met her or had ever had anything to do with her."

Having said her say, she stood waiting, a dignified, sturdy figure of an English spinster, a look of quiet resolution on her well-cut, weather-beaten features. Kean summed her up as a good friend and a bad enemy.

"This will mean a lot to Cynthia," he said warmly. "And I should like to thank you on her behalf. As for myself, I entirely agree with you; but, as you know, we may have to convince people who do not know Leslie, and, however strongly we may feel ourselves on the subject, we have no real proof to offer. Frankly, I came here in the hope that you might have some evidence that would help us. You say you are practically certain that Leslie never knew your sister. Is this only conjecture?"

"Mr. Leslie told me himself that he had never met her when I spoke to him about her visit to me; but that, I suppose," she went on with a rather grim smile, "is hardly sufficient for you lawyers! But, as a matter of fact, by sheer luck, my sister happened to pick up a snapshot of Cynthia and Mr. Leslie the morning she arrived. She recognized Cynthia from a photograph she had seen in some paper and asked who the attractive boy was with her. When I told her his name she said she had heard him spoken of at Staveley, but had never met him. Now, if what these idiots seem to suspect were true, John Leslie might have his reasons for keeping their acquaintance dark, but my sister could have had no objection to saying she knew him. Besides, from her manner, I am sure she did not recognize the photograph."

"Could you let me have this snapshot, Miss Allen?"

"It is on the mantelpiece behind you. Keep it, if you think it will be of any use."

"You will forgive me if I seem insistent," he went on. "But, as you know, this is a very serious matter for Leslie. Can you think of any one, in the past, who might possibly have harboured a grudge against your sister?"

Miss Allen hesitated, her clear eyes very troubled.

"I'd better be frank with you," she said at last. "You'll probably think what I am about to say almost indecent, but I've never shirked the truth in my life and I want to leave no stone unturned to help that boy. You met my sister at Staveley, I believe, Sir Edward, and I think you will understand what I am trying to tell you. You may not know that she was divorced by her first husband and would have been divorced by her second if he had not died in the nick of time. It isn't pleasant for me to say this and I hope it need not go any further, but that is the kind of woman she was. I don't judge her, and I suppose it was largely a matter of temperament. She was spoiled, too, as a child. But she was a woman who was bound to have enemies, both male and female, and she had some queer friends, too. If her first husband were not dead I should have been very much inclined to put this down to him. He went to pieces, altogether, after she left him, and became just the kind of half-mad, reckless creature that might end in the dock. Thank goodness, he is out of it, but she has made many friends and many enemies since his day."

"You know of no one in particular?" pressed Kean eagerly. "Is there nothing she said, at any time, that would suggest any one?"

But Miss Allen shook her head.

"You must remember that I was not in her confidence. We have never been intimate, and for the last ten years I have seen very little of her. I did not like her ways or her friends and I told her so. As a matter of fact, I was surprised when she proposed this visit herself. She told me when she arrived that she was economizing and wanted to put in a week somewhere in between two visits."

"She said nothing else that might possibly be a clue? Will you search your memory very carefully, Miss Allen? There may be something that seemed quite unimportant at the time."

He leaned forward, watching her anxiously.

"There was one thing. I didn't take much account of it at the time and I don't now. It was her way to make exaggerated statements. But, when she spoke of economizing, she said that, anyhow, it wouldn't last long. She was out to make a lot of money; in fact, was practically certain of it. I asked her whether it wasn't just another of her 'sure things,' for she was a born gambler, you know. And she said it was as sure as death. I've remembered her words since."

"As sure as death," echoed Kean softly. "What irony!"

"I took it for granted that she was talking either of racing or of some speculation she was mixed up in. She had a lot of queer people in tow, bookies and the sort of shady-looking men who are supposed to be something in the city. Looked like criminals, most of them, and I told her so, more than once. But I dare say they were harmless enough, really. I met her once in Paris with a man she told me was a well-known French bookie and I wouldn't have trusted him alone in a room with my purse. They fleeced her a lot, one way and another."

"There was nothing among her papers that pointed to any big transaction?"

Miss Allen shook her head.

"I went through them carefully yesterday. There was nothing. As I said, I don't believe John Leslie had anything to do with this and I should like to see him cleared, but I am not so heartless as I may have sounded. I don't say that we got on well together, but she was my sister, when all's said and done, and I find myself regretting many things now. Perhaps if I had taken the trouble I might have been of some influence in her life. I don't know. But I should like to see the man who did this brought to book."

Her voice was wrung with emotion and Kean could see that she had been tried more hardly than she realized in the past few days.

"I don't think I had ever understood the strength of blood-relationship until I saw her lying in that horrible place at Whitbury," she muttered almost in-audibly.

Kean waited in silence. There seemed nothing he could say. She pulled herself together with a pluck that roused his admiration and turned to him.

"I'm afraid I've helped you very little," she said regretfully.

"I'm not so sure. Anything may turn out to be important in a case like this. In the meantime, I am more than grateful to you, Miss Allen, for your frankness. Cynthia will no doubt see you very soon and thank you herself. In view of the fact that she may have to appear at the inquest this afternoon I considered it better that she should not be known to have been in touch with you. She saw my point; otherwise she would have come in answer to your note; this morning."

Miss Allen nodded.

"I'm very glad she has got you to turn to, Sir Edward. If there is anything more I can tell you at any time I will let you know."

Kean paused in the act of shaking hands.

"One thing more," he said. "You have no reason to suspect that your sister went out with the intention of meeting anybody on Monday night?"

"I hadn't at the time, but I have wondered since. I was writing letters in the little room I call my study when she went out. I shut myself up there directly after tea, to get through some troublesome correspondence, and left her comfortably settled in front of the fire in here. When I came back about half-past six she was gone and the maid told me she had seen her go out. I was surprised, because she hated walking and it was not the sort of weather to tempt her out of the house, but I did not get anxious until after the arrival of Cynthia. We waited dinner for her until past eight, and after dinner I sent the groom down to Keys to ask if she had been seen there. When he returned and said he could get no trace of her I began to get really anxious. Until then I had simply thought she had lost her way, and was in hopes that she might have telephoned to the inn at Keys, leaving a message for me saying she was hung up somewhere. I have no telephone here, you see, and she knew that the people at The Boar sometimes take messages for me. I sent my man straight back to Keys, telling him to see Gunnet, the constable there. But Gunnet was out and his wife did not know when he would be back. Of course, I know now that he was at the farm. Cynthia was just trying to persuade me to let her take her car and scour the lanes when the police arrived with the news of what had happened."

"You have no idea what could have taken her to Leslie's farm?"

"None whatever. I should certainly never have dreamed of looking for her there. By ten o'clock I had made up my mind that she had either lost her way or had an accident. There was a gale blowing that night and a good many trees were down, and I was afraid she might have been hit and be lying helpless somewhere. Thinking it over, I feel certain of one thing."

Kean looked up quickly.

"Yes?"

"She never meant to go to the farm. It is two miles the other side of Keys and forty minutes' walk from here. She was wearing an old pair of evening shoes and she hadn't troubled to change them. No sane woman would walk even a mile on a country road in thin slippers."

CHAPTER VI

KEAN FOUND FAYRE waiting for him when he reached the hotel at Whitbury. Cynthia, he learned, had taken the car to the garage to fill up and Leslie had accompanied her.

"With consummate tact, I said I should prefer to be dropped here to wait for you," explained Fayre. "Heaven knows how much more time they'll have together. It strikes me as a black outlook, Edward."

His kindly face was grave and troubled.

Kean nodded.

"I haven't been able to get much out of Miss Allen. She is convinced that Leslie had nothing to do with it, and I believe she is right. All the same, his story is weak."

"It's the most infernal bad luck! If only he'd gone up to London as he intended! What do you suppose induced poor Mrs. Draycott to go to the farm?"

"If we knew that, Leslie could snap his fingers at them," answered Kean sombrely.

He pulled out his handkerchief from his pocket as he spoke, and a small red stylographic pen came with it and rolled on the floor at Fayre's feet. He picked it up and examined it. The cap was missing and, half concealed beneath the mud with which it was plastered, was an inkstain, running right round the pen.

"Hullo! This is the fellow I picked up!" he exclaimed.

Kean took it from him and slipped it into the pocket of his coat.

"Our one clue," he assented dryly. "And we shall probably trace that to one of the reporters. I don't think we need build on it."

He pulled off his heavy coat and threw it over a chair. Then he turned and faced Fayre squarely.

"I'm going to save that boy if I can, Hatter, if things go against him," he said. "You can tell Cynthia that, if I don't have an opportunity myself after the inquest. We'll hope it won't come to that, but, frankly, I'm not sanguine."

"Neither am I. It looks almost as if suspicion had been deliberately thrown on Leslie. It's an inconceivably devilish scheme, if it is so. There's no earthly reason, as far as we know, why Mrs. Draycott should have gone to his farm at all, unless she were decoyed there, and, if she were, why choose that spot? Surely it would have been as easy to shoot the poor creature in the open. It looks uncommonly as if some one had tried to plant the murder on John Leslie."

Kean walked over to the window and stood there looking out, his hands deep in his pockets.

"It hasn't occurred to you," he said slowly, "that whoever did it may have known that Leslie had been subpoenaed as a witness and was due in London on Tuesday. Remember, he should, by rights, have been in the train at the time Mrs. Draycott was killed. I don't suppose he made any secret of the fact that he was going, and news travels fast in a small country place."

Fayre stared at him for a moment then, with a sudden look of comprehension:

"By Jove! That narrows things down a bit! If there is anything in your theory, we shall find the man is some one who either lives in the neighbourhood or who was there for a time, at least, before the crime was committed."

Kean turned to him with a smile.

"Come to that, why 'the man'? Women have been known to shoot people before now."

"Women!"

Fayre stopped, appalled. There was only one woman who, so far, could be said to have any connection with the case. Cynthia had, according to her own account, gone straight home when she parted from Leslie at five-thirty. She was fairly certain to have been seen by some member of her father's household. Supposing that, by some evil chance she hadn't been seen? Fayre gazed at Kean with something like horror in his eyes.

"Not Cynthia?"

Kean's smile vanished.

"Thank goodness, we can rule Cynthia out. The lodge gates are kept closed at Galston and, unless we are up against another piece of unheard-of bad luck, the lodge-keeper must have let her in. As a matter of fact, I had nobody in mind when I spoke. You were theorizing so smoothly that I couldn't resist the temptation to point to at least one weak point in your argument. After all, as you say, the murderer may have deliberately planted the whole thing on Leslie. It is as good an explanation as any, considering how little we have to go on."

"If it wasn't a plant, why did he take the trouble to get her to the farm?"

Kean had turned again to the window.

"The sound of a shot carries a good way in the open air, remember. I can see our young couple. I suggest that we drop the subject, as far as possible, during lunch. I can give Leslie a few hints on the correct behaviour for witnesses afterwards. I fancy he's a hotheaded young beggar and he mustn't be allowed to lose his temper."

Kean could be a delightful and interesting companion when he chose and on this occasion he laid himself out to keep Leslie's mind off the coming ordeal, with the result that even the two people most concerned found the meal a pleasant one. After it was over Kean drew the boy aside and spoke to him very seriously while Fayre did his best to keep the ball of conversation rolling with Cynthia. She had conquered her agitation and was facing things with a pluck that did her credit; but, in spite of both their efforts, the time dragged heavily and he was glad when the suspense was over and they started for the Town Hall where the inquest was to be held.

At Kean's suggestion they separated and he and Fayre joined the crowd in the body of the Court. Though one or two people looked curiously at the two strangers, it is doubtful whether anybody recognized the lean man with the keen eyes and hawk-like face, though his photographs had appeared often enough in the press. Their interest was focused on Leslie and on Miss Allen, who came in just before the proceedings opened and took her seat on the opposite side of the Court.

Fayre looked at her with interest. She was dressed in a black coat and skirt and a small black felt hat, of the kind affected by the more downright type of middle-aged spinster. She was pale, but composed, and was apparently oblivious of the little stir occasioned by her entrance. Catching sight of Leslie, she bowed to him, gravely, but with marked friendliness.

The Jury filed in, followed by the Coroner, an elderly man whose practise lay on the other side of Whitbury. His address to the Jury was short and to the point.

"You have inspected the body of this lady," he concluded, "and have been shown the cause of death, a bullet-wound in the left temple. The body, as you know, has already been identified. After hearing the evidence which will be brought before you, you are called on to settle in your minds in what way the deceased came by her death."

The proceedings opened with the evidence of Gunnet and Sergeant Brace. Brace described his visit, to the farm and the discovery of the footsteps under the window and in the barn. He reported his conversation with Leslie concerning them.

"You have not, so far, been able to trace them to any definite person?" suggested the Coroner.

"We are making inquiries," answered Brace evasively. "At present we have nothing to report."

One of the jurors, a tradesman whose shop was on the outskirts of Whitbury, cleared his throat nervously.

"There was a tramp passed my place on Monday afternoon," he volunteered.

There was a slight delay while he was sworn in.

"What time did you see this man?"

"Round about four. I was dressing the window, that's how I happened to remember the time. He was going in the direction of Keys, all right."

"Could you describe him?"

"A smallish man. Thin, with a reddish face. That's all I can remember. Don't know as I should recognize him if I saw him again. I just noticed him in passing."

The Coroner recalled Brace.

"I understand that the deceased was identified on the Monday night?"

"I went straight from Mr. Leslie's farm to Greycross, where I interviewed Miss Allen. At my suggestion she came at once with me to the mortuary. The body had arrived there about half an hour before and she identified it as that of her sister, Mrs. Henry Draycott, who was staying at her house."

The Coroner dismissed Brace and called Miss Allen.

"I am sorry to have to ask these questions, Miss Allen," he said. "I will be as brief as possible. Will you tell us the circumstances in which your sister left your house on Monday night. Was it usual for her to take a walk at this hour?"

"Very unusual, I should say. It was a long time since she had stayed with me and she had only arrived the night before, but she had never been a walker and did not care for exercise, especially in bad weather."

"Can you think of anything which could have drawn her out on such a night?"

"Nothing. I did not see her leave the house and was surprised when I discovered she was out. She had said nothing about going."

"You can think of no reason why she should have gone to Mr. Leslie's farm?"

"None. She did not know Mr. Leslie and, to the best of my belief, could have had no possible reason for going there."

The Coroner leaned forward.

"I am sorry to have to touch on such a subject, but did your sister speak openly to you about her affairs? Supposing she had gone out with the intention of meeting some one, would she be likely to mention it to you?"

Miss Allen hesitated for a moment.

"I was not in my sister's confidence," she said at last. "We have seen little of each other in the last few years and, though she was very frank as a rule about her affairs, I do not think she would have chosen me for her confidante in the case of any intimate business."

"So that she might quite well have left your house to keep an appointment without consulting you?"

"It is more than likely."

"You know of no message or letter which might have had some bearing on a possible appointment?"

"No. As soon as I became alarmed at her absence I questioned the servants as to whether any message had come for her, and found there had been nothing of the sort. I have since looked through her letters, but can find nothing. She had only arrived the day before and had received no letters through the post."

Miss Allen returned to her seat with the same quiet dignity she had shown all through the examination. Fayre, watching her closely, was astonished at the perfection of her poise; but now that she was off her guard for a moment it was easy to see that only the most iron self-control had enabled her to go through the ordeal. She was no longer young and her sister's death had evidently shocked her deeply, but he doubted, having known Mrs. Draycott, whether there could have been any real affection between the two women. Mrs. Draycott, shallow, yet astute enough in her small way, a born huntress of men, but only of those men she considered worth while, could have had nothing in common with Miss Allen, who, after all, had been almost disconcertingly frank in her description of her relations with her sister. She had stated plainly that she had never been in her confidence and he suspected that she had probably actually disliked her and was generous enough to feel repentant now of her attitude towards her.

Dr. Gregg was called next. He gave his evidence clearly and straightforwardly, but with an awkwardness of manner that amounted almost to surliness. Fayre had the impression that he was either shy or bad-tempered, possibly both. He expressed his opinion that the deceased had been dead for about four hours at the time of his examination. Asked whether the wound might have been self-inflicted, he said that such a thing would be practically impossible, even in the case of a left-handed person, as the shot had been fired at arm's-length, a feat so difficult as to be almost out of the question. In answer to a question by the Coroner, he stated that death would have been instantaneous and that, in the case of suicide, the weapon would undoubtedly have fallen either on the table or on the floor close to the chair. He gave his answers grudgingly, as though he resented having been drawn into the affair at all. His evidence was corroborated by the police surgeon who had been summoned from Carlisle.

There was a little stir in the court as John Leslie stepped forward. Kean had drilled him well in the few minutes he had had at his disposal and he gave his evidence in a clear, audible voice, confining himself to the bare facts of the case. He described his return to the farm and the finding of the body and stated emphatically that he had never met Mrs. Draycott and had no idea of her identity until Gunnet recognized her. Asked to account for his movements, he said that he had left the farm at about four o'clock and that from five until just before eight he had been walking.

"That leaves a certain period of time unaccounted for. Where did you go when you left the farm?" asked the Coroner.

"I walked to the edge of the Galston copse. I had an appointment there at four-thirty."

"Did you keep that appointment?"

"I did, leaving there at five and walking straight across the fields in the direction of Besley. When I was almost in sight of the village I turned off and made a wide detour and arrived back at the' farm from the Whitbury side."

"You did not stop at any inn or speak to any one in the course of your walk?"

"No. I was in the fields practically all the time. I hardly saw a soul. It was dark before seven and pitch-black by the time I got home."

"Then I understand that you spoke to no one except the person with whom you had the appointment?"

"No one."

"Who was that person, Mr. Leslie?"

"Lady Cynthia Bell."

Leslie spoke with obvious reluctance and there was a rustle as the crowd turned, sheep-like, to stare at Cynthia.

"And you parted at five o'clock?"

"Thereabouts."

"Why didn't you return to the farm after leaving the Galston copse?"

"I had been working all day and I needed exercise."

"Farm work is fairly heavy work, Mr. Leslie, even at this time of year. According to your account, you must have walked a good twelve miles between five o'clock and eight. Had you no other reason for making such a wide detour?"

Leslie's eyes flashed and for a moment it seemed as if Kean's admonitions were to go for naught, then he controlled himself with an effort.

"I was annoyed and wanted to walk it off."

"What had happened to upset you?"

"I had had a difference of opinion with Lady Cynthia. We had been going for a walk together, but, owing to this, we parted, rather suddenly. I'd got the walk in my mind, I suppose, so when that happened I just went on by myself and tried to walk my temper off."

"You are engaged to Lady Cynthia Bell, I believe?"

"Yes."

"Was the difference of opinion you mentioned just now due to attentions you had been paying to another lady? Mrs. Draycott, for instance?"

Leslie stared blankly at his interrogator, a dark flush slowly mounting to his forehead.

"Good Lord, no!" he ejaculated.

"You say that you tried to walk off your anger. Was that anger directed against anybody in particular?"

"I was annoyed with Lady Cynthia at first, in the way one is annoyed with any one one has had an argument with. But after that I was angry, principally, with myself for being such an ass as to quarrel."

"There was no third person involved either in the quarrel or in your thoughts afterwards?"

"Of course not. Who should there be?"

"You are sure that you did not go back to the farm after leaving Lady Cynthia Bell for the purpose of keeping an appointment you had made with the deceased?"

Fayre heard the sharp hiss of Kean's breath between his teeth, followed by a whisper:

"Then they have got something up their sleeves, after all."

Leslie, after the first blank stare of astonishment, flushed with anger as he realized the full force of the insinuation.

"Of course not," he said curtly. "I have told you that I didn't know Mrs. Draycott."

"You are certain that you did not meet Mrs. Draycott at all that evening?"

"I never saw Mrs. Draycott in my life until I found her body at the farm."

"Thank you, Mr. Leslie. Sergeant Brace!" Sergeant Brace took his stand, very erect and soldierly in his blue uniform.

"On the day after the murder you visited Mr. Leslie's farm, I believe."

"I went to the farm on Tuesday, the twenty-fourth, in company with Police-Constable Collins, and made a thorough search of the premises. In a drawer in Mr. Leslie's bedroom I found a Webley Service revolver, one chamber of which had been discharged. The other chambers were loaded and the gun had not been cleaned since it had last been fired."

"You have the bullet which killed Mrs. Draycott?" Brace held out his hand and displayed a bullet lying in the palm.

"Does it correspond with those used in the weapon you found at the farm?"

"It does."

"You have the revolver in court?"

Police-Constable Collins stepped forward and handed a heavy Service revolver to the Coroner. "Thank you. Call Mr. Leslie."

Leslie's expression was one of blank consternation.

"Do you recognize this, Mr. Leslie?"

Leslie examined the revolver.

"It belongs to me," he said simply. "I keep it in the drawer of the dressing-table in my bedroom. I suppose Sergeant Brace found it there."

"When did you last fire it?"

"About a week ago. I found a poor beast of a cat in a trap in Smith's field, just across the lane from me. It was past saving, so I went home and fetched this and shot it through the head."

"You have not used it since then?"

"No. I haven't had it out of the drawer since."

"Was any one present when you shot the cat?"

"No. I was alone."

"Did you speak to anybody afterwards of what you had done?"

"No. If I'd run across Smith I should probably have mentioned it to him, but I haven't seen him."

"Was there any one who could have heard the shot?"

"There might have been. Quite likely not. My man had gone home and Smith's farm lies a good way back from the lane."

"Why did you hide the revolver at the back of the drawer?"

Leslie coloured hotly.

"I've never hidden it. The drawer's full of mufflers and silk handkerchiefs and things and I keep it at the back for fear Mrs. Grey, who does my room, should get monkeying with it. She puts my handkerchiefs back when she brings them from the wash and I didn't want to run any risk with the revolver."

"You persist in your statement that you did not return to the farm till eight o'clock?"

"I went for a long walk, as I have said, and did not get back till close on eight. Hang it all, if I'd killed Mrs. Draycott do you suppose I'd have left my revolver in a drawer where any one could find it? Without cleaning it or reloading it either?"

Leslie's quick temper had got the better of him at last.

"That is for the Jury to decide, Mr. Leslie," said the Coroner. There was a sharp note of reproof in his voice and Fayre realized that, in a moment of irritation, Leslie had gone a long way towards effacing the good impression he had made in the beginning.

"You have no explanation as to why Mrs. Draycott went to the farm?"

"As I've already said, I didn't know Mrs. Draycott. Why she should have gone there is a mystery to me."

Leslie went back to his seat to the accompaniment of a low murmur of voices, as the crowds composed mostly of his own friends and neighbours, exchanged their whispered comments on the unexpected turn the inquiry had taken. He was popular in the district and Fayre noticed that, in spite of the damning evidence the police had brought forward, there was little hostility, so far, in the faces that were turned so eagerly in Leslie's direction. His heart sank when Cynthia was called. He had hoped that she might escape this ordeal.

"Will you tell us in your own words exactly what happened on the evening of March 23rd?" said the Coroner.

Cynthia's colour was a little deeper, her eyes a trifle brighter, than usual; otherwise she showed no embarrassment at the position in which she found herself.

"I met Mr. Leslie, as we had arranged, on the edge of the Galston copse ..." she began.

"What time was that?" interrupted the Coroner.

"About a quarter past four. We talked for about three-quarters of an hour and then I went back to Galston and Mr. Leslie walked away through the copse in the direction of Besley."

"Good girl," murmured Kean in Fayre's ear. "She's got her wits about her."

"You are sure you noticed the direction in which Mr. Leslie went?"

"Quite sure. After I had gone a few yards I turned round, meaning to say something to him, but he was walking so quickly that I gave up the idea. He was going in the opposite direction to the farm then."

The Coroner leaned forward.

"You were not on friendly terms with Mr. Leslie when you parted, I understand?"

"I was furious with him at the moment and I expect he loathed me. I got over it almost at once. That's why I turned round, meaning to call to him."

"You considered that he had treated you badly?"

"It wasn't that, exactly. I was angry because he would go on trying to treat me too well, or at least what he thought was well. I didn't agree with him and lost my temper. He'd got into his head that because he'd no prospects and couldn't marry for a long time he was putting me in a false position and that he ought to break off the engagement."

"Was this the first time he had made the suggestion to break off the engagement?"

"O dear, no. He began worrying about it ten minutes after we first became engaged."

A ripple of nervous laughter ran through the court and the Jury, who had pricked up their ears at the Coroner's question, relapsed into somewhat amused languor.

"Was it an old argument between you?"

"Oh, yes. That's why I was annoyed. We'd had it out so often that I was tired of the subject."

"So that, when Mr. Leslie wished to break off the engagement, you refused and held him to it?"

The colour flooded Cynthia's cheeks, but she was too wise to take offense at the suggestion. She looked at the Coroner with disarming frankness.

"He didn't wish to break off the engagement. That was why the whole argument was so silly. He went on suggesting it simply from a sense of duty. I shouldn't have held him to his word if I'd thought he wanted to go."

"Was he more insistent than usual on this occasion?"

"No. He didn't have time. I lost my temper almost at once."

"Are you sure that the presence of Mrs. Draycott in the neighbourhood was not one of the causes of this quarrel?"

"Perfectly certain. I had never heard of Mrs. Draycott. Miss Allen told me her sister was coming and asked me to meet her at dinner that night, but I didn't know then that that was her name."

"Had you never heard her name coupled with that of Mr. Leslie?"

"Never."

Lady Cynthia was the last witness. She returned to her seat, her head held high and her cheeks flaming, but she had done better work than she knew, for her gallant bearing had won the sympathy, not only of the spectators, but of the Jury, two of whom were her father's tenants and had known her since childhood.

There was an expectant hush as the Coroner rose to address the Jury. Fayre summed him up as a man of mediocre intelligence, slow, but conscientious, and perhaps a little over-conscious of the importance of his own position.

"Gentlemen of the Jury," he began. "You have heard the evidence put before you and are now called upon to consider your verdict. If there is anything that you have not fully understood I am here to help you. As to the manner in which the deceased met her death, you will have seen from the doctor's evidence how unlikely it is that she died by her own hand. You must not, however, entirely disregard the possibility of suicide. Unlikely as it may seem, it is not absolutely impossible that she herself fired the fatal shot. If, however, you decide that the deceased did not voluntarily cause her own death you must state whether she died at the hand of any person known to you or at the hand of some person unknown. I take it that you are ready to consider your verdict now, gentlemen."

The Jury filed out of the court and Fayre, after a word with Kean, crossed over to a chair by the side of Cynthia. He found her pale, but composed, talking quietly with Leslie. To his surprise they were discussing the farm and the steps to be taken should Leslie find himself unable to return there immediately, and his sympathy and admiration for these two increased as he realized the pluck with which they were facing an almost unbearable situation. Kean remained in his old place in the body of the court, deep in his own thoughts. He had little doubt as to what the verdict would be, in the face of the unexpected evidence brought forward by the police.

Indeed, the Jury was not absent for more than twenty minutes. Fayre watched them, trying to judge from their faces what line they would take. The Coroner addressed them.

"Well, gentlemen, have you considered your verdict?"

And even before the foreman spoke, Fayre knew what was coming.

They found that Mrs. Draycott had been murdered, and John Leslie left the court in the custody of the police.

CHAPTER VII

THE DRIVE BACK to Staveley was a silent one. Cynthia had been allowed to see Leslie for a few minutes before he was removed to the police station and had taken friendly and reassuring messages from both Kean and Fayre with her. She found him cheerful and, apparently, undismayed, but even her pluck had not been proof against the sordid atmosphere of the dingy little waiting-room and the menace of the two policemen who remained within earshot all through the interview, and she could no longer conceal her weariness and depression.

Miss Allen, who had waited at the entrance to the Town Hall, begged for a lift to Greycross, thereby earning the gratitude of the two men, who were in dread of collapse now that the strain was over. But Cynthia had not the smallest intention of breaking down; her whole mind was centred on Leslie and the necessity for instant action. What form this was to take she had no idea, but inactivity had always irked her and now, in the face of Leslie's danger, she found it almost unbearable. She sat huddled in a corner of the car, her mind working feverishly, barely hearing the low-voiced conversation of the two men and Miss Allen. With the wisdom of true sympathy they left her alone with her thoughts, knowing that even a chance word might undermine her control.

They dropped Miss Allen at Greycross. As the car started again, Fayre glanced at Cynthia.

"All right?" he asked kindly.

She nodded.

"Quite. Only thinking. There must be something we can do, Uncle Fayre!"

Kean roused himself from his abstraction.

"Want to get moving, eh?" he said in his incisive way. "I know how you feel, but it's no good trying to rush things. You did more for Leslie than you realized at the inquest to-day. I've seldom heard a more satisfactory witness. I congratulate you." Cynthia's eyes shone with pleasure. As he had intended, his praise supplied just the tonic she needed.

"I'll tell you exactly what I propose to do," he went on. "Then you won't feel that we are being idle. Directly I get back to town to-morrow I will see the man I have in mind for Leslie. He is a young solicitor I've had my eye on for some time. As keen as mustard and with his name to make. He'll do better for Leslie than one of the older fellows who've settled into their grooves long ago. He'll probably come down here at once and see Leslie. Then, later, he'll brief me and if we don't get your young man off between us, I shall be surprised. Your job is to stand by and keep a brave face on things. Let Leslie know that you believe in him and see that other people realize it too. You've got Miss Allen on your side and, from the look of it, a good portion of the people who were present to-day. That sort of thing helps more than you may realize. See any reporters who may approach you and talk to them. You've got nothing to hide, remember. You won't like it, of course, but keep in mind that the more confidence you manage to inspire, the better, and you can do that best by publicly advertising your own belief in Leslie. Make a point of the fact that he had no motive for the crime. In short, carry on on the lines you took at the inquest. The press can be an abominable nuisance, but, fortunately, it can be used too. I leave that part of the business in your hands. You've no idea how important it is."

Later, after they had handed the girl over to Lady Staveley and were sitting over the fire with Sybil Kean in the deserted billiard-room, Fayre went back to the subject.

"That was clever of you, Edward," he said. "And merciful. The inaction was driving the child frantic. Now you have given her something to do and made her feel that she has actually helped already."

Lady Kean's eyes stole to her husband's face. To her, his tact and consideration had always been unfailing, but it had never been his way to show much kindness to others and she had often been half amused, half exasperated, by the cold courtesy with which he had treated even her closest friends. She felt very grateful to him now for his gentleness to Cynthia.

"As a matter of fact," he said slowly, "it wasn't all eyewash. She can be quite useful and it will keep her out of mischief. She's got a head on her shoulders and plenty of grit. Leslie's a lucky man."

"I only hope his luck won't fail him now," put in his wife.

"Don't you worry, my dear," Kean assured her. "We'll pull him through, all right. You needn't lose any sleep over him!"

His hand was on hers and Fayre, after a glance at them, slipped out of the room and settled himself by the fire in his bedroom. For one thing, he wanted to think; for another, he possessed tact enough to leave these two to their own devices till the time came for Kean to catch the London train.

With a smile at his own childishness, he fell back on the time-honoured method of all detectives of fiction and set to work with a pencil and paper to get his thoughts in order.

According to Gregg, Mrs. Draycott had been shot some two hours before Leslie discovered her body in the sitting-room at the farm. Going on this assumption Fayre headed his paper:

"March 23rd. Between six and seven, Mrs. Draycott shot."

When he had finished, half an hour later, his notes ran as follows:

"John Leslie. According to his own account at six o'clock was walking across the fields in the direction of Besley. Motive: apparently none. Have only his own explanation of his movements and of the empty chamber in his revolver."

"Tramp seen by juryman outside Whitbury: May have no connection with the person whose footsteps were found by the police

outside the sitting-room window at Leslie's farm. Some one un-doubtedly slept in the barn on the day of the murder and this man was passing through Whitbury at four o'clock. This would get him to the farm before six. Motive: Robbery? May have been scared away by Leslie or the police."

"Cynthia Bell. Was at Galston Manor by six. Note: See lodge-keeper at Galston for corroboration. Motive: None, unless she and Leslie are keeping back Leslie's possible connection with Mrs. Draycott in the past. This is unlikely, as Mrs. Draycott herself stated that she had never met Leslie."

Fayre sat back in his chair and contemplated his handiwork. He did not seem to have got very far. Then he picked up his pencil again.

"May as well go through the lot of them," he muttered, out of patience with his own futility.

"Miss Allen. Was writing letters in her study at Grey cross at six o'clock. Motive: None, unless her disapproval of her sister's mode of life amounted to insanity. Does not impress one as a person likely to go to extremes. Note: Find out whether she benefits to any extent financially by her sister's death, also whether she was seen by any of the servants at Greycross round about six o'clock."

While he was in the act of writing the last entry Kean's words at the hotel recurred to his mind: "Why 'the man'?" Had he had Miss Allen in his thoughts then, Fayre wondered?

He sat over the fire for a long time, his thoughts busy with the problem of Miss Allen. He recalled her emphatic denial that her sister had ever had any dealings with John Leslie, her letter to Cynthia. Kean's suggestion that Mrs. Draycott might have died at the hand of a woman had come hot on his return from his visit to Miss Allen. Fayre wished with all his heart that he had been present at that interview. What had she told him?

As he dressed for dinner he was conscious of a growing resentment against Kean. The more he pondered on his manner at the hotel, the more he suspected that Kean had discovered something of importance at Miss Allen's, something, Fayre told himself with growing exasperation, that to-morrow he would pass on as a matter of course to Leslie's solicitor. He did not blame Kean. He knew him well enough by now to accept his methods, however annoying and inhuman they might seem; but there was a streak of obstinacy in

Fayre's nature which responded to just such treatment as he had received from his old friend and he felt more than ever determined to take a hand in the game. He had offered to meet Grey, the solicitor, at the station and Kean had not demurred. He made up his mind to get as much out of him as possible and then work on his own lines. He realized that these were disconcertingly vague, so far.

The events of the next morning, however, opened out a possible field of action. Crossing the hall, he ran into Dr. Gregg on his way to visit Lady Kean. The doctor's greeting was curt, but friendly.

"Have you heard that they've got our friend, the tramp, who was at the farm that night?" he said. "The police seem to have moved fairly quickly, for once."

"Have they got anything out of him?"

"I don't know. Except for old Gunnet, they're a close-mouthed lot. The fellow's safe enough, at all events. Literally tied by the leg in the infirmary at Whitbury. He was run down by a silly young ass on a motor bike and got his ankle badly smashed. I gather that he was up at the farm that night, meant to sleep there. Something seems to have frightened him off at the last minute. Probably the arrival of the police. If he does turn out to be the chap that did it, Leslie's troubles are over."

"Leslie's solicitor is coming to-day and I'm by way of meeting him. I suppose he will be allowed access to this man if he wants to see him?"

"I imagine so. Can I be of any use? I'm for Whitbury after this and can run you over in about half an hour's time."

Fayre accepted the invitation, glad of the chance to talk to the man, of all others, most likely to know the neighbourhood well. Gregg had not impressed him very favourably at the inquest and he did not take to him now. As a witness he had seemed almost surly; to-day, no doubt in an effort to be agreeable, he was garrulous and, at the same time, ill at ease. Fayre knew that he had the reputation of being a clever doctor, though something of a vulgarian.

Lord Staveley joined him as he was collecting his hat and coat in the hall and confirmed his impression of the man.

"Clever chap, Gregg," he said. "To tell you the truth, I'm not sorry to have, him on hand when Sybil's here. It's always a bit of a responsibility and I sometimes think Kean would murder us if anything happened to her. Amazing, the way the fellow's wrapped up in her. Never would have thought he was that sort. My wife's about the one person he'll trust to look after her. Thank goodness, Gregg's dependable."

"A queer fellow," commented Fayre thoughtfully. "A bit of a rough diamond, isn't he?"

Lord Staveley laughed.

"Very much so. Didn't get on with the old women round here at all at first. However, the old chap at Whitbury is such a dud that they had to come round. Now they swear by him. He's a self-made man. Son of a vet up in the North, so they say."

As he spoke, Gregg appeared at the top of the staircase and he and Fayre were soon on their way to the Junction.

"A bad business, this of Leslie's, if they find they haven't got their man, after all," said Gregg in his abrupt way. "I met Lady Cynthia on the stairs and she looked pretty hipped. It isn't doing my patient any good, either."

"You're not anxious about her?" put in Fayre quickly.

"She's no worse, if that's what you mean, but she can't stand worry. I should be better pleased if she was out of all this. If I had my way she'd be in her bed in London now."

"What do you think of Leslie's chances?"

"Bad. You and I know he isn't the sort to do a thing like that, but the evidence is strong against him. Depends what sort of old women they get on the Jury, if it comes to that. I hope it won't, now they've got this tramp."

"There's the lack of motive. Personally, I don't believe he ever saw Mrs. Draycott in his life until that night. You were there, weren't you? How did he impress you?"

"He was speaking the truth, all right. He behaved just as you or I would have done under the circumstances. It's a nasty jar to find the body of a strange lady in your sitting-room. On the whole, he took it very well."

"I wish they could find some clue as to why Mrs. Draycott ever went to the farm. I believe the secret of the whole wretched business lies there."

"It's a mystery. Though, from what I've heard of the lady, that's not the queerest of the many queer things she seems to have been up to," said Gregg dryly.

"There's been gossip already, has there? Bound to be, I suppose. Still, they might have let the poor creature rest in peace."

"If you lived in this neighbourhood you'd know that that was the last thing they'd be likely to do. If what they're saying is true, she was no loss."

Fayre was struck by the bitterness of his tone.

"You never met her, did you?" he asked.

"I must have paid a couple of calls at Staveley while she was there, but I did not run across her. From all accounts, though, she was a pretty average rotter."

Gregg's tone was brutal and Fayre felt his instinctive dislike for the man increase.

"I've come across that type once or twice in the course of my life and I don't blame the man that killed her," Gregg went on. "She probably richly deserved it."

"Well, the poor woman's dead and, unfortunately, her secret, whatever it was, has died with her," answered Fayre, in a voice calculated to put an end to the discussion.

But Gregg was not so easily quenched.

"Very pretty sentiment," he allowed, with something very like a sneer. "But it's neither just nor logical. It's a hard fact that the evil people do lives after them and I don't believe in the whitewashing process myself. The world's the better for her removal, so why not say so?"

"That's a strong thing to say of a woman who, at the worst, was only heartless and calculating, and, considering that I only knew her slightly and you not at all, it seems a good deal to assume," Fayre reminded him. He was interested, in spite of himself, in the viewpoint of a man who could work himself up to such a pitch of resentment against a woman who, after all, was a stranger to him. His first instinct had been to drop the subject, but now he found himself trying to draw out the doctor.

"In my experience, it's the stupid, greedy people who do the real harm in this world, not the wicked ones. The bad man works with an object and, once that's gained, is usually content to let his neighbour alone. The stupid man blunders on in his imbecile way, leaving a trail of mischief behind him."

"You would put down Mrs. Draycott as a stupid woman?"

Fayre had been struck himself by the dense strata of obtuseness that lay beneath Mrs. Draycott's surface acuteness and he was surprised at the accuracy with which Gregg seemed to have diagnosed her.

"From what I hear, she was of the blunt-fingered, blunt-minded type and a born petty schemer. However, I may be wrong. I'm going by hearsay, you know."

"It's curious how people get hold of their information," said Fayre thoughtfully. "I don't suppose more than half a dozen people in this neighbourhood had ever met her."

"They read their papers, though, and she's been before the public more than once, you must remember. Also, the mere fact that she was Miss Allen's sister would be enough to draw attention to her. After all, there was the Dare Case."

"She was mixed up in that, was she? I've been out of England for so long that I've missed things."

"She was called as a witness and came out of it pretty badly, as far as I can remember. I don't read those things much myself."

"All the same, you seem to have got your knife into her pretty thoroughly," remarked Fayre dryly.

The doctor sat silent for a moment.

"I'm afraid I rather let myself go on the subject of stupidity," he said at last. "It's a thing we doctors are always up against and we get to hate it. I was probably doing Mrs. Draycott a gross injustice."

He seemed to realize that he had said too much, for, in spite of Fayre's attempts to get out of him the exact form the gossip had taken, he kept resolutely off the subject during the rest of the drive to the station.

The London train was late and as Fayre sat waiting on the platform he read over the notes he had made the night before. After some thought, he added a memorandum on Dr. Gregg.

"Seems curiously well-informed as to Mrs. Draycott's past and general characteristics and is almost vindictive in his attitude towards her. Did not reach the scene of the murder till ten o'clock. Up till then, movements unknown, but was probably with patients. If

possible, find out from Leslie whether he noticed anything unusual in his manner at the farm."

Grey, the solicitor, turned out to be an even younger man than Fayre had expected, but he was, as Kean had predicted, very much on the spot and not only ready, but anxious, to discuss the case. His first object was to see Leslie, and he arranged to go straight to the police station and meet Fayre at the hotel on his return. Fayre told him of the arrest of the tramp, and Grey undertook to procure a permit to visit the infirmary. He did not imagine that any objection would be raised to Fayre's presence at the interview with the patient.

They parted in High Street and, as luck would have it, Fayre almost immediately ran into Gunnet, the constable from Keys. Fayre was known to him, both as a friend of Lady Cynthia's and as a guest at Staveley, and, being off duty, he saw no objection to stepping into the hotel and accepting the offer of a glass of beer. He had little of interest to relate. Two things he did say which had some bearing on Fayre's notes of the evening before.

"I stepped up to Galston yesterday," he remarked, "and had a few words with Doggett, the lodge-keeper there. He informed me that he let the young lady in at the gates shortly before five-thirty and she did not go out again till she passed through in the motor on her way to Miss Allen's."

"That tallies with what she and Mr. Leslie said at the inquest."

"It does. Come to that, beggin' your pardon, sir, I've known her ladyship since she was so high and she wasn't never one to tell a crooked story. I'd take her word anywhere, and so would any one in Keys. What I did, I had to do, in the way of duty, if you understand me."

Fayre nodded.

"Anything settled about the funeral?" he asked.

"The body's to be moved to Hampshire, I understand. The family grave is there and Miss Allen wished it. Very trying for Miss Allen, the whole thing, though they do say she's come into a bit of money as next of kin, seeing as the deceased left no will."

Gunnet departed, leaving Fayre with further food for reflection. He was very thoughtful as he strolled through the little town, whiling away the time until Grey should return from his visit to Leslie. By the time the solicitor joined him, armed with the permit, he had decided that, reluctant as he felt to do so, he would have to place Miss Allen in his category of suspected persons.

They found the tramp, a small, grey, shrunken individual, neatly tucked up in the accident ward of the infirmary with a cradle over his injured leg. As a potential murderer Fayre found him disappointing. He had already gathered from Gunnet that the police were inclined to accept his statement that he was not at the farm at the time the crime was committed. At the same time he seemed unable to produce a satisfactory alibi. One thing was obvious, the man was scared, though he tried to hide it under an assumption of indifference.

Grey questioned him closely as to his movements on the night of the twenty-third. He admitted that he had intended to sleep at the farm and described how he had looked through the window into the sitting-room and been frightened away by what he had seen there. He corroborated the statement of the juryman that he had left Whitbury about four in the afternoon, arriving at the corner of the lane leading to the farm at about five-thirty. According to his statement he then rested for about an hour on the grass by the roadside, not wishing to try the farm while any one was likely to be about in the yard. He had then retraced his steps down the highroad, intending to try his luck at the Lodge at Galston in the hope of begging some food. Here, however, he was frightened away by the barking of a dog and returned to the lane, this time going up to the farm. Finding no one about, he made his way to the barn and crept into the loft, meaning to stay the night there. He remained in the barn till about eight, when he was driven out by hunger. Then it was that he made the discovery that resulted in his abrupt departure from the neighbourhood of the farm.

"It wasn't likely I should stay there, after what I'd seen, now was it?" he demanded indignantly.

"You might have informed the police," suggested Grey.

"The police! Not me! Let them find out for themselves. It's what they're paid for!"

"Then from five-thirty to six-thirty, according to your account, you were lying in the grass at the corner of the lane," said Grey, consulting his notes.

"As true as I lie 'ere. I never went near the place till I went up to the loft at seven or thereabouts."

"No one saw you? You didn't beg from any one while you were at the corner of the lane and the highroad?"

"Not a soul come near me save a car or two. Not a soul that'd speak for me. I ain't got no luck, I 'aven't. Never 'ad!" The little man's voice was bitter.

Fayre bent over him, struck by a sudden idea.

"Nothing turned up the lane to the farm while you were lying there, did it?" he asked.

A gleam of suspicion crept into the tramp's furtive eyes. He distrusted everybody on principle, especially people who asked abrupt questions, but he had not the courage or the intelligence to lie.

"There was one car," he admitted cautiously. "They wouldn't 'ave seen me, though. It was dark and I was out of range of the lights."

Grey took up the interrogation eagerly, speaking softly so that his words should not reach the ears of the policeman sitting in the chair by the window.

"Can you remember what the car was like? Was it too dark to see who was in it?"

The little man looked at him with weary scorn. He was tired of being on the defensive and wanted, above all things, to be left alone.

"Pitch-dark, it was, nearly. I couldn't 'ave recognized the Prince of Wales in all 'is feathers."

"You've no idea of the colour of the car, or how many people were in it?" persisted Grey.

"You can't see no colours in the dark. There was two people in it, though, unless one was the shofer. It come close to me, takin' the turn, and I see the two heads. I did think one was a woman, but I don't know why. It was pretty dark."

"It went up to the farm, you say?"

"I don't know where it went. How should I? It went up the lane, like I told you."

"What time was this?"

"Just before I went along the road to the Lodge. About an hour after I lay down at the corner."

"You are sure of the time, more or less?"

The tramp groaned.

"I don't carry no watch, mister. Anyway, they couldn't 'ave seen me, so it don't prove nothing, either way."

Fayre hitched up his chair nearer to the bed, his friendly gaze on the man's face.

"I've been on trek myself without a watch," he said cheerily, "and had to go by the skies. It's a gift in itself and I'll wager you're as good a hand as any at calculating time. What time would you put it at, now?"

The man observed him shrewdly for a moment. Then:

"Seein' as you're the first as 'as spoke to me friendlylike since I've been 'ere I'll tell you as near as may be. Gettin' on for half-past six, I should say it was."

"And more likely right than a dozen watches. Can you remember if it was a big car?"

The tramp nodded.

"Goin' a lick of a pace, too. And what's more, I see it again, goin' back. And it was fair scorchin' then."

"Where was that?"

"On the road, just as I was comin' away from that there Lodge."

"Much later?"

"Twenty minutes or perhaps twenty-five, I'd put it."

Fayre's little bit of flattery had done its work and the man was now anxious to show off his ability to reckon time.

"It was going fast, you say?"

"Dangerous fast, I should call it. If I'd been a bit nearer the corner it'd 'ave caught me. As it was, it come near to smashin' up a farm-cart that was goin' peaceable and quiet down the main road. The carter didn't 'alf 'ave something to say about it and I don't blame 'im."

"Too dark to see the farm-cart, I suppose? You wouldn't know the carter?"

"Wouldn't reckernize 'im, though 'e passed me close a minute or two later. The cart 'ad a white 'orse, though. I see that in the light of the lamps. And I see the man in the car, too, when the light 'it 'im. He was alone then."

"You couldn't identify him?" asked Fayre quickly.

But the man shook his head.

"I only see 'im for a second," he said.

Fayre rose to his feet.

"We'll look up that carter," he said decisively. "After all, he may have seen *you* in the light of the lamps. If he did, you've got your alibi. Good-by and good luck. I hope your leg's mending."

For the first time the man's gloom lifted. Fayre's friendliness was, as usual, infectious and the tramp looked after him with something of the wistfulness of a stray dog.

"Good luck to *you*, mister," he croaked in his hoarse voice.

Back at the hotel Grey went carefully through his notes.

"Not a bad morning's work, on the whole," he said. "I shouldn't wonder if that car brought Mrs. Draycott."

Fayre nodded thoughtfully.

"It looks like it. She was in thin evening slippers when they found her and it struck me at the inquest that she could never have walked that distance in them. And it went back without her and that poor little beggar at the infirmary never grasped the importance of what he'd seen. I wonder if the police got as much out of him as we did!"

Grey laughed.

"I'm willing to bet they didn't. He's a suspicious customer and wouldn't say more than he was obliged and he obviously didn't think it worth the telling. What about tackling the carter? It shouldn't take long to run him to earth, given the white horse and the collision."

Fayre thought of Kean and the snubbing he had received at his hands and hugged himself. Now, at last, he had a definite plan of action.

"I'll tackle the carter," he said gleefully, "and let you know how I get on."

CHAPTER VIII

FAYRE AND GREY lunched at the station hotel, where the solicitor had booked a room for the night. From Fayre's point of view, the meal was more than satisfactory. Grey showed a keenness that was after his own heart and proved not only ready to impart information, but anxious to hear anything his companion might have to tell him that had any bearing on the case. He suggested that Fayre should make a note of any questions he wished put to Leslie and leave it in his hands. They agreed to meet at lunch on the following day and report progress.

Fayre's first act on parting with Grey was to hire a bicycle. It was a ramshackle affair with dubious tires, but it was the best the Whitbury dealer could provide, and at least it made Fayre independent of the Staveley motor. Lord Staveley had put his garage at his guest's disposal and had begged him to consider himself free to come and go as he pleased, but Fayre hesitated to take too great an advantage of his kindness. With the help of the bicycle he could pursue his investigations in peace, unhampered by the thought of a waiting chauffeur.

Mounted on the hireling, he set out for Keys, the first stage on his quest for the carter. It did not take him long to locate the village smithy, and the two men at work there looked with considerable curiosity at "the gentleman from Staveley" as he toiled past their door on an obviously inferior push-bike. A little farther on, on the opposite side of the road, was a small ironmonger's shop. Here he dismounted, propped the bicycle against the curb, and went in. A dusty-looking old man emerged from behind the counter and Fayre proffered his request. It appeared that the old man might or might not have a pair of trouser-clips. He would see, but it was a long time since he had been asked for any. While he was rummaging in a drawer, Fayre strolled to the window. From it there was, as he hoped, an excellent view of the smithy.

The trouser-clips materialized and Fayre explained that he had taken up cycling again after a lapse of years for the sake of exercise, and added the comment that he found the roads very different from what they had been when he was last in England.

"I reckon you got to have your wits about you nowadays, sure enough," agreed the shopkeeper. "I mind the day when a man might walk five mile round here and see nothing but a horse and cart, and a child could play in the lanes and its mother not give it a thought. It's a different story now."

"I suppose you get a lot of motors through here?"

"A goodish few. They got one of the red signs at the bend there, but it's little notice most of them takes of it."

"I saw a narrow shave the other day on the other side of the village," remarked Fayre conversationally. "A big car, coming round the corner too quickly, as nearly as anything ran down a farm-cart. I wonder the carter didn't summons him."

"Went off too quick, I reckon. That's their way. Main difficult to catch, they are."

"They were going too fast for me to see the number. I should know the cart, though. You don't often see a white horse, nowadays."

The old man's face lit up with the proverbial curiosity of the villager.

"That'll be George Sturrock's cart, I'm thinking. There's not a many white horses round about here, as you say. Or it might be Mr. Giles, the farmer over to Grantley. 'E got a white mare. In a fine way, 'e'd be, if anything 'appened to 'er."

"I expect you know most of the horses round here," observed Fayre. "Living where you do."

The old man chuckled.

"Always one for 'orses, I was. They've mostly got their allotted days for coming down to the farriers yonder. You wouldn't believe 'ow I notice if one of 'em misses. Them two white ones, I see 'em regular, the mare on a Monday and the 'orse Saturday."

"You'll see one of them to-morrow, then," said Fayre pleasantly.

"Saturday morning, regular as clockwork, 'e come. George 'as only got the one carter and 'e brings the old 'orse down afore 'e goes to 'is dinner."

Fayre paid for the clips and strolled out of the shop, well satisfied with his opening move. The storm of chaff that greeted him as, flushed and breathless, he peddled up the drive to Staveley nearly an hour later failed to disturb his equanimity. He said he needed exercise and, as Lord Staveley sapiently remarked, he seemed to be getting it.

Certainly he was markedly stiff the next morning and it required a certain amount of determination to unearth his steed once more from the garage and climb painfully into the saddle. He was rewarded, however, for March was going out gently indeed and the air was soft as spring. As he coasted quietly down the long slope to Keys he found himself wondering, for the hundredth time, at the beauty of England and regretting the long years he had wasted in the tropics.

He dismounted at the end of the road that led to the smithy and wheeled his bicycle slowly to the door. Here he paused and stood watching the smiths at work, one of a group of interested idlers. Out of the corner of his eye he kept a good lookout for the white horse.

He had been there about ten minutes when it came round the corner, led by a lanky, brown-faced farm labourer. Fayre noted with satisfaction that he did not belong to the heavy, bovine type so prevalent farther south. Here was a true North-countryman with the shrewd grey eyes and long upper lip of his kind.

Fayre moved aside to let him pass.

"I've seen you before, old fellow," he remarked pleasantly, addressing the horse.

The carter turned and summed him up silently.

"It was a bit dark and I didn't get a good look at him," Fayre went on, speaking to the carter directly this time. "But he's uncommonly like the horse I saw on the Whitbury road about a week ago. If he was, he's lucky to be here now, that's all I can say. There's one motorist near here that ought not to be allowed on the road."

The carter flushed a deep red under his tan.

"It wasn't no one round here or I'd 'a' let him hear of it. It was some damned stranger. I know the cars round here well enough. Ought to be hung, comin' round the corner like that, he ought!"

Fayre nodded.

"Lucky for me I hadn't reached the bend," he said. "I was walking carelessly and he'd probably have got me. You didn't take his number, I suppose? A fellow like that deserves to be hauled up."

"I got a bit of it," the man answered grimly, "but he was off too fast for me to catch the rest. *Y.0.7.* I did see, but I missed the rest of the number. Likely enough one of them chaps from Carlisle."

"Did he get you badly? I was too far off to see properly in the dark, but it seemed to me that he caught you a bit of a smack."

"It wasn't his fault that he didn't get us proper. Took a great splinter off the tailboard. I'll wager his mud-guard's caught it."

"That will give you something to go by if you see him again. Especially if he took a bit of your paint with him."

"Aye. He'll have a touch of red on him, all right. But I don't suppose I'll ever see him again. Likely he took the wrong turn up the lane and had to come back and was makin' up for lost time like. That's the way I figure it out."

"No doubt. If I see him about anywhere, I'll pass the word to you. He was driving himself, wasn't he? Or was there a chauffeur?"

"No, he was alone in the car. Joe Woodley, up to Mr. Sturrock's, will find me and I'd be glad to hear of him. He didn't do no damage, not to speak of, but that wasn't his fault and I'd like to have my say with him. On my right side, I was, and he can't question it."

The man moved forward into the smithy with the horse and Fayre retrieved his bicycle and pursued his way to Whitbury. He had not dared hope for so satisfactory an end to his investigations and was anxious to see Grey and make his report. That the carter should have noted even part of the number was an unlooked-for piece of good luck. That and an injured mud-guard, probably with a smear of red paint on it, was all they had to go on, but it was something, at least. If only Miss Allen had been more intimate with her sister's friends! Fayre felt that to apply to her would be worse than useless, but, on the impulse of the moment, he left the main road and swung round the bend that led to Greycross. Once more his luck held, for, almost within sight of the drive, he passed her, trudging sturdily along the road, evidently on her way home to lunch.

He jumped off his bicycle and waited till she overlook him.

"I'm afraid you won't remember me, Miss Allen," he said. "But we drove home from Whitbury together the other day."

For a moment she looked puzzled, then her face relaxed in a pleasant smile.

"Of course," she exclaimed. "You were with Lady Cynthia and Sir Edward Kean."

"I'm an old friend of hers, though I hadn't seen her for years till the other day. I could wish we hadn't renewed our acquaintance under such sad circumstances."

"Poor child, I'm afraid she's in for a bad time. I wish it was over, for all our sakes."

"It is as hard on you as on her," said Fayre sympathetically. "If you will forgive my saying so, it was very kind of you to write to her as you did."

"It was the least I could do. I was as convinced then, as I am now, that John Leslie had nothing to do with it and I felt it was my duty to say so."

"I wonder if I may ask you a question? Believe me, it is not from idle curiosity."

She looked both surprised and interested. "Certainly," she said. "But if it is about my sister, I am afraid I told Sir Edward all I knew when he came to see me the other day."

"Can you think of any one among your sister's friends who drives a large car with a touring body and who was likely to have been in this part of the world on the night of the tragedy?"

She shook her head.

"The trouble is that I knew so few of my sister's friends. I rarely go up to town and she lived almost entirely in London, except when she was abroad or visiting friends in the country. She had a very large circle of acquaintances, but they were not people I should be likely to meet down here. Why do you ask?"

She had hardly uttered the question when her own quick wits supplied the answer.

"Oh!" she exclaimed, her voice sharp with interest, "You think she was driven to the farm! I have known all along that she could never have walked there."

"You mean on account of her shoes?"

"Of course. I was surprised that no one at the inquest made any comment on it. I couldn't have walked that distance myself in thin evening slippers, and I am a good walker. My sister was a very bad one; she hated it. I have said from the beginning that I was sure she had no intention when she started of going to the farm. But, of course, if she expected to be driven there ..."

"You are sure she never mentioned any friend with a car whom she expected to meet in this neighbourhood?" persisted Fayre.

"Absolutely certain," was the decisive answer. "As a matter of fact, she hardly mentioned any of her own friends to me. We had not met for a long time and most of our talk was about various relations and acquaintances who belonged to the past. What had happened to them, and that sort of thing. You know how one goes over ancient history at those times. Besides, she knew I took very little interest in the people among whom she moved latterly. I wish now I had taken more!"

"Did anybody see her leave the house?"

"One of the maids saw her, through the scullery window, going down the drive. That was how I first knew she had gone out."

"When was this, Miss Allen?"

"About six, I gather, but the girl was a little vague about the exact time when I questioned her."

"And when did you first hear of it?"

"About half-past six. I went back to the drawing-room when I had finished my letters and did not find her there. The maid came in to make up the fire and I asked her if she had seen her. I was astonished to hear that she had gone out."

Fayre held out his hand.

"It is more than good of you to have been so frank with me," he said gratefully. "You have cleared up one or two points that were puzzling me. I am ashamed of myself for worrying you about such a painful subject. My only excuse is that I am lunching with Leslie's solicitor and all is grist that comes to his mill just now."

"I am only too glad to be of help. You must remember that I, too, have my reasons for wishing to see this matter cleared up. Give my love to Cynthia when you see her."

Fayre rode on to Whitbury with one load, at least, off his mind. Miss Allen, quite unconsciously, had cleared herself definitely of suspicion. Just about the time Mrs. Draycott must have reached the farm her sister was questioning the servant concerning her. With a sigh of relief he wiped Miss Allen off his list of suspects.

He found Grey hungrily awaiting his lunch. While they were eating Fayre gave him a brief account of his morning's work.

"We haven't done so badly," he finished. "We have corroborated the tramp's story of the car and, what is more, got at least part of the number. We know that the mud-guard was injured and is probably marked with red paint. We have established the fact that there was only one person, a man, in it when it returned and I see no reason to doubt the tramp's assertion that there were two people in it going. It looks very much as if one of those people was Mrs. Draycott. Anyhow, it is odd that the tramp should have had the impression that one was a woman. He made the suggestion on his own, without any prompting from us. Best of all, we have established the fact that Mrs. Draycott could not, according to the maid at Miss Allen's, have been shot before six-thirty. The doctor has put it down as not later than seven. That fits in, more or less, with the arrival and departure of the mysterious car."

Grey nodded.

"It's straightening itself out a little," he agreed. "But the car is a tough proposition! That number, by the way, is a London one, as you probably know, which widens our field considerably."

"Miss Allen, also, is convinced that her sister never walked to the farm."

"I know. I gather that she emphasized that point in her interview with Sir Edward. I have seen Leslie, by the way, and I put your questions to him. His description of the scene at the farm after the arrival of Gregg was very circumstantial. He told me one thing that rather struck me."

"Anything that bears on our friend the doctor?"

"Yes. It's small, but interesting. Fortunately for us, Leslie has got what is known as an oral memory. That is to say, he remembers things he has heard more easily than things he has read. With most people it is the other way round. He told me that, at school, he always had to say a thing out loud before he could learn it. The result is that he was able to repeat to me, almost word for word, everything that was said in his presence that night. Of course, the peculiar circumstances helped to impress it all on his memory. He shares your opinion of Gregg. Thinks him a tough customer and inclined to be brutal, at any rate in speech. This being the case, he was surprised at the emotion Gregg showed at the sight of Mrs. Draycott's body. He says it was slight, but quite apparent, and would have been perfectly natural in a layman. In Gregg, it struck him as curious. There was something curious, also, in the wording of Gregg's answer to the Sergeant when he asked him if he had ever seen the deceased. Leslie says he thought nothing of it at the time, but it remained in his memory and he is certain that he has it correct."

"I thought Gregg denied ever having met her."

"His exact words were that she was no friend of his. The Sergeant, very naturally, accepted it as a denial."

CHAPTER IX

WHEN FAYRE GOT BACK to Staveley he found a tea-party in full swing and spent the rest of the afternoon trying to escape from various formidable old ladies, who picked his brains as tactfully as might be as to the way Leslie's affairs were shaping; how Cynthia was taking the whole affair and whether Sir Edward Kean was likely to be briefed for the defence. He put them off as best he could with noncommittal answers and felt thankful, for Cynthia's sake, that she had decided earlier in the day to drive over to Galston and spend the afternoon at home.

Lady Staveley, realizing that the girl was dreading her mother's comments on the situation, had been over the day before and persuaded Lady Galston to let her keep Cynthia with her for the present. Fortunately, that lady had not realized that Staveley was a stronghold of the enemy and that Cynthia's loyalty to the man she had promised to marry would meet with nothing but encouragement there and was only too glad to feel, as she artlessly put it, that Cynthia would be out of mischief for a day or two.

The Staveleys had decided to wipe off two irksome duties in one day and Fayre found himself let in for a big dinner-party of county worthies. He was still stiff and tired from his unwonted exertions and was heartily glad when the evening was over. He managed, however, to glean a few facts about Gregg's past from people who,- on the arrival of the "new doctor," had made it their business to find out all about him and who responded only too readily to his adroit questions. He also discovered that the local vicar's wife had known the Allens in Hampshire in years gone by and had followed Mrs. Draycott's career from the beginning with considerable interest. In her capacity as vicar's wife she could not approve of her, but Fayre detected a touch of envy in her voice as she recounted some of the episodes in the dead woman's chequered past. According to her, Mrs. Draycott had managed to "have a good time," as she expressed it, from the moment she left the schoolroom and, at one time, in spite of her divorce from her first husband, had moved in a smart, but quite reputable, set in London. Of late years, however, she had undoubtedly gone down in the social scale. The Dare Divorce Suit had done her reputation irretrievable damage and she spent most of her time abroad when she was not staying with people who, for old times' sake or because they were less squeamish than the rest, were still willing to ask her to their houses. Lady Staveley's invitation, he gathered, had been the result of a large charity entertainment in which they had both been involved and in connection with which Mrs. Draycott had made herself very useful. Unfortunately, when it came to her associates in the last few years, the vicar's wife proved a broken reed. She knew as little as Miss Allen of the set in which Mrs. Draycott had been moving when she died.

Gregg's record, allowing for certain embroideries at the hands of the local gossips, proved slightly more enlightening. He had arrived in the neighbourhood about three years before, having come straight from a large, but very poor, practise in London. His predecessor, from whom he had bought his present practise, was retiring, after a long and popular career, and, having weathered a short period of unpopularity due to his brusque manner, Gregg stepped into his shoes as a matter of course. Of his skill there was no question, and, according to Fayre's informants, he hid a kind heart under a rough exterior. He was unmarried and lived alone, his women-folk being a cook-housekeeper and a maid. He kept one car, which was looked after by the cook's husband, who combined the duties of chauffeur and gardener. He had the reputation of being a good bridge player, but cared little for society and was not often to be seen at the local entertainments.

On one point Fayre's informants were unanimous: that never, at any time, could he have been a lady's man, and the general opinion was that he had once suffered at the hands of a woman. Certainly, his opinion of the sex was unflatteringly small and he made no secret of his views. Fayre began to modify the conclusions he had drawn from Gregg's antagonistic attitude towards Mrs. Draycott; in the light of what he had just heard, it seemed a fairly natural one.

Cynthia returned just as the party was dispersing and slipped up to her room, so that he had no opportunity of speaking to her that evening. He sent a message by Lady Staveley to the effect that Grey had seen Leslie that morning and that he had found him well and cheerful, and then went to bed himself, feeling more tired than he had been for many a long day.

The fine weather held and the next morning he basely turned a deaf ear to the bells of the little church at Keys and, having seen the Staveleys off to the pursuance of their Sunday duties, went in search of his fellow-truants, Lady Kean and Cynthia. He found them, wrapped in furs, in a sunny corner of the terrace.

Cynthia greeted him eagerly.

"I very nearly came to your room and heaved you out of bed, Uncle Fayre, last night," she exclaimed. "I did so want to know what you'd been up to. Only Eve said you were too tired. She declared you'd been bicycling!"

Fayre laughed outright at the horror of her tone.

"Why not?" he retorted. "When I left England all the best people bicycled and it seemed to me as good a way to get exercise as any. It never occurred to me that it would make such a sensation. Even the villagers look at me as if I'd suddenly gone mad!"

"You probably have," said Cynthia severely. "If you've really started careering about the country on a push-bike."

"Anyhow, I careered to some purpose. For one thing, Grey and I have pretty well established the fact that Mrs. Draycott was taken to the farm by some one in a car and that person was actually seen leaving, alone, after the murder."

He had made his point as effectively as a good actor, and his audience responded to the full. Even Sybil Kean's habitual languor deserted her and she leaned forward in her chair, her fine eyes alight with interest.

"Am I on in this scene?" she asked almost eagerly. "Or must I do the correct and tactful thing and drift away down the terrace as if I hadn't heard a word of what you've just said? I expect you do want to talk to Cynthia alone."

Cynthia turned on her indignantly.

"We want you, don't we, Uncle Fayre?"

"Of course. I was counting on your advice. For one thing, you must have a closer acquaintance with the person I want to discuss, than any one else in this house."

For a moment she looked puzzled. Then:

"Dr. Gregg?" she said quietly.

"How did you know? There are times when you're uncanny, Sybil."

"There's nothing uncanny about this. I'll tell you later, but get on with your story first. It's brutal to keep us in suspense."

"Begin at the very beginning, Uncle Fayre. And, please, what did Mr. Grey say, exactly, about John? Was he really cheerful and is he desperately uncomfortable?"

Fayre told her all he had been able to gather from Grey.

"He's going to try to get you an interview again next week. It's a bit of a strain for you, my dear, I'm afraid, but it means a lot to Leslie."

Cynthia's almost boyish youth seemed to fall from her like a garment and Fayre, watching her, had a sudden vision of what a charming woman she would make in the days to come.

Sybil Kean looked meaningly across at him.

"Get on with your story, Hatter," she said gently, and he knew that she did not want the girl's emotions played on at this juncture.

He told them in as few words as possible of the tramp's disclosures and his own subsequent investigations.

"The probability is," he finished, "that Mrs. Draycott was picked up at the bottom of the lane leading to Greycross—whether by appointment or not we do not know—and driven to the farm. Why she was taken to the farm is a mystery, unless it was part of a deliberate attempt to cast suspicion on Leslie. It certainly looks as if there was an appointment and she left Greycross to keep it. She was hardly the kind of woman to go for a stroll on a cold, windy night in such unsuitable clothing."

"It was a queer kind of appointment if she did not tell her sister about it," said Sybil Kean thoughtfully.

"It may have been with one of the many friends of whom she knew her sister would disapprove. In fact, that's pretty obvious, or she'd have asked him to the house instead of slipping out to meet him."

"I suppose Miss Allen can't suggest anybody?" put in Cynthia.

"Useless. I've asked her. She did her best—and sent a lot of messages to you, by the way, Cynthia—but she says she knows very little of her sister's friends. I gather they weren't a very reputable lot."

"Somebody else may have seen the car," suggested Cynthia.

"There's always a bare chance," agreed Fayre. "If our luck holds we may come across some one. You mustn't forget that the tramp's not out of the reckoning yet. He admits to being in the immediate neighbourhood of the farm at the time the crime was committed and we've no proof that he wasn't actually present."

"What he said fitted in very well with the carter's story, though."

"It did, but that doesn't alter the fact that he might have been actually *at* the farm when he saw the car the first time. We've only his word for it that he was at the corner of the lane. Personally, I don't think he's got brains enough to invent such an ingenious defence or enough pluck to commit a murder; but one never knows. A timid man sometimes kills in a moment of panic, from sheer fright at being discovered. We can't afford to rule him out yet. Mrs. Draycott may have gone to the farm on her own account and been surprised there by the tramp; and he, in his turn, may have been surprised by the arrival of the man in the car and have killed her to stop her mouth."

"But there were two people in the car, going, and only one coming back."

"Remember, that's according to the tramp himself. He's the only person who saw the car the first time."

"Then we get back to the original problem," said Sybil Kean. "Why did Mrs. Draycott go to the farm at all?"

Fayre nodded.

"That's the real snag," he agreed. "Still, I can't help thinking that it all points to an appointment, probably with the driver of the car. Given that the tramp killed her, the man with the car may have kept his appointment, found her dead and cleared off, hence his haste."

"And where does Dr. Gregg come into all this?" asked Sybil Kean.

"On very flimsy grounds at present, I'm glad to say, for the sake of your peace of mind! I can imagine it would be a little disquieting to find you'd got a murderer as your medical attendant!"

Sybil Kean smiled lazily.

"Poor Dr. Gregg! He is rather a bear, on the surface, but you'd be surprised how gentle he can be. You've got to be ill to see the best side of him. He's not cold-blooded enough for a murderer."

Fayre looked at her in surprise.

"Then what made you pitch on him as the person in whom I was interested? You said there was a reason."

"A very vague one. And I may be absolutely mistaken. It was more an impression I had."

"Let's have it, anyway; then I'll tell you what's been worrying me. We may make something of it between us."

"It was really Mrs. Draycott. As soon as she heard his name she did nothing but ask questions about him. When he came here; where he came from; what was he like, and that sort of thing. I may have been wrong, but I had a distinct impression that she had met him before."

"Why didn't she see for herself? She had plenty of opportunities. He came two or three times while she was staying here, didn't he?"

"That was the funny thing. I don't believe she wanted to meet him. As a matter of fact, I chaffed her about her curiosity and suggested she should stroll casually into my room and have a look at him. She laughed and seemed quite ready to fall in with the idea, but she never came."

"Did you ever tackle him on the subject?"

"Yes. On one occasion, I asked him point-blank if he had ever met her. He laughed and said that, unless she had ever been addicted to slumming, she was the last person he was likely to meet. All the same, I had an odd conviction that they had come across each other at some time or other and that neither was anxious to renew the acquaintance. Of course, I've nothing to go on but my own very vague impressions. That and the fact that I see more of him than most of the people here made me suspect that you had him in your mind."

"It's funny how it fits in with what I was going to tell you. My suspicions were roused in very much the same way. When he drove me to the station to meet Grey we discussed Mrs. Draycott and he seemed quite extraordinarily bitter against her, considering they had never met. Also, he struck me as knowing a good deal about her, nothing that gossip and newspaper reports would not account for, but enough to show that he had followed her career with considerable interest. Unfortunately I said something that put him on his guard and he shut up like a clam. Mine, like yours, was only a vague impression, but, oddly enough, Leslie seems to have been struck by the same idea. It's only fair to say, though, that Leslie may have been influenced by certain leading questions Grey put to him at my request."

"What roused John's suspicions?" asked Cynthia.

"Gregg's manner when he was called to view the body. Also, according to him, Gregg did not actually deny having met Mrs. Draycott when he was questioned by the police. He said, apparently, that she was 'no friend of his' and the police naturally took it to mean that he did not know her. It may have been merely his way of putting it. We've none of us really got anything to go on."

"Also, if he's got anything to hide, he's giving himself away rather stupidly, isn't he?" suggested Sybil Kean.

"He's apparently being criminally careless and he's not a stupid man. I admit to being puzzled by him, he's such a queer mixture of bluntness and reserve."

"And so you want me to do a little Sherlock Holmes work while he's taking my temperature! Cynthia can play Watson! Joking apart, though, I like Dr. Gregg and I can't believe he's got any real connection with the murder. He's a much better sort than people think."

"Probably," said Fayre. "Though I don't care for the chap myself. But it doesn't follow that he mayn't have a shrewd idea who did commit the murder and be shielding him for some reason of his own."

Sybil Kean laughed.

"Edward would say we were a lot of old women, with our impressions and deductions. Still, considering the paucity of clues, it seems a pity to disregard anything."

"*Y.o.7.*" admitted Fayre ruefully. "It's not much to go on."

Sybil Kean looked up quickly.

"What's that?" she asked.

"All we have got of the number of the car. That and a stylographic pen that might have been lying in the grass for ages."

"A pen!" exclaimed Cynthia. "This is quite new. You've been keeping it up your sleeve all this time, Uncle Fayre!"

"Didn't Edward tell you? I suppose he hadn't time. I picked up a red stylographic pen—a 'Red Dwarf,' I think they used to be called—by the gate the first time we went to the farm. The day we were there with you and Leslie. As I say, it may have been there for ages or, more probably still, was dropped by one of the reporters after the murder. I know he didn't consider it of much importance."

Sybil Kean rose to her feet.

"I must leave you, my children," she said regretfully. "If I don't go and rest, that sinister man, Gregg, will have my blood. If Hatter comes out with any more interesting revelations, mind you report to me, Cynthia."

She moved slowly towards the house. Cynthia looked after her with a little frown of mingled pity and anxiety.

"She doesn't seem to get any better," she said. "I hope we haven't tired her. She looked all in, just now."

"I wonder what Gregg's opinion really is ..." began Fayre; then broke off with a sudden exclamation and sprang to his feet.

But he was too late. Sybil Kean had wavered for a moment, recovered herself, and then, before he or Cynthia could reach her, sunk in a huddled heap by the door leading from the terrace to the drawing-room.

Cynthia was by her side in an instant.

"Ring for her maid, quick!" she commanded. "And then get Dr. Gregg on the telephone. It's her heart again!"

Fortunately the maid proved efficient and, while Fayre was ringing up the doctor, she and Cynthia got the unconscious woman to bed between them. Gregg was not at his house, but at the Cottage Hospital, where Fayre eventually ran him to earth and managed to get him on the end of the telephone. He promised to come at once and Fayre was waiting impatiently in the hall for his arrival when Cynthia joined him, looking worried and anxious.

"She's still unconscious," she said. "Her maid's splendid—she seems to know exactly what to do; but I wish Dr. Gregg would come!"

"Do you think all that stuff about Gregg could have upset her?" asked Fayre, his conscience smiting him. "I could kick myself for being such a fool. After all, she's entirely dependent on him while she's here."

Cynthia laid a reassuring hand on his arm.

"Nonsense, Uncle Fayre! Sybil's got much too much sense for that. You're not to blame. She gets attacks like this and they've been getting worse, her maid says. Probably the dinner-party last night knocked her up. It was pretty awful, according to Eve."

Gregg arrived sooner than they had dared hope. He was upstairs for a long time and Fayre hung about miserably, wishing most heartily that the Staveleys would return from church, for Eve

Staveley was one of those cheerfully competent people who are invaluable in a case of illness. He waylaid Gregg on his way out.

"She'll do," was his verdict in answer to Fayre's inquiry. "But she won't weather many more attacks like this. Each one is a fresh drain on her vitality. Blast that dinner-party!"

"You think that did it?"

"Sure. A stuffy dining-room and the effort of talking to a lot of stodgy people would be quite enough." Fayre looked him squarely in the eyes.

"Is she going to get any stronger?" he asked. "I'm one of the oldest friends they've got and I'd like to know how things really are."

Gregg shrugged his shoulders.

"The machine's worn out," he said. "We can patch it, of course, but every time we do, it becomes a bit weaker. Heart's always the devil, you know. I wish I could speak differently," he went on with a touch of real feeling in his voice. "She's one of the best and pluckiest patients I've ever had."

"Can nothing be done?"

Gregg shook his head.

"She couldn't be in the hands of a better man than Sir Victor, if that's what you mean. No one in Europe can beat him in his own line. I know, because I worked under him at St. Swithin's. He'll do all that's humanly possible. I must get back to the hospital. You can get me there or at home for the next few hours, but you probably won't need me. With rest and care she should do all right now. I'll drop in again this evening."

He hurried away, leaving Fayre to make the most of the small comfort he had given him.

He proved right. By that evening Sybil Kean was noticeably better and Fayre was able to fix his mind once more on his own, or rather Leslie's, affairs. As far as the tracing of the car was concerned, that was best left in Grey's hands and, in default of a better job, he decided to turn his attention to Gregg. The doctor had mentioned St. Swithin's and, for some reason he could not place, the name roused an illusive echo in his mind. For a long time he searched his memory in vain and it was not till he was in the act of getting into bed that he suddenly traced the connection. One Henderson, a man he had known well in his student days in London, had been at St. Swithin's. He did not know Gregg's age, but, from the look of him, they must have been contemporaries, more or less. It would do no harm to look the man up and ask him a few questions. In any case, he had been one of the many people he had meant to run to earth on his return to England and now, provided he was not in the Antipodes, would be as good a time as any. He made up his mind to get hold of a medical directory and write to Henderson at the first opportunity.

CHAPTER X

NEXT MORNING the report of Lady Kean was reassuring and Fayre felt at liberty to devote himself to his own business.

Immediately after breakfast he betook himself to the library in the vain hope of finding a medical directory. A brief survey of the rows of calf-bound volumes convinced him that his search was vain and he was obliged to fall back on the telephone-book. Here, rather, to his surprise, he found what he was looking for.

"L. S. P. Henderson, M.D. 24.a. Selkirk Road. Carlisle."

He scribbled the address and telephone number on the back of an old envelope, reflecting that, once more, his luck was in. He had not only found his man, but found him at Carlisle, of all convenient places. Things could not have fallen better to his hand. There was nothing to prevent his running over to Carlisle that morning and it struck him that, while he was about it, he might call at one or two of the big garages and try to find out if they had housed a car answering to the description of the one seen near the farm. Given the London number, it was on the cards that the man had made a bolt for the south in his flight from the scene of the murder. Unless he made an all-night job of it he would probably break the journey at Carlisle. At any rate, it would be worth trying.

His next step was to telephone. Here again he was fortunate, for Henderson himself answered the call. He was enthusiastic when he discovered Fayre at the other end of the line and pinned him down then and there for lunch at his house.

Lord Staveley, as soon as he heard his plans, insisted on his commandeering one of the cars for the day and by twelve o'clock he was in Carlisle. He chose a busy garage near the station as a likely place to start his inquiries.

He found the manager in the office and, on the plea that he was acting for a farmer whose cart had been run into on the evening of March the twenty-third, ascertained that no car answering to the very meagre description he was able to give had been garaged there on the night in question. He drew as complete a blank at three other garages he visited and was compelled at last to give up the quest in despair. In one case he did hit on a car with *Y.o.7.* as the beginning of the registered number, but the owner was well known to the garage proprietor and the car had been in his keeping for a week prior to the day of the murder and, to his knowledge, had not been outside the garage during that time.

Rather disheartened, he drove on to Henderson's and found the doctor and his wife awaiting him. They gave him a welcome that more than made up for his unsuccessful morning. Henderson, a huge, burly man with the strength of an ox and the gentlest of bed-side manners, had married in the interval and was evidently im-mensely proud of his tiny, very capable-looking Scotch wife. They entertained Fayre lavishly and, so infectious was their open-hearted friendliness, that, by the time lunch was over, he felt as though the intervening years had vanished like a dream and that he was back again in his old student days. Henderson was able to give him news of several old friends he had lost sight of and they were so deeply engaged in discussing the past that it was not until they were set-tled with their pipes beside the lire in the doctor's study that Fayre found an opportunity to bring up the subject of Gregg.

Henderson recognized the name at once as that of a man he had known fairly well at St. Swithin's and was interested to learn what had become of him.

"Very able chap, he was, but a bit of a roughneck. He was very raw when he first arrived, I remember, and had to put up with a good deal of chaff. Came from somewhere in the North, I believe, and had got most of his training from an old local doctor who took an interest in the boy. Apart from that he was mostly self-educated. Correspondence schools and that sort of thing. Rather an interest-ing fellow, in his way."

"Did you see anything of him after he left?"

"Lost sight of him entirely. I've a sort of idea that I heard a rumour at one time that he had a practise somewhere in London, but I'm rather hazy."

"Do you remember at all who his associates were at the hospital? I've an idea that he knew some one I'm interested in and I don't care to ask him point-blank."

"His great pal was a man named Baxter. They used to go about a good deal with a couple of nurses, one of whom was by way of being engaged to Baxter. I remember that because there was a certain amount of talk about it. The girl had the reputation of being hot stuff and Baxter was supposed to be making rather a fool of himself over her. It's extraordinary how it all comes back when one starts talking about old times. There was a St. Swithin's man here the other day and we began gassing and, I give you my word, I felt at the end as if it was yesterday that we were there together. We were talking about Baxter, among other things, so that he's fairly fresh in my memory."

"What happened to him?"

"According to Parry, the fellow who was here the other day, he married the girl and the thing proved a ghastly failure. Parry said he believed he was dead. Gregg would know, though; they were very thick with each other."

"You don't remember the names of the two girls? They may have been friends of the person I'm after."

Henderson shook his head.

"I haven't the remotest idea. They were pretty girls, I remember. The sort that take up nursing to get away from home and have a bit of fun."

Mrs. Henderson, who had been busy over the coffeepot, looked up suddenly.

"If you're wanting information about any of the nurses at St. Swithin's, why not go to Ella Benson?" she suggested.

Her husband brought his hand down on the arm of his chair with a whack which made the dust fly.

"By Jove, she's right! Mrs. Benson's a friend of my wife's and lives a few doors up this street. She was a nurse at St. Swithin's and she's up in all the gossip of her day. She's probably at home now."

"I'll stroll along and see when I've finished this," said his wife. "She often drops in after lunch. Her husband's a surgeon and we see a good deal of them, one way and another. She's a decent little body."

"Since when have you taken an interest in the medical profession?" asked Henderson lazily, his shrewd eyes on his friend.

Fayre laughed rather guiltily.

"It's curiosity, mostly, about Gregg. He's a queer stick and when he flatly denied having met some one I'm pretty sure used to know him in the past, it was too much for my inquisitive mind. I remembered that you were a St. Swithin's man and thought I'd sound you when I saw you. It's not important. The truth is, that I haven't got enough to do, nowadays, and I'm developing into a confirmed busybody."

Henderson grinned.

"Very good," he said appreciatively. "As far as it goes. But you weren't in the habit of doing things without a reason in the old days and you don't look as if you'd changed much."

Fayre felt himself redden.

"Confound you!" he said. "To be frank, it isn't all curiosity, but I've got so little to go on that I'd rather not say anything yet."

"Right," was Henderson's good-tempered answer. "That's good enough for me, but what are we going to say to Mrs. Benson? She's a lady with a very efficient tongue and not particularly lacking in imagination!"

"Why not leave Gregg out of it? Put it that I knew Baxter years ago and want to find out what has become of him. That ought to be enough to lead her onto the girls."

"Ella won't want much leading, if it's a question of St. Swithin's," remarked Mrs. Henderson, as she finished pouring out the coffee. She rose and slipped out of the room before Fayre could apologize for the trouble he was giving her.

"What's your program now?" asked Henderson.

"You'll find vegetation a bit of a bore, won't you?" Fayre settled himself luxuriously in his chair.

"I don't know about that. I've done my share of hard work and had one go of fever too many and I shan't be sorry to settle down. I shall loaf round for a bit, looking up old friends and that sort of thing, and then take a little place in the country with a spare bedroom or two and a bit of fishing. I might perpetrate a book. Like most of us who've been in the East, I've got ideas I shouldn't mind airing."

They chatted desultorily until Mrs. Henderson came back with Mrs. Benson, a plump, voluble little woman who seemed only too pleased to find a fresh audience for her reminiscences.

"It's funny you should mention Baxter," she said as she settled herself comfortably by the fire. "I turned up an old photograph of him only yesterday in a group taken just before I left the hospital. I'm afraid he made a mess of things, poor fellow."

"Do you know if he's alive? Henderson seems to think that he died."

"He went to pieces after his wife left him. He took to drink, I believe, and ended by drinking himself to death. He was a fool ever to have married her."

"There was a certain amount of gossip, I hear, over that affair."

"Gossip about her. She was a bad lot from the beginning. We nurses knew a thing or two, both about her and her great friend, a girl called Philips. They and Baxter and a man called Gregg were always about together and they got themselves a good deal talked about. We were all surprised when Baxter married her, not on his account, he was dotty about her, but because we all thought she was after bigger game. She was the sort of girl who's set on making a good marriage and generally succeeds in the end, too. Usually, she hooks a rich patient after she's left the hospital, and both she and the Philips girl were clever enough to do it."

"Was Gregg in love with either of them?" asked Fayre.

"I shouldn't think so. He amused himself with Philips all right, but he wasn't taken in by her. He was dead against Baxter's marriage, I know, and did his best to stop it. He wasn't a bad sort, old Gregg. He was surly and bad-tempered, but we liked working with him."

"What happened to Mrs. Baxter after she left her husband, do you know?"

"I've no idea. He divorced her in the end, I've been told. She was the sort to fall on her feet."

"What was her name before she married? It's funny I never heard it, but most of this happened after I had left England," explained Fayre, carefully avoiding Henderson's malicious eye.

"Tina Allen," answered Mrs. Benson. "She came of quite good stock, I believe. I heard once that her people were pretty sick at her taking up nursing at all."

For a moment Fayre was bereft of speech and, when he did speak, he controlled his voice with difficulty. That Mrs. Draycott should have started her career as a nurse at St. Swithin's was the last thing he had suspected.

"She knew this man Gregg well, you say," he asked at last.

"Must have. The four of them were always about together. I don't think he liked her much, though. As I said, he did his best to stop her marriage."

"You didn't keep up with any of them after you left, I suppose?"

She shook her head.

"I married, myself, and came up here. I used to get news of all the old lot from time to time, from a friend who stayed on at the hospital. There were some funny goings on there, I can tell you!"

She rambled on, but the flood of her reminiscences rolled over Fayre's head unheeded. He sat smoking, his thoughtful eyes fixed on the glowing fire, his mind full of Mrs. Benson's last revelation. "Christina Mary Draycott." The name had been given in full at the inquest. And Miss Allen had spoken of her sister as "Tina." The vicar's wife had alluded to her divorce from her first husband, but had not mentioned his name. Tina Allen, then Tina Baxter, and finally Tina Draycott! The whole thing fitted in with the precision of the pieces in a jigsaw-puzzle. Not only was her connection with Gregg explained at last, but his obvious venom was more than accounted for. And there was nothing surprising now in her curiosity concerning him, followed by her odd reluctance to meet him. Supposing they *had* come together at the farm that night! He could imagine what that meeting would be like and what it might lead to, given a man of Gregg's temperament. He collected his scattered thoughts with an effort and turned to Mrs. Benson, who had paused for a moment for sheer want of breath.

"Would it be giving you too much trouble if I asked for a look at that photograph you spoke of?" he asked. "I'd like to see one of Baxter again."

Mrs. Benson beat even her own record as a purveyor of information.

"I've got it here!" she announced triumphantly. "When I heard that you were an old friend of Baxter's I said to myself: 'I expect that photograph will amuse him.' It was lying on my table where I put it yesterday, so I just picked it up and brought it with me."

She fumbled in her bag and produced a photograph which she handed to Fayre. He looked at it eagerly and was at once confronted with an unforeseen difficulty. Gregg he spotted at once, younger and a trifle leaner, but unmistakable. He was sitting in the front row of a group of about fifteen men. Any one of the other fourteen might have been Baxter, for all Fayre knew. But which? And he did not dare ask!

It was Henderson who came to the rescue. He had risen and was leaning over the back of Fayre's chair, studying the photograph, and he grasped the situation almost immediately. Out of sheer devilry he allowed Fayre to sit for some minutes helpless, glowering at Gregg's not very pleasing features, racking his brains for a way out of the difficulty, before he placed a finger on the portrait of a dark, rather haggard-looking man at the end of the front row and remarked lazily:

"Baxter looks as if he'd been making a night of it! It's very like him, though."

"He was always a queer, nervous creature. But he was clever enough. I know they thought a lot of him at St. Swithin's," rattled on the unsuspecting Mrs. Benson.

Fayre was busy studying the photograph. The figures in the group were small, but very clearly defined, and Baxter's head stood out distinctly against the white overall of the man behind him. Fayre could place his type at a glance. Very dark, with a high, narrow forehead and deep-set eyes and the too sensitive mouth of a man whose nerves are perilously near the surface. The kind to fare badly at the hands of a woman like Mrs. Draycott. No wonder the marriage had ended in tragedy, he thought, and was not surprised that Gregg had done his best to spare his friend.

He returned the photograph to Mrs. Benson with a sigh. He could understand and sympathize now with many of the things Gregg had said during their drive to the station. He felt a sudden, rather disconcerting, sympathy for the man and was not sorry when

Mrs. Benson took herself off and gave him an opportunity to get away himself. He wanted to be alone with his thoughts.

By tea-time he was back at Staveley. During the drive he had had ample time for reflection, but it had not helped him much. He was still very much at sea as to his next move and realized that it would need considerable diplomacy to discover Gregg's whereabouts at the time of the murder without rousing his suspicions. And, keen as he was to clear Leslie, he now found himself almost dreading the answer to his thoughts.

Bill Staveley met him with the news that Leslie had appeared before the Magistrate and been committed for trial at the Carlisle Assizes.

CHAPTER XI

FAYRE WAS ONLY half-way through his first cup of tea when Cynthia cornered him.

"You look hipped, Uncle Fayre," she said, her sharp eyes on his face. "Didn't you like your old friend when you did find him? Or are you just fed up?"

He shook himself out of his abstraction.

"My old friend was excellent company, thank you, and very much his old self, plus a jolly little wife. But I do feel a bit weary. Too much bicycling, no doubt!" But Cynthia resolutely ignored the red herring so adroitly drawn across her path.

"It isn't anything new about John, is it?" she asked with a note of real terror in her voice. "You would tell me, wouldn't you?"

"My dear, of course not! Honestly, it's only the after-effects of the Hendersons' overpowering hospitality. They gave me the most enormous lunch and made me eat it, too. How have things been going here?"

"You're sure it's nothing else?" she urged doubtfully. "You wouldn't keep anything from me from a mistaken idea of kindness, would you, Uncle Fayre?" Fayre s eyes met hers with the blandest innocence. He could not take her into his confidence yet. Time enough when his suspicions were verified.

"The moment I discover anything definite, either for or against Leslie, I shall bring it to you, my dear," he said with complete sincerity. "You've got a right to know before any one else."

"Thank you," she answered simply. Then, with a return to her usual manner: "Sybil's much better. Dr. Gregg was here this afternoon and he says she may see people, in reason, if they don't stay too long. But she's not to be excited, so don't let her talk about Leslie's affairs, Uncle Fayre."

"I won't, if I can possibly help it," promised Fayre with all his heart. The last thing he wanted, at this juncture, was to share his knowledge with Sybil Fayre. He could not forget that, at any moment, her life might be in Gregg's hands and, so long as she was dependent on him, he resolved to do nothing to shake her confidence in him.

"She's anxious to see you," went on Cynthia. "But Eve and Bill have both been with her and they think she's had enough people for to-day. She wants to see you first thing to-morrow, though, and I'm afraid she means to go on with what we were saying on the day she was taken ill."

"She's a wilful woman, too," he said ruefully. "She'll probably have her way. I'm no match for her."

Cynthia laughed.

"You old fraud! Even I have seen you twiddle people round your finger before now. As for shutting up, you're like a clam when you choose!"

After tea Fayre joined his host in the library.

"I feel I owe you both thanks and an apology," he said slowly, as he filled his pipe. "You've been a brick over this business, Bill. You've let me have the car at all hours, and use your house like a hotel and you've never asked what I'm up to or even when I'm going! You must want to know that, I should think, by now!" Bill Staveley chucked a box of matches over to Fayre, who caught it neatly.

"That's the third! You've got two boxes of mine in your pocket now," he murmured. "I saw them go in."

Then, as Fayre turned out his pockets and sheepishly revealed three boxes of matches, he went on:

"Don't be an old ass, old man, and stop handing round compliments. I like watching you trotting about, so happy and busy! As for asking questions, I never believe in butting in on other people's affairs. So long as I know you're on the job, I'm satisfied. And stay as long as you like. If you don't know how Eve and I feel about that, I'm not going to indulge your vanity by telling you!"

"It's something to know that I've got you both behind me," said Fayre soberly.

"You can count on that, old chap."

Bill Staveley had abandoned his usual easy banter and spoke seriously enough now.

"Personally, I'd put my shirt on that boy's innocence, and I know Eve feels the same. Tell us as much or as little as you like; we don't care provided you clear him. And if any one can do it, I believe it's you. Only, if you've got any nefarious schemes up your sleeve, remember that I'm a J. P. and keep them to yourself. I don't want to know anything about them!" Fayre chuckled.

"I must say, you're a tophole-hogger! When I fall into the hands of the worthy Gunnet, I suppose you'll turn up looking as if butter wouldn't melt in your mouth and bail me out! If it's any comfort to you, I'm not contemplating anything of the sort at present. Cynthia may have told you that we've got hold of a couple of clues, but they may lead to nothing. Sometimes I think it's a hopeless business. The only thing I do feel sure of is Leslie's innocence."

Lord Staveley nodded.

"Same here, and if he is innocent it ought to be possible to prove it. Has any one thought of digging up that beastly cat?"

For a moment Fayre was puzzled; then his face cleared.

"The one Leslie shot? It appears that it was there, all right. According to Grey, Gunnet went off and did a bit of sleuthing of his own and he found the place and dug the cat up. Unfortunately it wasn't labelled like a pheasant with the day on which it had been killed and though I suppose they'll use it in the defence, it won't cut much ice with a jury. We want something more tangible than that."

"What you want is to produce the murderer, old man. That's your best defence and I don't see why you shouldn't do it if you're anything like the sticker you used to be."

Fayre's interview with Lady Kean the next morning proved far less easy. He found her lying on the sofa in her bedroom, looking pitifully frail and white. She was much weaker than she chose to admit and, at the first sight of her, he made up his mind to cut the interview as short as possible.

"Hatter dear," was her greeting, "I *am* sorry to have made such a fool of myself. I must have given you both a scare and I'm thoroughly ashamed of myself. I'd been feeling seedy all day and never dreamed when I started that I shouldn't manage to get to my room and collapse decently in private. Please forgive me for being such a nuisance."

Fayre pulled a chair up to her side and sat down.

"I think we were the culprits," he said gently. "We tired you out between us. It's something to see you up and dressed, but, for Heaven's sake, don't overdo it again like that. You don't look fit to be talking even now."

"Talking doesn't tire me," she assured him eagerly. "Hatter, please, I want to know what you've been doing. Is there any news? Cynthia says you went to Carlisle yesterday."

"I promised Cynthia I wouldn't let you discuss it," he answered reluctantly. "But if it will set your mind at rest, I'll give you my assurance that nothing definite has turned up since our last conversation. As a matter of fact, I went to Carlisle to look up an old friend and had very little time for anything else. I did go to one or two of the garages in the hope of finding some trace of the car that was seen that night, but I drew a complete blank."

"I had an idea that that's what had taken you to Carlisle," she murmured. "Thinking things over, it struck me the car might have stopped there. You found nothing?"

"Absolutely nothing. As far as I can see at present, it must have vanished into space. Grey did his best before he left, but could find no one who'd seen it."

"And Dr. Gregg?" she insisted and her tone was so urgent that he thought it better to humour her. "There's nothing new about him?"

"My dear Sybil, I was away all yesterday and Grey has gone back to London," he hedged. "Even if he's managed to stumble on something there, he hasn't had time to communicate with me. If anything turns up from him, I'll let you know, but don't worry your head about it now. Rest and get well."

She turned to him with a display of emotion quite foreign to her.

"I can't help thinking about it," she said piteously. "That boy shut up in prison haunts me! Just imagine, Hatter, what it must be. Alone, with nobody to reassure him, not knowing how it is all going to turn out! And Cynthia! Just at the beginning of her young life! It's cruel!"

He tried to soothe her.

"I know, Sybil, but it's no good for either of us to let it get on our nerves. Thank goodness, they *are* young and able to face things. Some day this will be like an evil dream to them and they'll be able to start afresh, with their whole lives before them. Don't waste your strength in futile pity, my dear!"

She managed to smile at him, though her face was still white and drawn.

"You're right, of course, and I know I'm being silly. It's only that when one's ill and helpless one loses one's sense of proportion. If I know how things are going, it won't be so bad. You will tell me, won't you? Don't keep things from me because of my rotten health, will you, Hatter?"

Her voice was very appealing and Fayre mentally cursed his luck. He had barely succeeded in heading off Cynthia and now here was Sybil Kean pressing him even more closely.

He rose and took both her hands in his.

"The moment anything definite happens, you shall know. Meanwhile, try to put it all out of your mind for a bit, anyhow till you're stronger. Edward was right when he said you ought never to have been mixed up in this."

She sank back on her pillows with a tired sigh.

"All right. I can rest more easily if I know that I can trust you to keep me posted. And come again soon, Hatter, please!"

He looked back as he reached the door and saw that her eyes were already closed. Evidently his visit, short as it had been, had taken what little strength she possessed.

He went straight from her room to the garage where he had housed his bicycle. One of the chauffeurs had cleaned and overhauled it and had it waiting in readiness. Now that his first stiffness was past Fayre was beginning to enjoy this despised method of getting about the country and he pedalled down the drive and out onto the highroad quite unperturbed by the grin on Bill Staveley's face as he rode past him on the chestnut mare he had put at Fayre's disposal at the beginning of his visit. Fayre, who had promised himself some hunting next winter, looked after him with only a passing feeling of regret. His mind was busily engaged with other things.

He kept a sharp lookout on the fields on either side of the road, but he had gone some distance before he found one that apparently interested him sufficiently to him dismount and stand for a minute or two looking into it.

Lord Staveley had been having the gates on the estate repainted and this one had evidently only been finished that day; nevertheless Fayre leaned heavily against it, with the result that, during his absorbed contemplation of three cows and a diminutive donkey, he managed to adorn his coat with a long smear of bright green paint. He took the misfortune with commendable fortitude and, picking up his bicycle, rode quickly off in the direction of Gregg's house.

Arrived there he went straight round to the garage at the back of the house. He found the doctor's man polishing the brass of a small two-seater.

"I don't know whether the doctor's in," he said genially. "If he is, I'll go round in a minute and have a few words with him, but I've just discovered this beastly stuff on my coat and I wondered if you could let me have a drop of petrol to clean it off with. I must have got it leaning over a gate near here."

The man touched the paint with his finger.

"You'll find the doctor in, sir, and this will come off easily enough while it's fresh," he said. "Lucky it's still wet."

He went into the garage and came out with a tin of petrol.

"If you'd got such a thing as a clean rag," suggested Fayre.

"If you'll wait a minute, sir, I'll get one from the kitchen."

He disappeared round the corner of the house and, as he did so, Fayre darted into the garage. It needed only a glance to see that there was room for but one car and that a small one. Fayre cast a quick look round the tiny garage and then made for a file of bills hanging from a hook against the wall. With one eye alert for the returning chauffeur he ran through them swiftly. Knowing the ways of small cars when left to the care of odd-jobmen he hoped that Gregg might on occasion be driven to hire a car from the local garage and there was a faint chance that the garage bill might be on this file. Fortunately for him it was not only there but near the top of the pile and he found it almost immediately. It took him but a second to find the entry he needed.

"*March 23rd. To hire..............................£0. 10*"

He slipped back into the yard just in time and was standing by the car, ruefully regarding his coat when the doctor's man returned.

"If you'll let me have the coat, sir, I'll have it off in a moment," he said, as he unscrewed the can of petrol.

While he was at work on the stain Fayre examined the car.

"Find her satisfactory?" he asked casually. "I'm thinking of getting a small car myself and I can't make up my mind about the make."

The man grunted.

"Been givin' a lot of trouble lately," he said. "Wants a thorough overhaul, but the doctor can't spare her."

"Always chooses the worst night to baulk on, I expect, if I know anything of cars."

"That's right. With the wind blowin' fit to knock you down and bitin' cold, she'll lay down on you proper."

"There was a night like that just after I got down to these parts," said Fayre reminiscently. "There were a lot of trees down, I was told."

"Night of the murder up to Mr. Leslie's farm. Awful night, that were. I was two hours workin' on this blessed car and then the doctor had to hire. I think you'll find that all right, sir."

Fayre thanked him and slipped a generous tip into his hand; then, getting into his coat, he made his way round to the front door.

The doctor was in, but was busy in the surgery. Fayre was shown into the study, an untidy, comfortable-looking room on the ground floor.

He took a quick inventory of the contents. A big desk piled with papers stood in the window. The fireplace was flanked by a couple of shabby, roomy armchairs. Fayre sat down in one of them and warmed his hands at the fire. As he did so, his eye fell on the mantelpiece and in a second he was on his feet again, examining a small framed photograph that stood there. He turned at the sound of the opening door to meet the steady gaze of Gregg.

"I haven't come to waste your time," he explained as he shook hands. "I know this is your busy time. I only wanted to explain that

I've made free with your petrol and the kind offices of your man in the most shameless way. I got some paint on my coat, leaning over a gate, and, as I was passing your house, I ventured to ask for some petrol to repair the damage."

"Very glad you did. I hope you got the stuff off," answered Gregg cordially. "Smoke?"

He handed a box of cigarettes to Fayre, who thanked him and took one.

"Sorry I can't be more hospitable," went on the doctor. "But I've got a pack of people waiting in the surgery and I sha'n't get rid of them for another hour, at least."

Fayre reached for a spill from a vase on the mantelpiece. As he did so his eye lighted on the photograph.

"That's an interesting head," he remarked.

"He was an interesting chap. He'd have gone a long way if he'd been allowed. One of the best fellows I ever knew."

"He looks it," said Fayre quietly, but with such obvious sincerity that Gregg was moved to enlarge on the subject.

"Got into the hands of a woman and she killed him as surely as if she'd murdered him. He died of alcoholic poisoning, the worst case I've ever seen. Trying to forget, he called it."

Gregg's voice was rough with emotion and, for the first time, Fayre felt really drawn towards him.

"What happened to the woman?" he asked carelessly.

Gregg turned away to light his cigarette. Fayre, watching him closely, noticed that his hand was steady as a rock, but his voice was not quite so certain as he answered.

"I lost sight of her," he said; "but, judging from the pace she was going, she's probably got her deserts by now."

He accompanied his guest to the door and stood chatting with him for a moment. He had regained his usual bluff manner; but Fayre, for all his quiet cordiality, was sick at heart. For the photograph was that of Baxter, and Gregg had once more flatly denied all knowledge of the identity of Mrs. Draycott.

CHAPTER XII

FAYRE DID NOT turn back to Staveley when he left Gregg's house, but rode straight on to Whitbury and lunched at the hotel there.

For one thing he did not feel equal just at that moment to facing any of the members of the Staveley party and, for another, the heading on the bill in Gregg's garage had been that of the Station Garage at Whitbury and he had a weakness for tackling nasty jobs at once and getting them over as quickly as possible. He did not conceal from himself that he dreaded the result of this next step.

He did not linger over his solitary meal, and by two o'clock he had already broached the subject of the car to the owner of the garage, a good-natured, chatty little man who seemed anxious to give him any information within his power. He adopted much the same story that he had used at Carlisle, only that, in this case, taking into account the manner in which news flies in a small town, he did not rely on the carter, but explained that he was acting for a friend in London whose motorcycle had been run down by a car on the night of the twenty-third, and who had narrowly escaped serious injury. The manager led him into the hutch that served him for an office and produced a ledger.

"A big, closed car, make unknown," he muttered. "London number with a seven in it."

He ran his finger down the page.

"Nothing of the sort in that night. It was the day of the murder, wasn't it? Blowing big guns and bitterly cold and there weren't many people out. We had nothing in at all, from lunch-time onwards, and I'm not surprised."

"You didn't let out any car answering to that description?"

"It's not much of description, if you'll excuse me!" said the man with a friendly grin. "You can't say you've given us much to go by! I've only two cars for hire and naturally neither of them has got a London number. One's too small for you and the other's well known round here."

He referred to his book again.

"Dr. Gregg had it that night. His own car was laid up. He took it out about five-thirty."

"Is it in now?" asked Fayre. "I know the doctor and I certainly don't suspect him of careless driving, but I promised my friend I'd have a thorough look round."

"Righto, I'll show it to you. If it was anybody but the doctor I might suspect a faked number. It's been done often enough. Except for the number, the car answers to your description, such as it is. So do half the other cars in this county, for the matter of that."

He was closing the book when his eye fell on another entry and he gave a sudden exclamation.

"Wait a minute! There was a car went out on the evening of the twenty-third, at about six o'clock. I've a kind of feeling it was a London car, too. Owner's name, Page. The number ought to have been entered, but my wife evidently forgot to do it. She's usually in charge of the desk here, and you know what women are!"

"Then six o'clock was the last you saw of it?"

"Yes. It didn't come back."

He was looking through the back pages of the book.

"Here it is. It came in on March 14th, and was fetched out on March 23rd. It's a pity we haven't got the number. I'll see if my wife remembers anything about it and I can show you the other car on the way."

He led the way to a somewhat weather-beaten, but still presentable, Daimler and Fayre gave the mudguards a keen, but hasty, scrutiny.

"You haven't had this repaired at all lately, I suppose?" he asked. "My friend's pretty certain that he injured the paint on the mud-guard."

"Haven't had this touched for over a year. Besides, it was all right when the doctor brought it back. I always look over them pretty carefully, even when it's a customer I know who's had them out. You never know what damage you'll find. No, I'll vouch for it that car hasn't been messed up in any way since I've had it."

He went off to find his wife, leaving Fayre battling with mingled feelings of relief and disappointment. Search as he might, he could find no trace of red paint on any of the mud-guards and they were quite intact. He seemed to have run into a blind alley, after all, unless the doctor were even cleverer than he had supposed. It was still within the bounds of possibility that he had changed cars again after leaving the garage in the hireling. If so, where? Fayre made up his mind to find that second car, if there was one, even if he had to search every garage in the county.

His thoughts were broken into by the arrival of the manager and his wife.

"It's no good, I'm afraid," he announced. "The wife, here, says she can't recall the number, even if she ever noted it, which is doubtful, seeing that she forgot to put it down. She says she does remember the owner, though, if that's any use to you."

Fayre started.

"You remember the man who brought it in? That's capital!"

She shook her head.

"Not the man who brought it in," she said. "That's too long ago, but I do remember the man who took it out that night. You see, what with it being the night of the murder and such awful weather, added to the fact that my sister and her husband came over from Carlisle for the night, that evening seems to stand out more clearly than most. Then, there were very few people in and out that day, so that one noticed a stranger. Not that I really saw him, though, if you understand me."

Fayre didn't, but he showed exemplary patience and left her to tell her story in her own way.

"I can remember it as if it was yesterday," she went on. "My sister was sitting at the desk with me, just chatting, and we watched him come in. As I say, he was the only one we'd had that afternoon and we were naturally interested and passed one or two remarks about him. He spoke about the car and then came over to the desk to pay his bill. What struck me was that he never took off his goggles. You know the way most people push them up on their foreheads, even if they don't take them off, but he didn't even take the trouble to do that. They were those big ones with the leather nose-flap and they pretty well covered his whole face. That's why I said I'd never seen him, really. My sister joked about it afterwards."

"What sort of man was he?" asked Fayre. "Well-to-do, I should say. Tall and thin, and he had a big motoring coat and a cap with a peak. I remember that, because it and the goggles hid nearly the whole of his face."

"You didn't notice his voice, I suppose?"

"No. I don't think he spoke except just to ask for the bill. He may not have done that. A lot of people just stand and wait till I give it to them. He must have given his name when he brought the car in because it's down in the book there. Page, wasn't it?" Her husband nodded.

"Was there nothing else you noticed about him? I'm in luck's way to have hit off such an observant person as yourself," said Fayre with a smile.

"I was always one to take an interest in things and, what with so many coming in and out here, you find yourself wondering about them. I do remember one thing, now you mention it: his hands. He took off his gloves to pay the bill, and I noticed how thin they were and yet how strong-looking. I was in the manicure before I married and I suppose that's why I'm such a one to notice hands. My husband's always laughing at me about it. I said something about it at supper that night and I remember them all laughing."

"Quite true," put in her husband. "I remember it now. It's always been a joke of ours, but we chaffed her a lot that night about one thing and another and that was one of them. There was another joke Lotty had that night, too, about a bottle. Do you remember?"

"Rather! That was that particular man, too. When he turned away from the desk his coat swung against the corner and something heavy came an awful thump up against the wood. Lotty said: 'Well, he's got his little drop of comfort with him, anyway,' meaning it sounded like a bottle. That was what she was laughing over at supper. She was always one for a joke and she'll make one over anything."

"Well, thanks to you, I've got some idea what the chap was like and he may be the one my friend's after. Page by name, tall and thin, with a bottle in his pocket! And if my friend can find him he may get the money for his broken lamp out of him! It doesn't sound a hopeful prospect, does it! I'm deeply grateful to you, all the same. I wish everybody had a memory like yours!"

"I'm sorry about that number," she said regretfully. "It isn't often I forget, but I must have been taken up with my sister."

Fayre rode back to Staveley very much divided in his mind between the mysterious Mr. Page and Gregg. Of the two, he was inclined to suspect the doctor, who seemed to be getting more and more involved in the whole business and for whose brains he had already conceived a wholesome respect. The other man was probably nothing but a harmless motorist who wanted his car badly enough to brave the weather and fetch it.

He found Cynthia writing letters in the drawing-room and gave her a short account of his visit to the garage.

She fastened onto the Page episode with an enthusiasm Fayre found pathetic. He told her frankly that he considered it of minor importance.

"You must remember that there may have been any number of people fetching their cars from garages just about that time. It isn't as if we'd been able to trace the number of the car. There is nothing except its size that answers to the carter's description."

"Still, that's about all we've got to go on anyway, Uncle Fayre, and the time does fit in. He could have gone round by Miss Allen's and reached the farm just about the time the tramp saw him. I know, because I've done it in a car myself."

"And the bottle in his pocket was a revolver, I suppose?" laughed Fayre, knowing the disappointment that lay in store for her if the whole thing petered out and determined not to encourage her in a false hope.

"Why not?" she said seriously. "And why did he keep his goggles down all the time? That woman was right: it *is* unusual."

"All right, my dear, we'll add him to our list of suspects; but I don't quite see what we're going to do about it."

"I do," was Cynthia's decisive answer. "I'm going to put the garages at Carlisle through a small sieve. I'll bet he did stay there, if he was going south, and, if he did, he must have garaged the car."

"But I told you I'd drawn Carlisle the other day. It was hopeless."

"What did you do?" she burst out scornfully. "You went to three or four of the big, obvious places. That's not where I'd park my car if I were trying to get away on the quiet. You wait, Uncle Fayre. If he went there at all, I'll run him to earth, you'll see!"

"And what do you propose to do? You can't go sleuthing about Carlisle all by yourself. They must know you pretty well there and we don't want this affair talked about."

"I'm not going by myself. I'm going with Tubby Campbell."

"Tubby Campbell?" murmured Fayre helplessly.

"If you weren't just a measly bicyclist you'd know his name at Brooklands," she scoffed. "He married the clergyman's daughter at Galston and they've settled at Carlisle. I've always promised I'd stay with them. I'll ring them up and go over for a few days and see what Tubby can do. If anybody will know how to set about it, he will. It's a gorgeous idea, Uncle Fayre; you must admit it!"

"You'll probably do the thing much more efficiently than I did, I admit that. But don't let your enthusiasm run away with you. Don't forget that it is probably a very forlorn hope!"

"If you think that, really, it means that you've got something else up your sleeve," was Cynthia's shrewd and unexpected comment. "What is it? Is it Dr. Gregg?"

Fayre was taken unawares.

"I have got an idea," he said slowly. "But it's so vague at present that I tell you frankly I'm going to keep it to myself. If it comes to anything, you shall be the first to know, but, so far, it's only fair to say that I've come up against a blank wall. I think your field of investigation is likely to prove quite as fruitful as mine."

For a moment she looked disappointed. Then:

"All right," she agreed. "You get to work at your end and I'll see what I can do at mine. If you only knew the relief it is to do something instead of sitting watching other people!"

The cry came so straight from her heart that Fayre was glad he had not succeeded better in his efforts to discourage her. At least the search would keep her employed during a very anxious period and he felt, too, that he could tackle Sybil and her questions better without Cynthia. He had been dreading the time when the two would get their heads together over Dr. Gregg and begin putting two and two together in earnest. Cynthia, he knew, already suspected that there was something behind his own visit to Carlisle. He would be able to pursue his investigations more freely in her absence.

CHAPTER XIII

HAVING AT LAST found something definite to do Cynthia proved herself a very able organizer. By lunch-time the next day she had extracted an invitation from the Campbells, squared Lady Stave-ley and packed her trunk. Directly the meal was over she started for Carlisle, brimming with enthusiasm for the task she had set herself.

Her departure was followed almost immediately by the arrival of Gregg on his daily visit to Lady Kean. He had barely turned the first bend on the wide oak staircase before Fayre was on his bicycle, riding his hardest in the direction of Gregg's house.

His disappointment at finding the doctor out was convincing enough to impress the maid, who showed him into the little surgery, assuring him that her master was certain to be in soon, as he was always at home to patients from four to six in the afternoon. Fayre, after a moment of apparent hesitation, decided to await his return and settled down to the inspection of the very stale literature provided by Gregg for the use of his patients. The maid, recognizing him as the gentleman who had called on a previous occasion, departed with a clear conscience to the back regions, leaving him to his own devices. He waited till she was out of sight and then, with a rather guilty smile at the thought of Lord Staveley's injunctions of the day before, cautiously opened the door leading into the study. A quick glance through the window assured him that the small front garden was deserted and that he could carry out his plans unobserved. The farther door, which led into the front hall, was shut and he opened it carefully, leaving it ajar, that he might be sure of hearing the footsteps of the maid should she return. Then he sat down at the writing-table and went quickly, but efficiently, through the mass of papers with which it was littered. As he expected, none of them had any bearing on the subject he had in mind. Neither was there anything of interest to be found in the top drawer, which he found unlocked.

The desk was of a standard make and closely resembled one he had used in his office in India, the key of which he still carried on a ring in his pocket. He tried this key and, to his relief, it fitted the two rows of drawers on each side of the knee-hole. The first two drawers proved disappointing, but at the back of the third he found a packet of letters, tied together and docketed: "Baxter." He glanced hastily out of the window once more, but there was no sign of Gregg and, slipping out the first envelope in the pile, he opened it.

It contained a letter from Baxter to Gregg and, as Fayre read it, he felt himself grow hot with shame at the part he was playing.

If it had not been for Leslie's danger and the unworthy part he believed Gregg to be playing in this game of life and death, he would have bundled the letters back into the drawer and locked it, for the letter was that of a broken man to a friend from whom he had no reservations. It seemed to have been written more in grief than in anger and in it Baxter said that he had traced his wife to Brighton, where she had been staying openly with Captain Draycott End that he proposed to do his utmost to persuade her to return to him. It was evidently in answer to a letter from Gregg, urging him to take action. This, he declared, he did not intend to do unless he were persuaded that the step would insure his wife's happiness and then only on the undertaking from Draycott that, in the event of a divorce, he would marry her. It was an honest, straightforward letter, pathetic in its complete selflessness. On the envelope Gregg had scribbled a pencilled note:

"*L. has seen her in Paris several times with a man whose name he was unable to discover. Comparing dates I have ascertained that Draycott was in Egypt at the time. L., knowing I was interested, took the trouble to trace them to their hotel, but is convinced that they were staying there under an assumed name. Useful evidence, if she interferes with the boy and I shall not hesitate to use it. Draycott will not stand for that sort of thing!*"

This note had evidently been made after her divorce and subsequent marriage to Captain Draycott and suggested that, for some reason, Gregg was wishful to retain a hold over her and proposed to use this hold if necessary. It looked as if Gregg's power to harm her had ceased with Draycott's death, in which case he could hardly have used his knowledge to force her to meet him at the farm. At the same time, Fayre realized that he had at last stumbled on a possible motive for an assignation. Supposing that Gregg's power over her still held and that, for some reason, he had decided to put on the screw. Given the man's bitterness against her, combined with his obviously uneven temper, it was not outside the bounds of possibility that he had been exasperated beyond endurance at her refusal to accede to his demands and had shot her in a moment of blind rage. Fayre, knowing Gregg, could not bring himself to believe that the thing was premeditated. He did, on the other hand, consider him perfectly capable of using the revolver as a threat, probably with no intention of firing it.

Fayre slipped the letter back under the string before extracting the one underneath it and was glad he had done so for, while he was in the very act, his ear caught the sound of an approaching motor. Quick as lightning he threw the packet back into the drawer, closed and locked it and was back in the surgery before Gregg was out of his car.

He heard him open the front door and go down the passage, where he was evidently met by the maid, for, a few minutes later, he appeared at the surgery door and invited Fayre into the study.

His manner was no less cordial than it had been on the previous occasion, but, this time, Fayre had the impression that he was waiting rather sardonically for an explanation of his visit. He hastened to assure him that he had come as a patient and went on to describe certain perfectly genuine recurrent symptoms, the result of the heavy bouts of fever he had suffered from in the East, complaining that they seemed to be becoming more frequent, probably as the result of the English climate.

Gregg listened to him in silence and, when he had finished, asked him the usual questions, making notes on the pad at his elbow as he did so. He finished by subjecting him to a very thorough examination.

"You've taken up bicycling lately, I see," he said, as he thrust his stethoscope back into his pocket.

"Yes. Anything against it?" asked Fayre, who was standing before the glass over the mantelpiece, refastening his collar.

"Nothing. You're in as perfect a state of health as any one can expect to be who has lived the greater part of his life in the Tropics. In fact, you're an admirable example of what temperate living will do for a man in a hot climate. I congratulate you!"

The words were harmless enough, but Fayre, suddenly catching sight of Gregg's face in the glass, was not taken in by them. He realized, and the discovery was anything but pleasant, that the doctor was laughing at him in a grim way all his own.

"I'll make you up a prescription, if you like," he went on, unaware that Fayre was watching him, "but I warn you it will probably be the same as the one you've got already."

"Thanks," said Fayre warily. He was waiting for the other's next move. "I suppose I may count myself lucky to have got off so lightly."

"You can thank your own common sense," was Gregg's curt rejoinder, as he turned to his writing-table.

Fayre slipped his hand into his breast pocket and the doctor gave him a quick, sidelong glance.

"There's no fee," he said abruptly.

Fayre's colour deepened as he took out his note-case and opened it, but he waited in silence for Gregg's explanation. It came with startling clarity.

"You didn't come here to consult me, Mr. Fayre. You could have done that any day at Staveley. And I doubt if you took up bicycling for the sake of exercise. And that paint you got on your coat the other day was put there on purpose. Oh, I know it was paint, all right," he cut in, as Fayre opened his mouth to speak. "I verified that, as you thought I should. I also discovered that you went straight from here to Stockley's garage, as the result, I suppose, of something my man told you. He described you, by the way, as 'a very chatty gentleman'! It was unfortunate for you that I paid my bill at Stockley's that evening and had a word with him. Stockley is a chatty gentleman, too. The thing I want to know now is, what's it all about?"

He had risen and was sitting on the edge of the writing-table, his hands in his pockets and his truculent eyes on Fayre's.

"Leslie's your friend, I understand, and I can only imagine that you're working in his interests," he went on. "I should like to mention that he's also mine and that there's nothing that would give me greater pleasure than to hear that he's been cleared. That being the case, I should be obliged if you'd tell me your object in hanging about here and questioning my servants. Anything you wish to know I prefer to tell you myself."

Fayre was silent for a moment. When he spoke he chose his words carefully, but it was evident from his whole bearing that he was saying frankly what was in his mind.

"I'm not sorry it's come to this," he said, meeting Gregg's angry gaze squarely. "To tell you the truth, I'm not proud of the part I've been playing and it's relief to me to come out into the open. In answer to your question, let me put one to you. Why have you concealed the fact that Mrs. Draycott was an old acquaintance of yours?"

The doctor's eyes shifted ever so slightly. Evidently he was unprepared for so bold an attack.

"I had my own reasons," he said curtly, "and I'm not accountable to you or any one else for them, at present, at any rate."

"You admit that you did know her?"

"I admit nothing."

"And if I tell you that I have proof that you not only knew her but were intimate with both her and her husband at one time?"

"I still admit nothing and I deny your right to question me."

"Let me put it to you in another way, then," went on Fayre, firmly keeping a hold on his temper. "You say you are a friend of Leslie's. He is lying at this moment under the shadow of an accusation that we both know is totally unfounded. In the face of that, do you still refuse to say anything?"

Gregg laughed suddenly and bitterly.

"We both know! There's a sting there, isn't there? If by clearing him you mean confessing to a murder I didn't commit, I certainly do refuse. I suppose that's what you're driving at, but you're taking a good deal for granted, aren't you?"

Fayre suddenly lost patience.

"Good heavens, man," he cried, "if you had nothing to do with it, why not say so, and if you can prove it, so much the better. I've only one motive in all this, to clear Leslie. Why work against instead of with me?"

"Because I resent your insinuations. If you think you've got anything against me, prove it. You've apparently had the damned impertinence to rake up my past and pry into my private affairs and you've all but told me to my face that I killed Mrs. Draycott. Well, take your story to the police and see what ice it cuts with them! If they've any questions to ask me I'm ready to answer them. Meanwhile, I advise you to take your amateur detective work elsewhere."

Fayre hesitated for a moment; then he decided to make one more effort towards conciliation.

"I'm very sorry you've taken this line," he said. "Frankly, I have hoped all along that you would be able to give some satisfactory explanation of your attitude towards the whole affair. I can very well believe that the subject is a painful one to you and I can sympathize with your reluctance to drag it up again after all these years, but you must admit that your behaviour has been open to suspicion. Once more I appeal to you to act reasonably, if only for Leslie's sake."

Gregg's only answer was to stride heavily to the door and fling it open.

"I have already told you that I resent your interference," he said shortly. "If I make any statement, it will be to those who have a right to demand it. You can hardly be surprised if I don't consider you one of them. Take what steps you please, but I warn you that I am quite prepared to meet them."

Without a word Fayre took out his note-case once more. He walked over to the writing-table and picked up the prescription Gregg had written, leaving two guineas in its place. Then he took his hat and coat and left the room with such dignity as he could muster. As he passed through the hall he heard the crash of the study door as Gregg slammed it, and realized that in the first encounter, at any rate, the honours of war were to the doctor. Either the man was innocent or he had put up the most amazing bluff Fayre had ever encountered.

And the worst of it was that, as Gregg no doubt guessed, he was not in a position to act. His information, as far as it went, pointed to but one thing: Gregg's deliberate attempt to conceal from the police his former connection with Mrs. Draycott. Beyond this, Fayre had nothing to go on, unless he could trace the mysterious car to Gregg. According to Stockley, the proprietor of the garage, he had taken out the hired car at five-thirty. This would give him ample time to drive to one of the several other garages within a radius of ten to fifteen miles, change his car, pick up Mrs. Draycott and arrive at the farm at about the time the murder was presumably committed. But here the London number on the car described by the carter arose as a distinct stumbling-block, for it was extremely improbable that a local garage would have a London car for hire. On the other hand, if by some extraordinary chance one of them had let out such a car, it should be easy enough to get on the track of it; but Fayre realized that the doctor had him at a hopeless disadvantage unless he could manage to trace his movements on the night of the twenty-third, and he recognized the cleverness of the man in forcing his hand before his investigations were complete. And yet, for the life of him, he could not make up his mind whether Gregg's outburst had been mere bluff or the genuine anger of a man smarting under the sting of a false accusation. Either way Fayre had cut an uncommonly poor figure and he was painfully aware of the fact.

CHAPTER XIV

AFTER DINNER that night Lord Staveley, wishing to ring up his bookie, strolled into the little anteroom that housed the telephone. Here, to his surprise, he discovered Fayre. He had settled himself comfortably in the one armchair and, with the help of the local telephone directory, was busy compiling a list on a half-sheet of paper. Bill Staveley eyed him quizzically.

"Rotten place to spend the evening," he observed with cheerful scorn. "Looking for a good dentist, or is it Sherlock Holmes on the trail?"

"It's Holmes in the devil of a muddle," was Fayre's acid rejoinder. "I've come a cropper, Bill!"

"In other words, you've met your match. Who's the local genius?"

"Gregg. I started out to pump him according to the most approved methods and he pumped me instead and very efficiently too! And he was uncommonly disagreeable about it."

"He would be. What have you got against him? I suppose you know that, amongst other things, he's the Police Surgeon?"

"I don't care if he's the Prime Minister!" snapped Fayre, still hot from his gruelling at Gregg's hands. "But I'd give something to know where he was on the night of Mrs. Draycott's death!"

Bill Staveley gave a low whistle.

"As bad as that, is it? Why, he was at the farm, wasn't he? I thought he gave evidence."

"He turned up at the farm soon after ten o'clock, after the police had been trying to get him for nearly an hour. The assumption was that he had come in late from a case and, as far as I know, he has never been asked to give an account of his movements. All I do know is that he left the Whitbury garage at five-thirty in a hired car and, apparently, did not get home till about nine-thirty, when he found the police call waiting for him."

Staveley's eyes narrowed as he stared at Fayre.

"You don't seriously mean that you suspect Gregg of Mrs. Draycott's murder?" he ejaculated.

"On my word, I don't know what to think. If the fellow was bluffing this afternoon he did it uncommonly well. If he wasn't, why didn't he clear himself? He could have done it easily."

"What line did he take?"

"Told me to go to the devil—in other words, the police—and flatly refused to give any account of himself whatever. The worst of it is, he's in a very strong position. Practically the only thing I've got to go on at present is the fact that he undoubtedly knew Mrs. Draycott at one time and has gone out of his way to lie to the police about it. You must admit it looks fishy."

"The devil he did! Do the police know?"

Fayre looked rather sheepish.

"Unless they've been pursuing the same lines of investigation as myself, they don't. I kept quiet about it in the hope that it might lead to something."

"Being naturally afraid that the Force, in its naïve way, would blunder. Oh, Hatter, Hatter, this comes of reading detective stories!"

"I know; you needn't rub it in. I've made an infernal hash of the whole thing."

"How much did you tell the fellow?"

"Quite enough to put him on his guard, unfortunately."

"What's your theory about the whole thing?"

"Somebody picked up Mrs. Draycott in a car and drove her to Leslie's farm. Everything points to that. We've got good reason to believe that we've got part of the number of the car. It ran into a farm-cart and the carter took what he could see of it. If the man in the car was Gregg he must have done one of two things. Either he deliberately faked the number of the car he hired from the Whitbury garage, or he changed cars somewhere before he picked up Mrs. Draycott. There is, of course, the possibility that he picked her up in the hired car and somehow managed to reach the farm and get away again without being seen. In the light of what we know, this is extremely unlikely."

"If he's got an alibi, why on earth doesn't the fellow produce it?"

"Either because he's so sure of his position that he can afford not to or for the more simple reason that he hasn't got one. Meanwhile, I'm left kicking my heels. I've got a list here of the garages in this neighbourhood within a radius of fifteen miles or so. If he did change cars, it will be bound to have been at one of them."

"Touching spectacle of Mr. Fayre, late of the Indian Civil, peddling on his little push-bike within a radius of fifteen miles!" mused Bill Staveley. "Poor old Hatter! I can let you off that, though. You don't know Foot, do you?"

"That's the chap who drove me the other day, isn't it?"

"Probably. He was my batman in France and, after the war, I gave him a driver's course. He took to it like a duck to water and he's a first-rate chauffeur and an uncommonly intelligent chap. He's bought himself a motor-bike and takes it to pieces every Saturday night just for fun and I'll bet there isn't a garage round here where he hasn't talked motor for hours. Give him the description of the car you want and he'll find it for you if it's anywhere in this part of the country."

"The question is, will he talk?"

"Not if I give him a hint. You can leave that part of the job to him quite safely. On the other hand, if we could get onto the case Gregg was called to that night we could keep Foot out of it altogether. Even if he was at the farm that night he must have gone on somewhere afterwards. He's not such a fool as to drive vaguely round the country for three solid hours before going home. You may be pretty certain he looked up a patient, even if he wasn't called to one."

"None of the tenants been ill or injured, I suppose?"

"Not that I know of, but we might go through the local rag. I've got it in my room and it's one of those conscientious papers that puts in catchy little comments on old Mrs. Snook's chilblains and that sort of thing. It doesn't miss much and if any one hurt himself that night, we shall find it there."

They adjourned to the library, where they spent a fruitless half-hour searching the columns of the local paper. They were about to give it up in despair when Fayre, who had reached the last page, gave a cry.

"What about this?" he asked, pointing to the *Births* column. *"March 23rd. The wife of George Hammond of The Willow Farm, Besley, of a son."*

"Would Gregg be their man?"

"Sure to be. He attends all the farmers round here. Hammond's a tenant of mine and I can ride over tomorrow, if you like, and do the heavy landlord. As a matter of fact, it'll probably be expected of me, sooner or later, so it won't rouse any comment. I take it that you want to know what time Gregg was sent for, what time he arrived, and when he left, with a description of his car, if I can get it without rousing too much curiosity. Anything else?"

"No. I think that covers it. How long ought it to take him to reach the Hammonds?"

"If he left Whitbury at five-thirty he should arrive at Besley at five to six, and the farm is, roughly, five to ten minutes' run from Besley. Say thirty to thirty-five minutes."

"And if he took the corner of the lane running to Greycross and then Leslie's farm on the way?"

"Give me a minute. That's considerably more complicated."

He took a pencil and made some notes on an old envelope.

"Just under the hour, I should say. Perhaps longer. That's not allowing for getting out and going into the farm."

"In that case, we'll give the garages the go-by for the moment," decided Fayre. "Time enough for them when we've discovered whether Gregg was at the Hammonds' or not. It will be just as well to keep your man out of it, if possible."

"Good. Then I'll ride over to Willow Farm tomorrow and see what I can find out. By the way, did I tell you that Kean is coming down to-night? You can have the whole thing out with him to-morrow. He ought to be able to suggest something."

Fayre gave an exclamation of surprise.

"Sybil said nothing when I saw her."

"She did not know. He telephoned yesterday saying he could get away earlier than he had expected and was going to motor straight through. I gather that he's going to take Sybil back to town by car as soon as she's fit to travel. He'll be on tenter-hooks till she's seen her own doctor, and I don't blame him. I should feel the same myself.

To tell you the truth, fond as I am of her, I shall be relieved to get rid of the responsibility. It's touch-and-go when she has these attacks."

"She's better away from this business," said Fayre thoughtfully. "I'd no idea until I saw her on Tuesday how much she's taking it to heart."

"She's got a very weak spot for Cynthia. She's a fascinating little minx and I fancy Sybil would have given a lot to have had a daughter of her own. What about Bridge, eh?"

Lady Staveley's brother and a nephew had arrived the day before and they played until the arrival of Kean shortly before midnight. He had come without a chauffeur and had driven his car himself all that day and through a good portion of the night before. Fayre was amazed at his powers of endurance. If he were exhausted he certainly did not show it in the few minutes that he stood chatting with the four men, but he was impatient to see his wife and went upstairs almost immediately and Fayre did not get a chance to talk to him until after breakfast the next day, when he found him on the terrace, waiting for Gregg to put in an appearance. He was intent on getting his wife up to London as soon as the doctor would allow her to travel. It was evident that her collapse had been a severe shock to him and only her insistent messages on the telephone through Lady Staveley had prevented him from throwing up his work and traveling down post-haste to see for himself how she was. Even now his mind was full of her and Fayre was aware that his interest in what he had to relate was purely perfunctory.

It appeared that he had seen Grey and was fairly well posted as to what had transpired since his departure. Fayre told him the result of his inquiries about Gregg.

"I think you're barking up the wrong tree," said Kean frankly when he had finished. "The fact that the fellow knew Mrs. Draycott does not necessarily point to him as her murderer."

"On the other hand, he's the only person we have been able to discover who had a definite grudge against her."

"Come to that, she was hardly popular with a good many people. And there's the difficulty of the motor. You'll find it a hard job to connect him with that."

"Unless he faked the number on Stockley's motor or changed cars somewhere."

"In which case the crime was premeditated and, on your own showing, that is unlikely. A man does not detest a woman for years and take no steps about it and then, just because he happens to run across her staying in the same neighbourhood, devise an elaborate scheme to murder her. Psychologically, your theory doesn't hang together unless we can discover some better motive than that of mere dislike. The best thing you can do is to take the story to the police; he will then be obliged to tell them where he was that night. He can't take the line with them that he took with you, and I've a strong conviction that he will be able to produce a perfectly satisfactory alibi."

"You advise me not to waste time in following it up, then?" asked Fayre, feeling more than a little damped.

Kean's smile was so friendly that it was impossible to take offence.

"If you want my real advice, old chap," he said, "I should say drop the whole thing and leave it to Grey and the police. Let Grey have a clear account of what you've done and he will deal with it. I'm not belittling your work: it's been uncommonly good as far as it goes, and if Gregg *is* concerned it may prove invaluable; but it's useless to pit yourself against experts or to try to act without proper authority. How did you get hold of this letter to Gregg?"

The question came with startling abruptness and Fayre stifled a sudden spasm of amusement as he realized that Kean was using professional methods on him.

"I took it out of his desk when I was waiting for him the other day," he answered with rather exaggerated meekness.

"And put yourself in a very nasty position if he finds out, apart from the fact that, if he jumps to the fact that you searched his desk, it will be the easiest thing in the world for him to destroy any evidence it contains."

"Do you suggest that I should have kept it?" asked Fayre, with a mischievous twinkle in his eye.

"I certainly don't," was Kean's dry rejoinder. "But I should like to point out that if his desk had been searched officially the police would have kept the letter and we should have had our evidence to hand if we'd needed it. That sort of amateur detective work is all right in fiction, but it's dangerous in practise."

Fayre was left feeling rather sheepish and distinctly obstinate. He had taken his dressing-down meekly enough and, on the whole, he felt bound to admit that it was not undeserved, but he hadn't the smallest intention of being warned off the course by Kean or any one else. And he still held to his theory about Gregg.

The rest of his day was spent as harmlessly as even Kean could have wished. Fayre sat for a time with Sybil, who was up and dressed and so much better that the doctor had sanctioned her removal, by easy stages, to London the following day. The various members of the house-party were in and out of the room most of the time, so that, to Fayre's relief, there was no opportunity to broach the subject of the murder.

As he was dressing for dinner he received a visit from Bill Staveley. He was still in riding kit and had just returned from his call at Hammond's farm.

"I've got your times for you," he began, "and I found out what car Gregg was driving. A very cunning bit of work, I may tell you, on my part! I'm beginning to think I've got a natural gift for this sort of thing! If you imagine I'm just a sort of Watson, my dear Holmes, you're entirely mistaken."

"If you want real appreciation and encouragement let me suggest that you go and tell Edward all about it," advised Fayre dryly. "Meanwhile, when you've finished wagging your tail, you might produce the proofs of your genius."

Lord Staveley chuckled.

"So that's how the land lies, is it? Was he very down on our little efforts? He always was a damned superior beggar."

"I kept you out of it, which is more than you deserve. What did you find at the Hammonds'?"

"A brand-new baby, among other things, which was brought into the world by Gregg at eight-fifteen precisely, on the night of the twenty-third. They telephoned to him between four-thirty and five and he must have started almost at once and walked over to Whitbury for the car. And I've no doubt he used some language, too, considering what a beastly night it was. After that things get more interesting. You say he left Stockley's at five-thirty. Well, he didn't get to Hammond's till close on seven. Hammond was quite definite about that. He was in a bit of a stew because Gregg was so late."

Fayre, who was busy with his tie, spun round with an exclamation. Staveley nodded.

"That's a fact," he said quietly. "An hour and a half to do thirty minutes' run. Of course, he may have called somewhere else on the way, but, considering that Hammond's message was urgent, it doesn't seem likely."

"What excuse did he give Hammond?"

"None, I gather, but I imagine things were pretty urgent by the time he got there. He just said he was sorry he was late and they were all in such a state of nerves by that time that nothing more was said. It's the chap's first baby and he seems to have thought the world was coming to an end. Gregg left about nine, which would bring him home just in time to get the police call."

"Did you find out what car he turned up in?"

"Stockley's. Hammond knows it well because they take in lodgers in the summer and they use Stockley's cars. I couldn't very well ask him about the number, but he didn't seem to have noticed anything unusual."

"I wonder if the carter could have made a mistake?"

"Not likely. He probably knows Stockley's cars. Every one does round here and he'd be practically certain to know Gregg, even if it was dark. You'll have to rule out the garage car, I suspect. That is, if Gregg's really implicated."

Fayre sighed.

"Well, we seem to be getting somewhere at last," he said. "Though Heaven knows what it's going to lead to."

"Do we break the glad news to Edward or not?" asked Staveley mischievously.

"I'm blessed if we do!" answered Fayre, with unexpected heat. "After all, it's Grey's job at present. I'll write to him to-night."

He kept his word and sent the solicitor a clear and concise account of all that had happened.

He was hardly to be blamed if there was a spark of malice in his eyes the next morning as he stood on the steps with the rest of the house-party watching the departure of the Keans. Sir Edward was too absorbed in the task of making his wife comfortable for the journey to notice anything unusual in his friend's manner, but Sybil Kean gave him a moment of discomfort as she said good-by.

"I believe you and Bill are up to some mischief," she said jestingly. "I advise you to keep an eye on them, Eve! They had their heads together after breakfast this morning—and look at them now!"

Fayre managed to retain an expression of bland innocence, but Bill Staveley was grinning openly.

"I thought so," she went on quietly. "Always distrust Hatter, Eve, when he looks as if butter wouldn't melt in his mouth."

At this moment, to Fayre's relief, Kean joined her, his arms full of cushions, and together they went down the steps to the car.

They had hardly disappeared round the bend at the end of the long drive when Fayre was rung up by Cynthia.

"Tubby's done it, Uncle Fayre! Didn't I tell you he would?" Her voice was breathless with excitement. "I'm coming back this afternoon on the two-thirty. Will you ask Eve to have me met? I'll tell you all about it when I see you, but we've traced the car, broken mudguard and everything!"

CHAPTER XV

WHEN CYNTHIA stepped out of the train at Staveley Grange she found Fayre waiting on the platform. The station-master, an old friend of her childhood, bustled forward to receive her and she did not have an opportunity of unburdening herself of her news till she found herself alone with Fayre in the car on their way to Staveley.

"I've one disappointment for you, Uncle Fayre," she began. "We've traced the car, but we haven't got the rest of the number."

For a moment he could not conceal his chagrin. He had been counting on that one invaluable piece of information ever since he had received her message the night before.

"Do you mean to say that two garages can have housed the car and neither have taken the number? It's incredible!"

"This time it wasn't there for them to take. The man said that the car came in with half the numberplate missing! It was broken clean across just after the number 7, and the owner said that he had been run into from behind by a lorry just outside Carlisle. Tubby had a talk with one of the cleaners who had had a good look at the car while he was working on it and he said that the number-plate was an aluminium one, the sort that will snap easily with a smart blow from a hammer. Except for the cracked mudguard there were no other signs of a collision, but there was paint, red paint, on the mudguard. He remembered trying to get it off. Tubby thinks it possible that the man broke the plate himself and that's why the carter couldn't see more than half."

"Looks as if our friend, Mr. Page, must have done it soon after he left Stockley's garage. They certainly said nothing about a broken number-plate there."

"Tubby says he wouldn't get far with only half a number-plate and, if he were stopped, we ought to be able to trace him."

"Did the garage people describe the man at all?"

"If you can call it a description. It was very like Stockley's. I think it must have been the same man. Tall and thin, with a heavy coat and goggles that he did not take off. He brought in the car on the evening of the twenty-third, about eight-thirty and took it out again on the twenty-sixth, but they are not certain of the time. Tubby says he's sure that the man was trying to avoid observation or he wouldn't have gone to that garage. It's a rotten little place almost on the outskirts of Carlisle and it's not near a hotel or on any of the direct routes north and south. It's the last place any one would leave a car if he were just passing through. Tubby had an awful hunt before he found it."

"Page must have been in Carlisle from the twenty-third till the twenty-sixth, then. I wonder where he went after that? Probably south to London. The chances are that he didn't dare risk having the mudguard mended in Carlisle, in which case there is a bare chance that we may trace him by it on the London route. And, as you say, he'd have to do something about the number."

"As for that, he could use a temporary number, but it would be more noticeable than an ordinary number-plate."

"I'll send a line to Grey to-night and see if he can get onto anything at his end. He'll know better how to set about it than I do. Frankly, I still think this man, Page, may have nothing whatever to do with the affair. He may have had his own reasons for lying low. After all, there've been several cars stolen in the north during the last few weeks. It's becoming a regular profession and he may have been working his way to London with some car he had taken. We've got very little to go on."

Having decided not to take Cynthia into his confidence on the subject of Gregg's complicity, he could not give her his real reason for doubting the importance of the Page clue. Argue as he might, he could not manage to connect the doctor with the strange car, and if he was at the Hammonds' farm from seven till nine on the twenty-third he could not possibly have been in Carlisle at eight-thirty.

Cynthia was gazing at him in astonishment.

"But, Uncle Fayre, the car was seen coming away from the farm just after the murder was committed, and you know that that lane doesn't go beyond the farm. It must have been coming from there and there are hardly liked to have been two cars with *Y.0.7.* on the number-plate and a cracked mudguard. You can't rule the car out altogether!"

"The tramp may have been lying. We haven't cleared him yet, remember," objected Fayre.

"The carter's honest enough, anyway, and he backed up everything the tramp said. After all, the real description of the car came from him. And you've always said you were sure Mrs. Draycott was driven to John's."

"I still think she was driven there, but we can't afford to ignore the fact that cars have been known before now to turn up a blind lane and come back in a hurry, after finding out their mistake and that's what this car may very well have done. I'm all for tracing this man Page, if we can, but I shouldn't be surprised to hear that he found a car already at the gate of the farm when he got there and that all he did was to turn round and go back the way he had come. I'm only trying to save you from possible disappointment, my dear."

"In that case, we're just where we were before," sighed the girl, her hopes cruelly dashed.

Fayre suddenly realized that, in his determination not to be diverted from his pursuit of Gregg, he had allowed himself to wound and discourage Cynthia. He was conscious, too, that his case against the doctor was getting lamentably weak and that only his native obstinacy prevented him from admitting it.

"My dear, what nonsense!" he exclaimed remorsefully. "Don't you see the immense importance of getting in touch with the one person who was actually on the spot at the time of the murder, even if he didn't actually commit it, and, mind you, I don't say that he didn't. For all we know, though, he may have seen the thing happen and it's hardly possible that he didn't hear the shot. If we do get him, it will be your doing. You've been invaluable."

Cynthia had been watching him closely.

"I believe you do mean it," she said at last, "and are not saying it just to comfort me."

The car drew up before the broad double flight of steps that led to the great oak doors of Staveley, and Cynthia prepared to get out.

"But I would most awfully like to know," she added over her shoulder, "what you've got up your funny old sleeve."

With that she ran up the steps and disappeared into the house, leaving Fayre staring in front of him, a comic picture of dismay.

"Bless the women!" he ejaculated as he prepared to follow her.

He made for the library and entrenched himself firmly behind the *Times*; but he wasn't to escape for long. Less than ten minutes later he heard Cynthia's voice in the hall and then her quick, light step as she came into the room. He buried his nose deeper in the leading article.

There was a protesting creak from his chair as she settled herself comfortably on the arm and placed a slim white hand between his eyes and the print.

"I did play the game, didn't I, Uncle Fayre?" she murmured softly. "I never asked a single question. Don't you think I deserve a lump of sugar?"

"What do you want now?" he asked, trying in vain to speak gruffly. Cynthia in her wheedling moods was doubly dangerous.

"Supposing we were to nip back into the car and run over to the Cottage Hospital, just you and me.

If we go at once we shall be back in plenty of time for tea."

"And may I ask what you propose to do there?"

"Sit in the car while you go in and see the tramp. Please, Uncle Fayre! If you do I promise I won't bother you to tell me anything you don't want to."

"What do you suggest that I should say to the tramp when I do see him? He's told us all he knows already."

"I don't believe he has. I've been thinking that, if he was really lying there all that time, he must have seen any one else who came up the lane and, if you really think the Page man hasn't got anything to do with it, then somebody else must have driven to the farm while the tramp was there. How did Mrs. Draycott get there, if the Page car didn't bring her?"

"If you can answer that, my child, you've all but solved the mystery," sighed Fayre.

"Well, if the tramp can't answer it, who can?" demanded Cynthia. "You said he was frightened and suspicious and on his guard against the police. Why shouldn't he have been keeping back something? I've got a hunch that if you treat him like a human being and get him to believe that you're not his enemy like the rest, you may get something out of him. Anyway, it's worth trying. Just to please me, Uncle Fayre! His leg's getting better and once he's out and in the hands of the police you won't have a chance to get at him."

Fayre knew that he was weakening, but he made a determined effort to retain his comfortable seat by the fire.

"It's an absolutely forlorn hope, you know," he urged. "And the chances are that they won't let us see him when we get there. You must remember that I went with Grey last time. Besides, by the time we get the car ..."

"The car's there now," stated Cynthia calmly. "I ordered it as I was coming through the hall just now. I told them I'd drive myself. Please, Uncle Fayre!" With a sigh Fayre heaved himself out of his chair. "You're a nuisance and a bully and you don't play fair," he complained, with a smile that belied his words. "But I suppose if I'm to have my tea in peace, I shall have to humour you."

Cynthia drove with her usual cheerful abandon and they arrived at the police station at Whitbury in record time. Fayre had insisted on going there for a pass before attempting to storm the hospital and was glad he had done so, for the Inspector recognized Cynthia as the daughter of a J. P. and was ready to oblige her.

"As a matter of fact, we've withdrawn our man," he said. "The hospital authorities are quite capable of looking after their, patient. He can't walk on that leg yet and nobody except yourself and your friend has visited him so far, Mr. Fayre. He's still under suspicion, of course, but it's ten to one against his having anything to do with the murder."

They drove on to the hospital and Fayre presented his pass, leaving Cynthia in the car outside.

He found his man sitting up in bed reading the paper. His appearance had improved considerably in the interval, owing, no doubt, to good food and soap and water. He received Fayre's friendly greeting with the reserve of one who has learned to put his trust in no one.

"Glad to see you looking so fit," said Fayre. "I was passing and thought I'd look in and see how you were doing. Also, I wanted to thank you."

The man observed him warily.

"I ain't done nothing for you that I know of," he volunteered grudgingly.

"On the contrary, you've helped me and my friend very considerably and we're grateful to you. The fact is, this man they've arrested in connection with the farm murder is a pal of mine and I'm doing what I can to help him. If it hadn't been for you, I should never have got onto that car you saw, and that car may mean a lot to us. If there's anything I can do for you when you get about again, let me know. You won't be fit for the road yet awhile, you know."

The hunted look came back into the tramp's face. "I wish to God I was back on the road!" he burst out. "Fat chance I've got of ever gettin' there, it seems to me. I ain't blind nor deaf neither. The police 'ave got it in for me proper. I know where I'm goin' from 'ere, right enough. And me got no more to do with it than a babe unborn!"

"I believe you," said Fayre simply. "It's just a bit of bad luck that you and Mr. Leslie got dragged in at all. It's the third person that's responsible for all this that I'm anxious to find."

The man gave him a quick, sidelong glance.

"Is Mr. Leslie the gent what found the body?" he asked.

Fayre nodded.

"'E didn't do it," affirmed the man with surprising conviction. "I see 'im through the winder when 'e found 'er, like I told the police. Rare taken aback, 'e was. 'E didn't do it. I could've told them that if they'd asked me. The police!"

He spoke with infinite scorn.

"I know he didn't; but the trouble is to prove it. And what clears him will probably clear you—that's why I wanted to have a chat with you. You haven't any theory of your own, I suppose?"

"Not me. I wasn't nowhere near the place when it 'appened. Didn't even 'ear the shot, for the matter of that."

He was talking freely now and Fayre could see that he had managed to gain the man's confidence and was quick to act on the discovery. He bent forward confidentially.

"There's absolutely nothing you can remember, no matter how small, that happened while you were waiting at the corner of the lane, is there? The murder was committed while you were lying there and there may be something you didn't think worth mentioning before. I give you my word I won't pass it on to the police, unless it's something that will go towards fastening the guilt on the right person."

"Come to that, 'ow am I to know as you don't think I'm the right person, mister?" queried the man shrewdly. "I was there all right, wasn't I?"

"I'm ready to take your word for it that you never budged from the corner of the lane, and I'm taking my chances there, you know. But if I'm straight with you I look to you to be straight with me."

The tramp leaned back on his pillows wearily. "What do you want me to say?" he asked bitterly. "That I saw the bloomin' murderer goin' up the lane with the weapon in 'is 'and? I tell you, I didn't see no one, 'cause there wasn't no one to see."

"You're certain of that?"

"As sure as I'm lyin' 'ere, which I wish I wasn't."

The conversation languished and Fayre had almost made up his mind to give it up as a bad job and depart when the man turned on him suddenly.

"What time would you say that there murder was committed, mister?" he asked.

"According to what little we have been able to find out, about six-thirty. It must have been then, if the car you saw had anything to do with it."

Fayre took some sheets of paper out of his pocket and looked up the notes he had made.

"Here you are. You saw the car going towards the farm at about six-twenty and you saw it again, coming away, at six-forty or thereabouts. At six-thirty you were at the Lodge gates of Galston. If you can prove that, I think you may consider yourself out of it altogether."

The man hesitated.

"'Ow can I prove it? What d'you think?" he said at last. "But I'll tell you this, though I wouldn't say it to no one else. And it's not for the police, mind you. You said as you wouldn't pass it on, mister?"

"I won't. Fire away."

"There was a woman as might 'ave seen me. She was comin' towards me on the Whitbury road and she turned into the Lodge just before I got there. Lodge-keeper's wife, I put her down to be."

Fayre stared at him in amazement.

"Good Lord, man!" he cried. "Why on earth didn't you say so when they questioned you? It's your one chance of clearing yourself. How do you know she didn't see you?"

"I 'ad me own reasons," stated the man stubbornly. "The cops won't get nothin' out of me I don't choose to tell."

Fayre shrugged his shoulders.

"Hanging's a nasty death," he suggested.

His curiosity was thoroughly roused, but he knew that his one chance of getting anything out of the man was not to seem too eager.

The tramp's face seemed to grow whiter and more pinched.

"They can't fix it onto me," he whispered doggedly.

"They can, unless you can prove that you were not at the farm at six-thirty. You don't seem to realize that you're in almost as bad a position as Mr. Leslie."

"Supposin' she didn't see me?" The man was evidently wavering.

"If you saw her she probably saw you."

The logic of this was so obvious that it reached the tramp's brain, warped though it was with suspicion. He considered it for a moment; then, raising himself on his elbow, brought his face close to Fayre's.

"I've been a fool," he whispered. "I see it now. But I was afraid of gettin' in bad with the police. Will you promise not to pass it on without I tell you?"

"I told you I wouldn't. Go on."

"It was this way. I see the woman, like I told you, and I watched her go into the Lodge. Then I went on to the Lodge, meanin' to ask for a bite of something. When I got there I see something lyin' in the road and I picks it up. It was a purse. It 'adn't got much in it, only a 'alf-crown."

He paused, evidently at a loss as to how to proceed.

"And you pocketed the half-crown and put the purse back where you found it," suggested Fayre calmly.

He knew now why the man had kept silence and marvelled at his mentality. Better, apparently, to risk the gallows for a crime he hadn't committed than risk "getting in bad with the police" for one he had. The one evil he understood, the other he hadn't sufficient imagination to realize.

"That's right, mister. But I wasn't goin' to tell the cops that, was I?"

"No, I suppose not. You can trust me, but, I warn you, you'll probably have to make a clean breast of it in the end if you want to clear yourself of something much more serious."

"Seems to me I'm for it, whether I tells 'em or whether I don't. Never did 'ave no blinkin' luck, did I?"

Fayre had risen to his feet and stood looking down at the man in the bed. He was not a prepossessing object, with his furtive eyes and weak chin. But probably, as he had said, he had never had any luck and Fayre was conscious of a sudden feeling of pity as he realized the utter friendlessness of this wretched, homeless creature who existed only on the sufferance of other men more fortunate and stronger than himself. No wonder he trusted no one and felt instinctively that every man's hand was against him.

"Look here," said Fayre, speaking on impulse. "I'll do this for you. I'll go to the Lodge myself and see the woman there. If she remembers you, well and good; you'll have your alibi ready then if you need it. As to the purse, I'll settle with her myself over the half-crown. You've spent it, I suppose?"

"Most of it, mister. The rest's there."

He jerked his head in the direction of the table by his bed. On it lay the contents of the dirty red handkerchief he had been carrying when he was picked up. The police had been through them and found nothing worth confiscating.

"Very well, I'll square you with her. I think I can undertake to do that without giving you away. If she's a decent woman she'll no doubt agree not to prosecute once she's got the money back. I will give you my word not to go to the police about it, but, if you take my advice, you'll make a clean breast of it to them as soon as you get on your feet again. Otherwise, you know where you'll find yourself. However, that's your affair. Anyway, I'll see to the purse business for you, which is more than you deserve, you know!"

If Fayre's last words were harsh his smile was very friendly as he extended his hand in farewell. Weakness had always irritated and, at the same time, appealed to him and he had only just begun to understand how peculiarly helpless the class to which this man belonged must be.

The tramp thrust a limp hand into his extended one. He was evidently struggling for expression.

"Thank you, mister; I shan't forget it," was all he said, but Fayre knew he spoke the truth.

He had reached the door when the man called him back.

"I say, mister, I reckon you'd best take these towards that there half-crown. It's all I got left."

He was holding out the small pile of coppers that had been on the table by his side. Fayre took them from him and gently laid them down again beside the folded red handkerchief. The man watched him and, as he did so, his eyes fell on a small object which lay among his pitiful possessions.

"I'd rather you took it, mister," he said half-heartedly.

Then, as Fayre shook his head: "Thank you kindly, all the same. You were askin' if there was anythin', no matter how small, as I could remember. There's that, if it's any use to you. It 'ad gone clean out of my 'ead. It won't 'elp you much, but if I'd remembered I'd 'a' give it to you. By the gate of the farm, it was. I stepped on it in the dark goin' in, when I was on my way to the barn."

He held out his hand and in the palm was lying the cap of a "Red Dwarf" stylographic pen.

CHAPTER XVI

As FAYRE PASSED down the broad staircase of the Cottage Hospital he reviewed his conversation with the tramp and decided that, considering the little he had gained by it, he might as well have stayed by the comfortable fireside in the library. Cynthia's "hunch" had not amounted to much, after all, and he was sorry, more on her account than his own, for he had not expected anything himself from the interview. It had, however, simplified matters, in so far as it had definitely wiped off the tramp from the possible list of suspects. He had a strong conviction that the man's story was true.

He suddenly became conscious of something hard pressing against the palm of his hand and remembered the little red cap the tramp had given him at parting. It belonged obviously to the pen he had picked up on his visit to the farm and he was in the act of slipping it into his pocket and dismissing it from his mind when a thought struck him which caused him to pause in his descent and stand gazing blankly into the hall below. He had suddenly realized that if the tramp had picked up the cap on the occasion of his arrival at the farm somewhere about seven o'clock the pen must have been dropped still earlier in the evening. Fayre's mind went back to the copper-coloured sequins he had found by the gate. They had been lying close to the pen and he found himself trying to picture what had happened.

If Mrs. Draycott's dress had caught in the gate in passing, the pen might have fallen from her companion's pocket while he was disentangling it. Or could the unhappy woman have been seized with a premonition of her fate and hesitated on the very threshold of the farm? At any rate, the finding of the cap by the tramp did away once for all with the possibility of the pen's having been dropped after the murder by a reporter, as Kean had suggested, and its proximity to the spangles from Mrs. Draycott's dress pointed to the possibility that she and her companion might have paused for a moment near the gate on their way to the house.

The pen had suddenly developed into a far more important link than they had supposed, and Fayre went on his way feeling that not only had his morning not been wasted, but that Cynthia, this time at least, had scored, not only against himself but against Kean, a fact which afforded him a certain amount of satisfaction.

He found Cynthia deep in conversation with the porter of the hospital.

"Cummin's son is our undergardener at Galston," she explained with a smile that included both men. "I was telling him that he's the only person who really understands Mother's beloved roses."

Fayre, watching her, understood why it was that she had, not only the estate, but the whole of the village of Galston, at her feet, and remembered how even Gunnet had dropped his official reserve when speaking of her. He climbed into the car and, after a few more friendly words to the porter, they drove off.

"Well?" she asked as they swept round the corner into the High Street of Whitbury. "Did he say anything?"

"He cleared himself, if what he says is true. Is there time to call on your lodge-keeper at Galston on the way back?"

She turned to him in surprise.

"Of course. It's a little out of the way, but not enough to matter. Why do you want to see him?"

"I want to see her, if there is a her."

"There is. His wife, Mrs. Doggett, is a dear old thing. If you want to get something out of her, you'd better leave it to me. I've known her all my life."

"I do. I want her to deal kindly with our friend, the tramp, for one thing."

He told her the story of the purse and then showed her the red cap the man had given him and explained its significance.

"Mrs. Doggett will be all right; I'll manage her. But the cap is important, Uncle Fayre! I'm glad you went!"

"So am I, now. You were quite right and it's decent of you not to rub it in!"

He waited while Cynthia went into the Lodge. After a short interval she came out, followed by a pleasant-looking old woman.

"This is Mrs. Doggett," she said. "Mr. Fayre's a great friend of mine, Mrs. Doggett, so you must be kind to him."

Mrs. Doggett's answer was a broad smile and an old-fashioned curtsey.

"It *was* her purse," went on Cynthia, "and she's going to be a brick and let the poor man off. Tell Mr. Fayre about it, Mrs. Doggett."

"I must 'a' dropped it just before I got to the gate, sir," explained the old woman. "I hadn't been home more than a few minutes when I missed it and went out again into the road to have a look. I found it almost at once, but it was empty. I was quite took aback, wondering who could 'a' cleaned it out in such a short time, when I remembered seein' some one comin' towards me as I neared the gate. I went up the road a bit, but I couldn't see no one, so I give it up. There wasn't only half-a-crown in it and, if he was in want, I'm glad he should have it, pore soul."

"Do you remember at all what time you reached home that night?" asked Fayre.

"I couldn't tell you to a minute, sir, but it must have been somewhere round about six-thirty, I should say. I'd been doin' me bit of shoppin' at Whitbury and I usually stay till the shops close at six and it's just about half an hour's walk home."

"How long were you in the house, do you think, before you discovered your loss?"

"I can't rightly say, but not more than a quarter of an hour. I hurried out as soon as I found it was gone. It wasn't long, because me 'usband come in for 'is supper at seven and I'd got it all cooked and ready for 'im by then. And *he* hasn't been late once this month, to my knowledge, sir."

"Then, that clears the tramp. You've done him more than one good turn to-day, Mrs. Doggett. Perhaps Lady Cynthia explained that I had promised not to report the theft to the police, so if you wouldn't mind keeping it dark ..."

"They won't hear nothing from me, sir! I don't want no traffic with them. Writin' everythin' down in their little books! Oh, I couldn't, sir, thankin' you kindly all the same," she finished, as Fayre slipped a note into her hand. "It wasn't only half-a-crown and I don't grudge it 'im."

"You've got to, Mrs. Doggett," called Cynthia over her shoulder as the car leaped forward. "And you deserve it for being such a brick."

"So that's that!" said Fayre, with striking lack of originality. "He's out of it. Now we can concentrate on the real culprits. It'll take us all our time, too!" he added ruefully.

He spoke more truly than he realized. They had only just passed the lane leading to Leslie's farm when a small two-seater turned out of a by-road on their right and sped past them on the way to Whitbury.

It was being driven by Gregg and by his side was the man who had cleaned the paint off Fayre's coat in the doctor's garage. At the sight of Cynthia Gregg raised his hand towards his hat, but his eyes were on Fayre and it seemed to the latter that his glance held both contempt and defiance.

He turned and looked after the car and, at the sight of the luggage-rack at the back, an exclamation broke from him. It was loaded with a portmanteau and a big suitcase.

"Good Lord, I might have guessed it! What an ass I was!" he muttered in consternation.

"What's the matter?" asked Cynthia, surprised at his tone.

"He's bolting! Idiot that I was not to have foreseen this!"

"Dr. Gregg? Then you really do suspect him?"

"I not only suspect him, but he knows it. Cynthia, I've made an unholy mess of this. The only thing to do now is to make for Staveley as quickly as possible. I must get into touch with Grey and warn him."

Cynthia wasted no time in asking questions. She did her best and Fayre made a mental note never again, when she was at the wheel, even to suggest to her that he was in a hurry. To do him justice he underwent three hairbreadth escapes without making a sound, but he thanked his stars that he was still alive as he tore up the steps and into the little room that housed the telephone at Staveley.

He got Grey with surprisingly little delay and told him what had happened.

"It's my fault, I'm afraid. If I hadn't shown my hand he'd never have taken fright. Can you do anything at your end?"

"I'll see to that if he makes for London. I can put a man onto the station here. What's he wearing, did you notice?"

"No idea. I was looking at his face. That wouldn't be enough, anyhow, for your man to go by. If only I could catch that train!"

"If you did you'd give the show away worse than ever. He's certain to be on the lookout. I wish to goodness we had a photograph! We must go by the ticket, that's all. I'll back my man to get onto him if it's humanly possible. Fortunately, he's on good terms with the station people. It'll be a bore if Gregg goes north, though!"

"It doesn't even follow that he's going by train. He was on his way to the Junction, but that means nothing. He's got his man with him, which looks as if he were sending the car home from the station.

The fellow's a sort of gardener as well, so he's not likely to take him with him if he's going far."

"That points to a train journey, so our luck may be in, after all. Look here, are you free to come up at any moment?"

"Quite. To-night, if you like."

"There's no great hurry, but you might run up in the course of the next day or two. There's nothing much you can do where you are now, and it's about time we compared notes again. I may have something for you by the time you get here."

Fayre calculated for a moment.

"I'll come up by the night train to-morrow, arriving Sunday morning. Then I can look you up on Monday."

"Good! Or, better still, lunch with me on Sunday at the Troc."

"Excellent! I'll be there at one. By the way, if Gregg was making the night train he'll get in about six-twenty. Tell your man to be careful. He's no fool, remember."

"Thanks. See you Sunday, then."

Fayre was hanging up the receiver when a voice at his elbow made him start.

"What's this? Not the naughty doctor doing a bunk? Now, that looks fishy, if you like!"

Bill Staveley had come in unperceived and had overheard Fayre's last sentence.

"He's off," answered Fayre. "Met him just now on the way to the Junction, luggage and all. It looks as if he'd got the wind up."

Staveley glanced at his watch.

"Even if you're only just back he was allowing time and to spare for the five-forty. What makes you think he was going to London?"

"Nothing. He may not have been going by train at all."

For answer Staveley pushed him gently to one side and, picking up the receiver, gave a number.

"That Whitbury station? That you, Millar? Lord Staveley speaking. Has the London train gone yet? Confound it, then, I've missed it. I wanted to catch Dr. Gregg about something. He was on that train, wasn't he? I thought so. You don't happen to know if he was going straight through to London, do you? If he's stopping at Carlisle, I might ring him up there. Thanks, I'll hold on."

There was a short pause while he waited, the receiver to his ear.

"Hullo. Yes. He booked through, did he? Yes, that settles it. Thanks very much."

He replaced the receiver and turned to Fayre.

"Booked to London and had his luggage labelled straight through. Want to let your man know?"

He stood waiting while Fayre put through the trunk call.

"What's the next move?" he asked. "By Jove, I'm beginning to think you're right about the doctor!"

"I'd better go up myself and see if Grey's got anything for me to do there. To-morrow night will be time enough."

"If it wasn't for this blessed Cattle Show on Monday I'd come myself. I'm beginning to enjoy this business. I wish it hadn't been Gregg, though."

"So do I," agreed Fayre heartily. "I disliked the fellow at first, I admit, but now I've got a sneaking sympathy for him. He's a loyal friend, whatever else he may be."

"He's a benighted idiot to cut and run now. I'd have given him credit for more sense. Was Cynthia with you when you saw him?"

"Yes. And I shall have my work cut out to prevent her from dashing up to town with me, I expect, once she knows what it all means. Which reminds me that if I don't go and make a clean breast of the whole thing at once I shall never hear the last of it. It's no good keeping it from her now."

He departed hastily in search of her, but she was nowhere to be found and he concluded that she must have gone straight to her room. When she failed to put in an appearance at tea he was really puzzled. He knew she must be waiting eagerly for his explanation and it was not like her to curb anything, least of all curiosity. He was relieved to find that the Staveleys took her defection very calmly.

"If you knew Cynthia better you'd take everything she did as a matter of course," announced Eve Staveley. "She's probably gone home to collect a few more oddments."

"If she hasn't made a dash for the five-forty and caught it!" suggested Bill Staveley with a wicked gleam in his eye. "She can twist old Millar round her little finger and if she told him to keep the train till she arrived, I wouldn't bank on his not doing it."

"My dear Bill, why on earth should she go off on the five-forty?" demanded his wife.

"Why shouldn't she? It's just the sort of Tom Fool thing she would do," he countered cheerfully.

The suggestion made Fayre uncomfortable and he went through a good deal of quite unnecessary worry before she walked calmly into the dining-room, ten minutes late for dinner, and apologized very prettily to her hostess for her unpunctuality.

Lady Staveley took it for granted that she had been to Galston and neither of the two men thought it wise to question the fact in public. After dinner, however, she found herself pinned into a corner of the big drawing-room, well out of hearing of her hostess, and made to give an account of herself.

"It's no good trying the happy home stunt on us," remarked Bill Staveley lazily. "We want to know where you've really been and what mischief you've been up to."

"I never said I'd been to Galston," protested Cynthia, the picture of injured innocence. "It was Eve who insisted on it."

"In spite of all your protestations," jibed Staveley. He and Cynthia were old sparring partners and he was a worthy match for her.

"Well, did you want me to give the show away?" she asked.

"Considering that we don't know what the show is!"

She cut him short and tackled Fayre direct.

"Did you manage to do anything about Dr. Gregg, Uncle Fayre?" she asked.

"I rang up Grey, and Bill got the station and discovered that he had caught the London train. Grey's going to try to keep him under observation at the other end. That was all we could do."

For answer Cynthia opened the little gold bag she carried and took from it a slip of paper. She handed it to Fayre and watched him in silence as he read it aloud.

"*Care of Dr. Graham, Brackley Mansions, Victoria Street,*" it ran.

For a moment he stared at the girl in utter bewilderment; then he broke into a low chuckle.

"She's beaten us, Bill!" he exclaimed. "It's Gregg's address, I'll be bound. How did you get it?"

"Ran the car over to his house and asked for it, of course. That's why I was late for dinner. I punctured on the way home. I told the maid that Lady Kean had written to say that she'd lost his prescription and had asked me to see him about it. They said that he always stays at that address when he's in London and that he'd told them to forward letters there, so he's sure to go to it if only to collect them."

There was a blank silence, broken eventually by Lord Staveley.

"Absurdly simple, my dear Watson, when you know how it's done. One up to you, Cynthia. He'll smell a rat, of course, when he gets back, but it probably won't matter then."

Fayre caught the night train for London on the following evening. Lord Staveley had offered to send him into Carlisle by car, thus saving the change at Whitbury, but he preferred to go from Staveley Grange.

"Both your chauffeurs must hate the sight of me by now, though why you persist in using that wretched little branch line is beyond me," he complained.

"Lord knows!" admitted Staveley frankly. "It's a bit of a way round to Whitbury, it's true, but that's nothing in a car. Of course, in the old horse days it was a consideration. That and the fact that they gave my grandfather the branch line as a special concession in days gone by and we've felt it our duty to use it ever since is the only reason I can think of why we stick to it still. We're a hide-bound lot, but I must admit I've got a weakness for that rotten little station. It reminds me of coming home for the holidays in my school days for one thing."

"And then we're surprised to find Americans laughing at us! We are a queer country, you know."

"Well, if you can find a better 'ole, go to it!" quoted Staveley cheerfully. "You can have the car to Carlisle if you like to-night, but I'm dashed if I'll send you to Whitbury now!"

So Fayre travelled from Staveley Grange after the approved Staveley fashion and was glad he had done so, for, as he was waiting for his train at Whitbury he was joined by Miss Allen, whom he would undoubtedly have missed in the crowd at Carlisle. She, too, was on her way to London and she and Fayre dined very pleasantly together in the restaurant car. He found, as he had suspected, that she improved on acquaintance and they sat talking for some time after the meal ended.

Fayre wondered later, as he sat huddled in his stuffy corner, waiting for the sleep that would not come, what she would have said if she had known the reason of his journey to town.

"The whole cast of the melodrama seems to be moving to London," he thought whimsically. "Though what we're all going to do there, goodness knows! It would be more satisfactory, too, if one knew which of us was the villain of the piece!"

CHAPTER XVII

FAYRE SAW MISS ALLEN into a cab and then drove straight to his club. After a hot bath and a leisurely breakfast he felt better able to face the world, but he was not sorry to spend a quiet Sunday morning drowsing in front of the smoking-room fire and it was with a distinct effort that he turned out, shortly before one, to keep his appointment with Grey at the Trocadero.

He found the solicitor already seated and busy studying the wine-card. At the sight of Fayre he sprang to his feet and greeted him with a mixture of enthusiasm and deference which the older man found refreshing in these casual days.

"How about a pick-me-up, sir?" he asked, with a keen glance at his guest. "Or do you despise cocktails?"

"They have their uses," admitted Fayre, a glint of mischief in his eyes, "especially after a long night in the train, but I'm not such a dug-out as you might think, you know!"

Grey laughed.

"I didn't mean that!" he apologized hastily. "Only you look a bit done up."

He ordered a couple of Martinis and then plunged at once into the business which was engrossing both their minds.

"My man rang up about an hour ago," he said. "He got onto Gregg all right. He managed to square the ticket-collector and stood by his side as the passengers passed through. The collector spotted the Whitbury ticket and gave him the tip and he followed the man. He says he answered to our description. I think it was Gregg all right."

"Where did he go?" asked Fayre.

His lips twitched involuntarily, for he guessed what was coming.

"To a doctor's house, or rather flat. Brackley Mansions, Victoria Street. He took his luggage in, so that looks as if he meant to stay there, unless it was a blind."

"Good work," was Fayre's only comment.

Grey looked at him sharply.

"What's the joke?" he asked.

"Nothing much, only we had our noses pulled rather thoroughly over that address by Lady Cynthia!"

He told Grey what had happened.

"I like that girl," was Grey's enthusiastic comment. "She's keen. We'll get Leslie off, if only for her sake."

"We don't look much like doing it at present," said Fayre rather hopelessly. "It seems to me that until we can get Gregg to account for that extra hour he spent getting from Whitbury to Hammond's farm we're pretty well stuck. And, if he won't speak we're not in a position to make him."

"I can't for the life of me see any connection between Gregg and the Page car," said Grey thoughtfully.

"There is none. Of that I feel convinced. My opinion is that Page simply turned up the lane and, finding it a cul-de-sac, came back again. He may have seen something, but I don't believe he took Mrs. Draycott to the farm."

"The tramp seemed to think there was a woman in the car, though, the first time it passed him."

"He was very vague about it and admitted he could hardly see the occupants. I believe we ought to concentrate on Gregg."

Grey deliberated for a moment.

"I'm not sure that I agree with you," he said at last. "Gregg's not behaving like a guilty man. I fully expected that he'd make a break for the boat-train, instead of which he's gone quite openly to the address at which he always stays, according to his servants, when he comes to town. He may have come up merely to get legal advice."

"Lady Cynthia's certainly got a strong feeling that this man Page is implicated," admitted Fayre.

"I think she's right and her suggestion that the car may have been stopped if it ran to London with a broken number-plate is quite sound. We can work on that, anyhow."

"In the meanwhile, is there anything I can do?"

"Yes," answered Grey decisively. "Get in touch with Sir Edward, if you can, and see if he won't arrange an interview with us. He's got one of the acutest brains in England and I'd welcome his advice. Besides, he's got a personal interest in the case."

Fayre laughed.

"He hasn't exactly encouraged my maiden efforts!" he complained. "In fact, he told me flatly to go to the police just before he left Staveley."

Grey nodded.

"That's the line he would take. Like all competent people he distrusts the capacity even of professionals; and amateurs simply don't exist for him. I don't think he'll take that line now, however, especially when he realizes how far we've got. He'll admit that we've every reason now to keep the thing in our own hands."

"I'll call on Lady Kean this afternoon and see if I can get hold of him. He's sure to be there unless they are week-ending out of town, and I don't think she's well enough yet for that."

"Any time he chooses to appoint will suit me. Meanwhile, if nothing further transpires as regards Gregg, I'll beard him myself. He may not resent my curiosity as much as yours, and if he has been to see his solicitor he'll no doubt have had it impressed upon him that his attitude is not only stupid but dangerous, if he's really got nothing to hide."

They lingered over lunch and again over their coffee. When they at last parted Fayre strolled down Piccadilly and across Green Park and it was close on four o'clock when he reached Kean's house in Westminster.

Two cars were standing before the door when he reached it. Evidently he was not the only caller, a discovery which afforded him a certain satisfaction. If there were other people there Sybil would have little opportunity for discussing the Draycott murder and he might manage to slip away and transact his business with Kean.

He had hardly taken his hand off the bell when the door was opened and, without waiting for his inquiry as to whether Lady Kean was at home, the butler stood aside for him to pass into the hall.

"Sir William is waiting for you, sir, if you'll step up," he said.

"Sir William?" repeated Fayre, puzzled. "Isn't this Sir Edward Kean's?"

For a moment the man seemed taken aback; then he realized his mistake.

"I beg your pardon, sir; I took you for the doctor the gentlemen are expecting. Lady Kean is very ill. The doctors are holding a consultation upstairs. Sir Edward is at home, but I don't know ..."

"I won't trouble him now, of course," said Fayre quickly. "I'm very sorry about this. When was she taken ill?"

"Her ladyship had a heart attack yesterday evening soon after she arrived from the North. The doctor thinks the journey was too much for her. We are very anxious about her, sir."

The man looked genuinely distressed. Evidently Sybil Kean was of those who endear themselves to their servants.

Fayre produced a card and scribbled the address of his club on it.

"Tell Sir Edward that this will find me if I can be of any use. I'll call again later in case there is better news."

As he went down the steps a car drove up, no doubt bearing the third doctor. His heart was very heavy as he made his way slowly back to his club. For the moment his mind was swept completely clear of the Draycott case and he could think of nothing but the Keans: the hushed house and the possibly fruitless consultation that was now taking place. Sybil Kean was the oldest of all his friends in England and he was very fond of her. Edward could, on occasion, exasperate him almost beyond endurance and he was an unsatisfactory companion in the sense that he gave little and asked for nothing where the ties of friendship were concerned, but Fayre had always both liked and admired him. He had struck him from the first as one of the loneliest beings in existence, a man fated to remain detached, too strong to invite sympathy and too engrossed in his own interests to offer it. Fayre pictured him, waiting alone for the verdict of the doctors, and wished he had had the courage to break in upon his privacy.

He dined at the club and, after a fruitless attempt to enjoy a quiet cigar, was driven by sheer anxiety to return to Westminster.

To his surprise he was told that Sir Edward wished to see him.

"It was good of you to call, Hatter," was Kean's brief comment as he rose to greet him.

His voice had lost none of its resonance, but Fayre thought he had never seen a man look so ill. His face was a grey mask and his eyes, bleak and lifeless, seemed literally to have receded into his head. Fayre cast a swift glance round the room.

"Look here, old man," he said, "have you dined?"

Kean stared at him vaguely.

The butler, who had been making up the fire and was about to leave the room, turned at his words.

"Sir Edward made a very poor dinner, sir," he ventured.

Kean swung round on him impatiently; but he was too exhausted to act with his customary vigour and Fayre forestalled him.

"Do you think you could raise a few sandwiches?" he asked the man pleasantly. "I see drinks are here."

The butler responded with alacrity.

"Cook did cut some, sir, on the chance."

He vanished, only too thankful to feel that Sir Edward was at last in the hands of some one who seemed able to influence him. He had hardly eaten or slept, in the opinion of his household, since his wife had been taken ill.

Fayre strolled over to the little table near the window, on which stood a tantalus and a couple of syphons. He poured out a stiff drink, but withheld it until the butler returned with a tray of fruit and sandwiches.

Kean sat gazing into the fire. He did not show the slightest interest in Fayre's movements and the fact that his old friend had coolly taken possession and was issuing orders to his servants seem to have escaped him.

Fayre moved the table with the tray to Kean's elbow.

"Is Sybil conscious?" he asked quietly and with what seemed deliberate cruelty.

Her name was enough to rouse Kean from his abstraction.

"Her mind's quite clear, but she's so weak she can hardly speak," he said. "The doctors won't say anything definite yet."

"Then, if she's able to think at all she's worrying about you. Don't give her more cause for anxiety than you can help, old chap. She'll need you as soon as she picks up a bit and what earthly use are you going to be to her if you let yourself go to pieces now?"

He held out the tumbler and Kean, after a moment's hesitation, took it and drank thirstily.

"I wanted that," he said.

For answer Fayre silently pushed over the plate of sandwiches. Then he sat quietly watching the dancing flames while Kean forced himself to eat. The self-discipline he had always practised stood him in good stead and the plate was half-empty before he leaned back in his chair and fumbled for his cigarette-case.

"Sorry, Hatter," he said with the ghost of a smile, "but that's the best I can do."

Fayre grinned back at him.

"Good enough," he answered. "Feel better?"

Kean nodded.

"I'd lost grip of myself for the moment, that's all. Those con-founded doctors took such a time this afternoon and then I couldn't get a thing worth having out of them. I suppose they couldn't help it, poor beggars, but it seemed a lifetime to me. It was decent of you to come, Hatter."

"I came because I couldn't stand the suspense any longer my-self. Glad I did, now."

"So am I. I'll tell you as much as I know myself. If she pulls through the night they think she'll do and she's no weaker than she was this morning. That's all I've got to go on. If there's any change the nurse will come for me, otherwise she's to see no one. The doc-tor's coming again in an hour's time."

"Thanks," said Fayre appreciatively. "I'm glad to know. It's not such a bad lookout as I feared. Like so many people with frail bod-ies, Sybil's always had more than her share of nervous vitality and I'm ready to bank on that. And you've given her an incentive to live, old man," he finished gently.

Kean stared at him for a moment without speaking. Then:

"I've done my best," he said with a curious grim note in his voice that made Fayre wonder whether, after all, he had not always re-alized how very little of her heart Sybil Kean had to give when she married him.

There was a pause; then Kean rose to his feet and thrust his hands into his pockets with the gesture that was so characteristic of him.

"I can't stand this," he said abruptly. "I must get my teeth into something or my imagination will get away with me. What have you and Grey been doing?"

"As a matter of fact, I came here to-day at Grey's request. He wants to consult you and suggested I should make an appointment. Of course, that's all off now."

"For the present, anyhow. But there's no reason why you shouldn't put me *au fait* with things. I should be grateful for anything to hitch my brain onto at this moment."

Fayre realized that he was actuated by sheer instinct for self-preservation and met him half-way by plunging at once into a recital of all that had happened in the last few days.

Kean listened attentively. Now and then he interrupted to ask a trenchant question; otherwise he heard him in silence. When he had finished Fayre handed him the little red cap the tramp had given him.

"This may as well go with the other exhibit," he said. "Anyhow, we know now that it was lost before, and not after, the murder."

Kean dropped it into the drawer of his writing-table and turned the key.

"It would be interesting to know how much that fellow, Gregg, really knows of Mrs. Draycott's past," he said slowly.

"Whatever it is, he's made up his mind not to speak."

Kean stood rocking backward and forward on his heels, lost in thought. Fayre watched him in amazement. Half an hour ago he had been a broken man. Not only had he pulled himself together by sheer force of will, but he was now giving his whole mind to the matter in hand with a lack of effort that seemed almost superhuman.

"Gregg ought to be get-at-able," he said at last. "His treatment of you was nothing but a display of bad temper. If he's innocent it ought to be possible to convince him of the folly of the line he's taking. If he's guilty, the only course will be to put the matter in the hands of the police. My own impression is that he's shielding some one. Miss Allen said that this man Baxter, Mrs. Draycott's first husband, was dead. She also went so far as to say that he was the one person she could think of connected with her sister's past who would have been capable of killing her. Have we any proof that the fellow *is* dead?"

"Gregg told me that he had died in his arms. We haven't followed the matter up, if that's what you mean."

"A statement of that sort, coming from Gregg, is of no value to us. Get Grey to look the thing up, will you?"

"It's an idea!" exclaimed Fayre. "I wonder we never thought of it! Baxter was Gregg's friend and Gregg hated Mrs. Draycott on his account. He'd certainly shield him if the necessity arose. And Baxter was a drunkard and half demented, at that, if the accounts be true. There may be something in it."

Kean made a gesture of impatience.

"Don't go off the deep end, Hatter. The man's probably dead and buried. It's worth investigating, though. And look here, Hatter, keep Grey off Gregg, will you? We don't want this thing muddled and if Grey's clumsy he'll do more harm than good. Tell him I'll make the doctor my business, that is ..."

He broke off and the lines on his face deepened. Fayre knew that his mind was back in the quiet, shaded room upstairs and that the words "if all goes well" had trembled on his lips and he had been afraid to utter them.

"I'll see to that, old chap," he broke in hastily, "and I'll put the Baxter theory to him at once."

Kean sank into a chair and closed his eyes. He looked mortally tired and Fayre forbore to disturb him. For a time they sat in silence; then Kean shook himself out of his abstraction.

"As regards the Page business," he began thoughtfully, "I doubt ..."

There was a sound in the hall and in a moment he was on his feet, everything but his wife forgotten. They heard the front door close, followed by the sound of subdued voices.

"It's the doctor. Wait here, old man, will you?" Kean flung the words over his shoulder as he left the room, and for the next half-hour or so Fayre, alone in the big shadowy library, gave himself up shamelessly to the depression which had haunted him all day.

He waited till the departure of the doctor and the return of Kean with the news that his wife was, if anything, a little stronger and then walked back through the quiet, lamplit streets to his club.

CHAPTER XVIII

BEFORE GOING OUT the next morning Fayre rang up Kean's house and ascertained that Sybil Kean had passed a good night and was appreciably stronger. The doctors were still unable to pronounce her definitely out of danger and had warned Kean that, at any moment, there might be a relapse, but Fayre was conscious of an immense relief as he set out for Grey's office in Chancery Lane.

He gave Grey the gist of his interview with Kean. The solicitor was inclined to be sceptical as to the existence of Baxter, but he admitted that, were the man still alive, Kean's suggestion would more than hold water and he promised to look into the matter at once. He smiled at Kean's offer to deal with Gregg himself if the occasion arose.

"Didn't I tell you that he trusted no one but himself in a matter of any real importance?" he exclaimed. "That's a part of the secret of his success. That and his amazing capacity for cramming two men's work into the twelve hours. He must be uncommonly keen on the case, though. Apart from Lady Kean's illness he's up to his eyes in work already."

"Which will be the saving of him if things go wrong with her," said Fayre. "I wish this next week were over."

Grey nodded.

"So do I, from our point of view as well as his. If Lady Kean dies Sir Edward will do one of two things: try to lose himself in work or chuck everything. It's a toss-up. If he were to throw up the sponge, I don't know what we should do. Even with the little we've got now, Kean might get Leslie off on insufficient evidence, but there's not another man at the Bar who could put it through. We're still in an uncommonly tight corner."

In the afternoon Fayre called on Kean and literally forced him into the open air. The two men walked across the Park as far as Bayswater. Once there, however, Kean fell into a panic and, refusing Fayre's offer to ring up his house at the nearest public telephone, jumped into a taxi and hurried home. Fayre turned back and strolled quietly along the Serpentine in the direction of Hyde Park Corner. He had not gone far when his eye fell on the figure of a woman walking just ahead of him. Something in the purposeful swing of her walk and the carriage of her erect figure struck him as familiar and he quickened his steps and was soon abreast of her.

She turned at the sound of his voice.

"Mr. Fayre! I was just thinking of you, curiously enough, and wishing I had asked you for your address the other day when we met in the train."

Fayre turned to her with a smile.

"If I were a more conceited man I should feel flattered, but I'm afraid you've got some annoyingly good reason for wishing to see me. Is there anything I can do?"

"It is only that you asked me once whether I could tell you anything about my sister's associates and I wondered if you would care to go through some papers of hers which have only just come into my possession.

They have been in a dispatch-box at her bank all this time and were handed over to me yesterday. I went through them cursorily and they seem to consist mostly of business papers, but there are one or two letters and photographs which might give you some hint as to the set she was moving in. They convey nothing to me, but you may know something about these people."

"It is more than good of you …" began Fayre.

"Nonsense, Mr. Fayre. I am as anxious to find out who killed my poor sister as you are to clear John Leslie and it struck me that two heads are better than one. Also, you may have arrived at certain conclusions already and these letters may throw some light on them. I warn you that there was nothing private, with the exception of certain letters which I have already destroyed or disposed of. They concerned only my sister and could have been of no use to you whatever, but I prefer to deal frankly with you."

Fayre's sharp eyes did not miss the sudden wave of colour that swept to the roots of her grey hair when she mentioned the letters and he made a shrewd guess as to the character of that portion of Mrs. Draycott's correspondence that her sister had found it better to destroy.

He hastened to reassure her.

"Of course I understand. Show me only what you care for an outsider to see. As you say, you may have something that confirms certain suspicions of mine. In any case, I am very grateful to you for giving me the opportunity to see them."

"Could you look at them to-morrow?" she suggested, coming to the point at once in her downright way. "I shall be in from four onwards."

"Delighted, and if you are going to walk back to your hotel, perhaps you'll let me take you to the door. You look as if, like myself, you were out for exercise."

"I am, and to tell you the truth, I was bored to death! It's a funny thing, but I can walk for miles alone in the country and enjoy every moment of it, but five minutes of it in London is enough to make me long for some one to grouse to. The crowds both worry and stifle me."

"I know what you mean; I feel the same myself. I put it down to the years I have been away. London's the one place where I feel really lonely nowadays." She nodded.

"I forgot you'd been abroad for so long. The truth is, I suppose we've both dropped out of things. It's dawning on me that I've turned into a regular country cousin. I'm not going straight back to my hotel, by the way. I've got a parcel to leave near Victoria. Is that out of your way?"

"Not a bit. The further, the better."

They walked on, chatting quietly. Their conversation ranged over a wide field and Fayre discovered that, though she was pleased to call herself a country cousin, she had not by any means lost touch with the outside world, for she was a voracious reader and had gathered a store of homely wisdom in the course of her quiet life. The time passed so pleasantly that he was surprised when he found himself at the corner of Grosvenor Place, facing Victoria Station.

"Where do we go now?" he asked idly.

Her answer took his breath away.

"I'm making for some flats behind the Cathedral. Brackley Mansions, they're called."

Gregg's headquarters in London! They crossed the road in silence, Fayre busily engaged in assuring him-self that there was nothing unusual in such coincidences.

"If you're really so keen on exercise and are not in a hurry we might stroll on to my hotel," pursued Miss Allen. "I'm only leaving this parcel. I can't offer you tea to-day, as I'm entertaining a dull batch of relations, but I shall be glad of your company to the door."

She took a small, flat package out of her bag and Fayre, glancing at it involuntarily, could not help seeing Dr. Gregg's name written across it in a clear, bold script, the type of handwriting he would have expected from Miss Allen.

They left the parcel with the porter and then strolled on to Miss Allen's hotel. Fayre's conversation was as intelligent as could be expected in the circumstances, but it was somewhat mechanical, for his mind was wrestling busily with this new problem. Until now it had not occurred to him to connect Miss Allen's visit to London with that of Gregg, but now he began to wonder. He had parted from her and was on his way back to his club when the probable explanation dawned on him. Did the parcel she had just left for Gregg contain some of the letters she had "disposed of"? It seemed more than likely. If so, Fayre would have given a good deal for a glance at the contents of the packet.

Events followed each other in an almost uncanny sequence. When he reached the club he was handed a card by the porter, who told him that a gentleman was waiting to see him, and the name on it, to his astonishment, was that of Gregg. Fayre found some difficulty in collecting his thoughts as he went in search of his visitor and led him to a secluded corner of the almost deserted library.

The conversation opened awkwardly, for Gregg seemed to be labouring under an acute attack of embarrassment.

"Very good of you to see me after what happened," he began clumsily, his manner even more abrupt than usual. "Fact is, I made a blithering ass of myself the other day and I've come to say so. Hope you'll accept an apology."

"That's all right. I expect I must have seemed an infernal busybody," said Fayre hastily. "I'm only too glad you've come to look on me in a more friendly light. Are you a tea-drinker or would you prefer something else?"

He waited impatiently while the servant supplied their needs. When he had gone Gregg, as he had hoped, came directly to the point.

"You asked for an explanation the other day," he said bluntly. "If it hadn't been for my infernally hot temper I should have given it and saved us both a lot of trouble. Well, I've come to give it now."

He shifted uncomfortably in his chair, his tea cooling unheeded by his side.

"It's a bit difficult to know where to begin, but you may as well have the whole story. I did know Mrs. Draycott, as you guessed, but that was before she married Draycott. I give you my word that, until I saw her lying dead at Leslie's farm, I'd never set eyes on her since the week after she ran away from Baxter in 1916. I knew she was staying at Staveley, of course, but I fancy she avoided me there. Anyhow, I never saw her and I was glad of it, for it wasn't an acquaintance I was anxious to renew. When that chap, Brace, asked me if I knew her, I denied it on impulse. If you ask me why, I'm blessed if I know. I hated her and everything to do with her and the time I had known her, and I suppose it was a sort of blind endeavour to put it all behind me. Anyway, as soon as I'd done it, I knew what a fool thing it was to do, but there was nothing for it then but to stick to what I'd said. How you got onto the fact that I'd ever had anything to do with her, I don't know, but it was cursed awkward for me and I'm not surprised you got the wind up."

"It was an accident, more or less, helped by your own obvious dislike of her. You made a mistake there."

"I know. I was rattled over the whole thing and I've no doubt I gave myself away. You see, I had more than one reason for wishing to keep out of it. For one thing, I knew that my statement that I had never seen her looked fishy, to say the least of it, and then there was the boy."

He paused, evidently trying to sort out his story. Then, catching sight of Fayre's face of bewilderment:

"I expect it all seems an unholy muddle to you. I'd better get back to the beginning. Miss Allen, as she was then, was at St. Swithin's with me, as you probably know by now. She married my special pal, Baxter, and I can assure you I did my best to put a spoke in her wheel there. It was no good, however; Baxter was almost insane about her and wouldn't listen to a thing against her, and, knowing what I knew about her, it made me pretty sick, as you may imagine. So much so that, after they married, I saw very little of them.

I'd got a big, very poor practise then and was too busy, anyway, to look up old friends. Then one day he turned up, half demented, and told me she'd gone off with Draycott and left him with their small boy on his hands. To make a long story short, he ended by divorcing her after trying in vain to get her back. I went to see her myself, much as I disliked her, the day after Baxter's visit to me. I found her at a hotel with Draycott and she laughed in my face when I tried to get her to return to her husband. After the divorce he went to pieces altogether and I had my hands full, I can tell you. When he got past work I persuaded him to come to me with the boy, and he died soon afterwards in my house. I'd got fond of the little chap by then, and I stuck to him, there being no other relations he could go to. He's at a preparatory school now and going to a public school next term. That's the principal reason why I didn't want my connection with this business to come out. I gave him my name and he's supposed to be my nephew and, for his sake, I don't want to drag up the past now."

"I see that," said Fayre sympathetically. "In fact, I'm beginning to realize now how you must have cursed my interference."

"Your butting in as you did was a calamity, from my point of view, and, like a fool, I lost my temper and tried to bluff it out. You see, I'd concealed his identity with a good deal of care and I began to see myself in the witness-box and photographs of the little chap in the papers, all my trouble gone for nothing, as it were, and I saw red."

"Does the boy know he's Baxter's son?"

"He knows his name was Baxter originally, but he wouldn't connect his mother with Mrs. Draycott. He thinks she died before he came to me with his father. I never tried to conceal his parentage from him; in fact, I've done my best to keep the memory of his father alive as he was before he let himself go to pieces. Fortunately the little chap was too young to notice much in those days. No, it was his mother I was afraid of. She'd got no legal claim on the boy, but I knew her. She was a greedy woman where money was concerned and an infernally clever one. Even when Draycott was alive she was eternally hard up and there was very little she'd stick at to raise money. I never saw her again, as I said, but I kept track of her and, from what I heard, I'm pretty certain that, if she'd known where to find the boy, she'd have put the screw on me, little as I should have been able to give her. She knew I'd do a good deal to prevent her from getting at him. She was an attractive woman and a good enough actress to make a very pretty and affecting scene if she'd chosen to look him up and play the fond mother. She'd have got round him, I've no doubt, and she knew I couldn't afford to risk that. That was why I changed his name and I was very careful not to talk openly of where he was. You must remember that she detested me and, apart from the money, she was quite capable of going and worrying the boy out of sheer spite."

"She wouldn't descend to blackmail, surely," protested Fayre.

He had disliked Mrs. Draycott and everything that he had since heard of her had been to her discredit, but he found it difficult to believe that a sister of Miss Allen should have sunk low enough for blackmail.

"I know what you're thinking," said Gregg shrewdly. "She came of good stock and was brought up according to the traditions of her class, but, believe me, when a woman's once started on the downward slope she gets pretty callous about what she does. I give you my word that, bad as the shock of finding her dead was, it had less effect on me that night than the discovery that she was Miss Allen's sister. I realized then, for the first time, the sort of people she had sprung from and I came very near to giving myself away, I was so surprised. Oddly enough, in spite of the name, I had never connected them with each other."

"You say you kept an eye on Mrs. Draycott. Does that mean that you were in touch with any of her associates? I don't mind telling you that we're still at sea as to the motive of the crime."

"I can't help you there, I'm afraid," answered Gregg frankly. "There was an old servant of hers who took up dressmaking and to whom she always went when she wanted anything of the sort. I believe she had some arrangement with her, too, by which she used to send her cast-off dresses to sell on commission. I used to go and see the woman every now and then and she'd give me the latest news of Mrs. Draycott. She worked for her, but she'd no reason to love her and she liked the boy and was ready to do him a good turn. But she only saw Mrs. Draycott at intervals and knew none of the people with whom she foregathered."

"You can think of no one yourself who owed her a grudge?"

"There must have been plenty, but I don't know of any one in particular. I've told you my reason for wishing to keep out of her clutches. She failed with me, but she probably succeeded with others. There's motive enough, if you want one."

"Blackmail!" said Fayre thoughtfully. "It seems incredible, but the idea has its possibilities. In that case, there ought to be papers of some sort among her effects."

"They're all in Miss Allen's hands now," volunteered Gregg. "And what's more, she's in town. She's been going through some things her sister kept at the bank and she wrote to me yesterday to say that there were some old letters of Baxter's that she thought I might like to have and offering to send them to me. From something she's found she's got onto the fact that I know where the boy is and she proposes to make over to him what money her sister left. As straight as a die, Miss Allen is, and I've written to thank her. It seems that she thought he was in the hands of Baxter's people until now. You might go and see her, but she's not the kind to give her sister away."

"I'm calling on her to-morrow, but, as you say, it's hardly a subject one can broach."

His heart sank as he remembered the papers Miss Allen had told him she had burned and the hot flush that had risen to her cheeks when she spoke of them.

Gregg buttoned his coat preparatory to departure.

"I've told you all I know," he said. "But I doubt if it's been much help to you. There's one thing more that you might think worth following up. A fellow I know saw Mrs. Draycott in Paris in 1920, three years after she married Draycott. Draycott was in Egypt at the time and she was with a man whom this friend of mine, Lloyd, was unable to identify. He was an old friend of Baxter's and knew that I should not be sorry to have a hold over her, so, after he'd run across them three or four times, he followed them to their hotel one night, but her name was not on the register and he couldn't trace the man. He believes they were staying together under assumed names. I kept his letter, thinking I might bluff her with it if we ever came up against each other. I give you the story for what it's worth and I'll write down Lloyd's address for you and send him a line asking him to tell you what he knows, if you think it's worth while to look him up. But I warn you, he doesn't know much. It's possible, however, that if she went to Paris with this man, she may have put the screw on him later."

He scribbled an address on the back of a card and placed it on the table.

Fayre picked it up and slipped it into his pocket-book.

"Anything's worth while at this stage of the game," he admitted thoughtfully.

He stood hesitating, considering his next move. Knowing Gregg's quick temper, he found considerable difficulty in clothing the question that was trembling on his lips in a form the other would not immediately resent, but he knew that he could not let the man go until he had an answer.

"I wish you'd tell me one thing," he said at last.

"Fire away. I'm not going off the deep end again, if that's what you're afraid of," answered Gregg with disconcerting intuition.

"Can you give me your movements from, say, five onwards on the evening of the murder? I've a good reason for asking."

Gregg looked genuinely surprised; then his lips parted in a rather grim smile.

"I'm blessed! You've got it all pat, haven't you? If was about five when I left the house and I bet you're perfectly aware that I went straight to Stockley's garage at Whitbury and hired a car. Mine was out of commission. You've been putting in some hard work, Mr. Fayre, and if you don't know already that I went on to Willow Farm on a maternity case, I'll eat my hat. However, you shall have the whole program. I picked up the car at Stockley's at about five-thirty and made straight for Hammond's, that is, the Willow Farm. There's a little village, you may or may not know, about three miles from Whitbury on the Besley road. I was going through when a boy ran out of one of the cottages and yelled something at me. I stopped the car and shouted back that, unless it was urgent, I could not see any one just then. Mrs. Hammond's a delicate little woman and I was anxious about her. However, it was urgent. A wretched baby had pulled over a kettle of boiling water and scalded its legs and one arm. It was in a bad way and it was over an hour before I got away, with the result that I didn't get to Willow Farm till close on seven. I left Hammond's somewhere about nine, drove home and went on, almost immediately, to Leslie's farm."

Fayre stood observing him with some chagrin. It was obvious that the man was speaking the truth, and, in any case, his story would be easy enough to verify. "I don't mind telling you," he said ruefully, "that you've just cheerfully demolished my best clue. If it wasn't for John Leslie I would tell you, quite honestly, that I'm uncommonly glad. As it is, I feel rather cheap. I'd got all your movements except for the hour lost on the way to Willow Farm. You must admit that it looked suspicious, taking into account the fact that Mrs. Draycott met her death somewhere about six-thirty."

Gregg stared at him for a moment.

"Good Lord!" he burst out. "I don't wonder you've been nosing about after my black past. I'd no idea you'd got me cornered like that!"

He dived into his pocket and produced a pencil and an old envelope.

"If you don't mind I'll add the name and address of that unfortunate baby! You'd better verify my statement and, while you're about it, have a look at the scar on the kid's arm. I'm proud of the way that healed, I can tell you."

He held out his hand with a friendly smile. Fayre took it, and as he did so, his old dislike for the man vanished once for all.

"By the way," he said, "what made you come along to-day to bury the hatchet?"

Gregg laughed.

"Because I made up my mind I wasn't going to be ballyragged by any damned lawyer! As you may imagine, it's not a story I care to dwell on and I decided that if I'd got to tell it it should be to a human being. And I was beginning to feel that I owed you an apology, too. So when Sir Edward Kean rang up this afternoon and tried to bully me into making an appointment I temporized and then, ten minutes later, rang up his house, feeling pretty sure a servant would answer. Luck was with me and I got the butler at the other end and he gave me your address, after which I came straight along to you. Pity you asked! I rather hoped you'd think it was spontaneous!"

So this was Kean's doing! Kean, who had requested Fayre to keep Grey from butting in and making a mess of things!

CHAPTER XIX

ON HIS WAY to keep his appointment with Miss Allen, Fayre called at Kean's house in Westminster, where he was assured by the butler that Lady Kean's improvement "was maintained." That solemn functionary had recovered his professional manner and looked a different person from the harassed and very human individual who had mistaken Fayre for a Harley Street specialist on the night of his mistress's illness. Fayre, observing his native pomposity for the first time, realized how complete his collapse had been and liked him the better for it.

Before going on to Miss Allen's hotel he dropped into a florist's and ordered a great sheaf of flowers to be sent to Lady Kean. Remembering their old days together in the country he chose simple, country flowers rather than the heavy-smelling hot-house blooms that were pressed on him by the saleswoman. He had an idea that they would please her and he knew that she would understand and appreciate the spirit that had caused him to select them. He enclosed a short note bearing his good wishes for her speedy recovery and then, on a sudden impulse, he bought another, smaller bunch and carried it away with him.

He produced his offering a little shyly on his arrival at Miss Allen's. It was a long time, he realized, since he had done this sort of thing and the very act seemed, somehow, to emphasize the fact that neither he nor the recipient were in their first youth. Miss Allen, however, was troubled with no such misgivings and was frankly delighted with the gift. Ringing for vases she set herself to arrange the flowers with the appreciative care of one who really loves them. Fayre sat watching her as she moved about the ugly hotel sitting-room and decided that Greycross must be a pleasant house to stay in and its owner a delightful hostess.

She was putting the finishing touches to her last vase when tea was brought in.

"Pour it out, will you, Mr. Fayre," she said in her decisive way, "while I clear up this mess. Lots of milk and no sugar for me, please."

She disappeared into the next room, her hands full of paper and wet foliage, and came back carrying a good-sized dispatch-box.

"We'll have a go at this after tea," she said as she sat down and observed the results of her handiwork. "Mercy, how different the room looks! Those flowers are a breath of the real country. You've chased London out of the window, Mr. Fayre!"

"London isn't so easily chased out as that, I'm afraid. It makes me ache to get away from it. It's all very well for the young, but for people like myself it's grown a little overwhelming. So many of the old landmarks are gone and life seems to have grown amazingly hectic in such a short time. I dare say it's partly a question of contrast. The East's noisy, but it's a place of leisure. I've lost the habit of moving quickly."

She nodded appreciatively.

"I know what you mean. It takes me the same way. I spend my life among plants and animals and I'm beginning to realize how slowly and surely nature progresses. Everything else, nowadays, seems anything hut slow and appallingly insecure. At least, that's my feeling, but then I've crossed Piccadilly at least half a dozen times to-day and I'm wondering why I'm still alive. The moment my business here is finished I shall make for home again. What are your plans, now that you are back in England for good?"

"A little place somewhere in the country, just large enough to hold a few friends and a dog or two. If possible, some fishing. Then I shall settle down and cultivate my garden and write a dull book about India."

"You won't be lonely?"

"Are you?" Fayre shot back at her.

She laughed.

"No, I must admit I'm not, but you must remember that I've got a small village on my hands and I'm on all sorts of queer little local committees and things. *You* don't propose to become the vicar's prop and stay, I presume?"

"Not exactly, but I've no doubt that some of the philanthropists of the neighbourhood will find a use for me. I've never met any one yet who escaped them."

"Oh, they'll get you," agreed Miss Allen cheerfully. "When I took Greycross, more years ago than I like to think of, I mapped out a neat little program for myself. Riding to hounds in winter and gardening and tennis in summer. I saw myself drifting into a healthy, mildly selfish old age, but the local busybodies got me before I'd been there a year. And you'll be easier to net than I was!"

"I'm not so sure," asserted Fayre grimly.

"I am. You're the sort that can't see a child fall down without crossing the road to pick it up. You won't have a chance!"

Fayre reddened as he caught the disarming twinkle in her eyes.

"Look at you now," she went on ruthlessly. "How long have you been home?"

"Three months, more or less," he informed her meekly.

"And you're up to your eyes in this affair of John Leslie's already. And, as soon as that's over, you'll find some one else in trouble."

"It's a depressing program for a man who has come home to enjoy a well-earned rest," he protested.

"It's the fate of all unattached people," she assured him briskly. "Don't you know that the spinster and the bachelor are at the mercy of their friends? I speak from personal experience."

"And you enjoy every moment of it!" put in Fayre shrewdly.

It was Miss Allen's turn to blush.

"Well, it keeps me busy and it may save me from becoming a selfish, cantankerous old woman."

She drew the dispatch-box to her and unlocked it.

"The private letters, such as they are, are at the bottom," she said, removing several bundles that were obviously bills and receipts. "Do any of these names suggest anything to you?"

She handed him a packet of letters and he went through them with the swiftness of one accustomed to handle papers. They seemed to consist mostly of old invitations. Why Mrs. Draycott should have kept them, it was difficult to imagine. Probably she had been too lazy to sort them out and had thrown them carelessly into the box with other papers, but they were useful inasmuch as they gave some clue as to the people she was in the habit of visiting. One or two of the signatures Fayre recognized as being well known in the City. He made a note of some of them in his pocketbook, meaning to ask Grey for information about them. As Miss Allen emptied the box his list grew longer, but even the few private letters which he read carefully from beginning to end, in the hope of finding at least some allusion to Mrs. Draycott's private affairs, failed to produce any enlightening information. There were several packets of photographs, some of which were signed and many of which bore inscriptions, but they conveyed nothing either to Fayre or Miss Allen.

"That's the lot," she said at last, beginning to stack the pile of papers back in the box. "I'm afraid it hasn't been much help."

Fayre rose to help her.

"It's given me a list of names that may prove useful and at least we know now what sort of set she was moving in. Any one of these people may be able to give us information as to some one who had reason to bear her a grudge."

He picked up an envelope which was lying at the top of a bundle of receipts and opened it idly. A snapshot fell out and dropped, face upwards, onto the table.

Fayre bent over it and, as he did so, the colour ebbed slowly from his face, leaving even his lips white.

He snatched the photograph up and walked quickly over to the electric-lamp that stood on the writing, table. Holding the snapshot just under the light, he studied it carefully.

Miss Allen, who was absorbed in fitting the papers back into the box, had not noticed his emotion. Now she suddenly became aware that he had found something that interested him.

"What have you got there?" she asked. Then, seeing the envelope on the table: "Is it that snapshot? It puzzled me, too. The odd thing is that it seems to have come from Germany, according to the inscription on the back."

Fayre turned it over. Stamped across the back were the words: "Staatsnarrenhaus, Schleefeldt."

"What do you make of it?" she went on. "I don't know a word of German, but it seems to be the name of a place."

Fayre came slowly back to the table and picked up the envelope. His face had regained its normal colour and there was nothing in his manner to show that he had just had, perhaps, the greatest shock of his life. He was a good German scholar, but he did not enlighten Miss Allen as to the full meaning of the inscription he had just read.

"It seems to have come from a place called Schleefeldt," he said, examining the envelope narrowly as he spoke. "You've no idea, I suppose, how your sister got it?"

"None. She had no connection with Germany that I know of, either before or after the war, though she may have been there when she was abroad. She was on the Continent a good deal and had a good many friends there. There was nothing in the box that seemed to have any connection with the photograph. It was lying on the top, in the envelope, just as you saw it, when I first came on it."

"We may take it, then, that it was probably one of the last things she put into the box," suggested Fayre.

"It looked like it, certainly."

Fayre picked up the topmost packet of receipts and pulled one out. It was dated 1926.

"You don't know at all when your sister last asked for this box at the bank?" he asked.

Miss Allen shook her head.

"I could find out, I suppose. But I do know that my sister only sent it to the bank with her plate when she left her London flat about two months ago, so that she had access to it up till then. I believe she stayed on in town for a bit after giving up her flat, so she may have had the box out again. Do you want me to find out?"

"It's very kind of you, but I don't think it's necessary. There's no date on the envelope; evidently it is just an unused one that she slipped the photograph into for safety and I was trying to get a clue as to when she is likely to have received the photograph. As it was at the top and as the receipts under it are for 1926, it looks as if she had put the photograph in fairly recently."

"Does it suggest anything to you?" she asked.

"It bears an extraordinary resemblance to a man I firmly believe to be dead," said Fayre slowly. "Of course, it probably is only a chance likeness, but it is so strong that I am going to ask you whether I may borrow the photograph for a day or two."

"Of course," agreed Miss Allen readily. "Keep it as long as you like. If, later, I come across anything that throws any light on it, I'll let you know, but I think I've been through all my sister's papers now." Fayre stowed the envelope and its content carefully away in his breast pocket. He stayed chatting with Miss Allen for a minute or two and then took his leave. As he was saying good-by he remembered a question he had meant to put to her.

"By the way, you could not tell me anything about the death of your sister's first husband, I suppose?"

"He died of drink, poor soul," she said bluntly. "He was a friend of Dr. Gregg's, you know, and the doctor was with him to the end. He was buried at Putney, I've never quite known why, and, as a matter of fact, I went to the funeral."

"You went to the funeral?" Fayre echoed her words mechanically in his surprise.

"I suppose it was rather an astonishing thing to do," she admitted, "considering what had happened, but I'd always liked him, though I'd never seen much of him. I had a very painful interview with him after my sister left him and was sorry for him. I was in London when he died and Dr. Gregg wrote to me about the funeral. I don't know quite why I went, but, somehow, it seemed the decent thing to do. My sister had a lot to answer for there, Mr. Fayre." Fayre could hear the pain and humiliation in her voice.

"I think you are right about unattached people," he said gently, "only you forgot to mention that some of them are apt to take the sins as well as the troubles of others on their shoulders."

"They get there of their own accord," she said with a rueful smile. "Believe me, they need no taking." As he was leaving, a thought struck him.

"Didn't Gregg's attitude at the inquest strike you as odd?" he asked. "You must have known that your sister was no stranger to him."

She shook her head.

"I took it for granted that he didn't recognize her. I always understood that he saw very little of the Baxters after their marriage and I don't suppose he ever saw her before. The name Draycott might have given him a clue, but, when he first saw her at the farm, he didn't know her name even."

Evidently Miss Allen was unaware of Gregg's connection with St. Swithin's and the fact that he had known Mrs. Draycott before her marriage.

On the way back to his club Fayre bought a powerful magnifying-glass. Armed with this he went to his room and examined the photograph closely under the light of a strong reading-lamp.

The snapshot was that of a man sitting on a bench in what looked like a private garden. He was staring straight in front of him, his face devoid of all expression, his hands hanging loosely between his knees. He was poorly dressed and his clothes looked shabby and ill cared-for. By his side, hanging over the edge of the bench, was a newspaper. Even without the glass, the name of the paper, printed in large type at the head of the first page, was decipherable. It was that of a well-known German daily. Underneath it was the date, in much smaller type, and Fayre had some difficulty in making it out, even with the aid of the glass he had bought. He did succeed at last. It was January 16th and the address, printed with an ordinary stamp on the back of the photograph, was that of the State Lunatic Asylum at Schleefeldt, a small town in north Germany.

When Fayre at last raised his head his face in the crude light of the electric-lamp was white and drawn. He seemed to have aged ten years in as many minutes.

CHAPTER XX

FAYRE SLEPT LITTLE that night and rose the next morning jaded and sick at heart. During the long hours in which he had tossed ceaselessly on his bed, wrestling in vain with the problem that was torturing him, he had been unable to come to any conclusion. If he did what he felt was his duty he would be the means of involving two, at least, of his dearest friends in dire trouble, besides running the risk of jeopardizing the cause he had most at heart. If, on the other hand, he held back the discovery he had just made he would be taking on his shoulders a responsibility so great that he hardly dared face it. He had confronted difficult problems in the course of his official life, but seldom one that touched him so nearly or made him feel so utterly helpless.

It was in this mood that Cynthia found him when she rang up from her aunt's house in Grosvenor Square and asked him to take her out to lunch. A troublesome tooth had given her the opportunity she longed for and she had hurried up to town, ostensibly to see the dentist, but really to find out what progress Fayre had made in his investigations.

For a moment Fayre was taken aback, then he found himself welcoming the prospect of her company for an entire afternoon. He feared her sharp eyes and direct mode of attack, but, more even than these, he dreaded his own thoughts. Cynthia was the embodiment of youth and courage and, after his night of miserable indecision, he felt a positive craving for the stimulus of her society.

As though in answer to his needs she seemed even more vividly alive than usual when he picked her up and carried her off to an unpretentious, but very select, little restaurant he and several of the older members of his club affected. Cynthia had stipulated for a quiet place where her ready tongue could wag freely. She had plenty to say. Bill Staveley had managed to procure her another interview with John Leslie and she reported him as cheerful and inclined to take a hopeful view of the future.

"He says that, so long as he knows he's innocent and that I believe in him, he doesn't mind what happens; but he doesn't realize how black things look against him," said Cynthia. "He's frightfully grateful to you and Edward Kean and full of faith in you both. I tried not to show how anxious I was. Uncle Fayre, they surely can't convict him if he's innocent, can they?"

On the face of this Fayre found it hard to break to her the news that Gregg had completely cleared himself. To his relief she took it more cheerfully than he had expected.

"I never really suspected him, you know," she said. "I suppose I should have been beast enough to be glad if he had done it, because it would have cleared John, but I should have been sorry, too. It would be too horrible if it was some one that one knew. It's a relief, in a way. Has Mr. Grey done anything about the Page clue? I always felt that that was where our hope lay."

"He's working on the Carlisle to London route, on the chance that the car may have got held up somewhere and, if that fails, he proposes to advertise openly for Page. If, as I still think, the man had nothing to do with the actual murder, he may come forward. On the other hand, it would be a mistake to warn him by advertising too soon. It is a last resort."

"I believe he did it," asserted Cynthia obstinately. "If we can find Page we shall get to the bottom of the whole thing. You know the police have let the tramp go? He ended by confessing that he took Mrs. Doggett's money and I made her go up to the station and speak for him. He's very lame still and the police want him to stay in the neighbourhood, so Bill found him a room in one of his cottages. I went to see him. He's a funny little man and we got quite chummy, but he's determined to go back to 'the road,' as he calls it, as soon as he can get away. He told me that he had been tramping for years and he's got all sorts of interesting stories about tramps and burglars and all kinds of queer people and he adores you. When I spoke about John he said: 'The gentleman'll get 'im off, you see,' as if you were a kind of Providence. He's rather a pet, really. What did you do to make him love you so?"

"Treated him like a human being, I suppose. He's not going back to the road, if I can help it, poor little beggar. He's never had a chance and I'd like to give him one."

"If we do get onto that man, Page, he'll deserve it. After all, it was through him that we first heard of the strange car."

"When I get my cottage I'll see what I can find for him to do. He's not a pleasing object at present, but he'll improve with prosperity."

"I can see your cottage!" observed Cynthia mischievously. "It'll be crammed with all sorts of derelicts and lame dogs and you'll go fussing round them like a hen with a lot of chickens. May I come and stay with you, Uncle Fayre?"

"As often and as long as you like. You'll be a respectable married woman by then and you can act as chaperone to Miss Allen."

"Is Miss Allen going to stay with you?"

"If she'll come. I haven't asked her yet."

"I'm glad you've made friends with her. She's a brick, isn't she?"

"A thorough good sort, I should say," assented Fayre rather cautiously. There was a gleam in Cynthia's eye he didn't quite like.

She flashed a sidelong glance at him.

"It's an awfully good idea; I wonder I never thought of it."

"What is?" asked Fayre suspiciously.

"Her coming to stay with you, of course," was Cynthia's innocent rejoinder.

After lunch they called at Grey's office.

"I'm glad you dropped in," he told Fayre. "We've got on the track of a car which was held up at York. It was traveling without a taillight. If it was our friend, Page, he was probably trying to conceal his broken number-plate. Anyway, I've sent a man up there to find out all the particulars and he'll be back early to-morrow. There's just a chance that we've got onto the right car."

"That'll please you, Cynthia. Lady Cynthia's always believed in the Page clue," explained Fayre.

"Now that Dr. Gregg's gone off with a clean sheet, it's all we've got to go on," said Grey. "It's a funny thing how he crops up all through this case. That fellow Baxter died in his house, you know, and Gregg signed the certificate. As far as we can make out, everything seems in order and, short of exhuming Baxter, we've done all that's necessary to prove his death."

"I've no reason to think that Gregg was concealing anything the other day. He seemed only too anxious to tell all he knew. If he's shielding any one he's doing it very cleverly."

"I think we may wipe out Dr. Gregg altogether now. After all, at the time, he'd have had no reason to conceal Baxter's death, whatever he may feel about it now."

"I've got a feeling in my bones about this Page business," said Cynthia, as they turned into the Strand after leaving Grey's office. "I believe we're going to find him and that things are going to be all right for John. You can call it imagination, if you like, but this is the first time I've felt really hopeful. Life seems quite different, all of a sudden!"

Fayre was suddenly afraid for her. There was something terribly pathetic in her optimism and he knew it was reared on a pitifully frail foundation.

"Don't build too much on it," he begged, ruefully aware that it was always his lot to throw cold water on her enthusiasm. "If may be nothing but a wild goose chase, after all."

"It isn't," she asserted positively. "I can't tell you why I know, but I do and you'll see I'm right. The funny thing is that Sybil Kean has had the same feeling all along. Did you know? She told me so when she was ill at Staveley."

The haggard look came back into Fayre's eyes. He had forgotten his own worries for the moment, carried away by Cynthia's enthusiasm, but now they returned to him, their strength in no wise diminished. Cynthia, intent on her own thoughts, did not notice his preoccupation.

"It was the night before I went to Carlisle to stay with the Campbells. I didn't tell her why I was going, because we'd agreed that it was better for her not to talk about the whole thing. We hadn't mentioned John or anything, but, when I said good night, she looked at me in such a queer way and said, somehow as if she knew it was true: 'Don't worry, Cynthia, John will never be convicted. I'm certain of it.'"

Fayre stared at her in astonishment.

"Sybil said that! Did she give any reason for it?"

"None, but she seemed so curiously certain. Almost as if she knew something. She didn't say any more and she looked so desperately ill and tired that I just went. Do you think she had some sort of second-sight, Uncle Fayre? People do do that sort of thing when they've been very ill, don't they? I'm certain she wasn't just saying it to reassure me."

The worried lines on Fayre's face deepened.

"I don't know," he said, "and I can't understand it. I was under the impression that she was worrying about the whole thing more than was good for her. It never occurred to me that she was in the least hopeful. I only hope she's right. You know she's been very ill again?"

"Yes. Edward wrote to Bill. He was a fool to whisk her off like that before she was really fit. It was Dr. Gregg's fault, really, for saying she could go. It's funny, but he felt just as you did about the case. He said she must be got away from the atmosphere of the whole thing because she was wearing herself to a thread over it and would never have a chance of pulling up unless she got right away. And she's the only person who's given me any real hope!"

"You're very fond of Sybil, aren't you?" asked Fayre thoughtfully.

Cynthia stared at him.

"Of course. She's been a perfect brick to me always and she's a dear, anyway. You know, whenever I've got hopelessly fed up with things at home she's had me in London for weeks together, and she was an angel about John from the beginning. I'd do a good deal for Sybil, and I'm not naturally an unselfish person," she finished frankly.

Fayre did not allude to the matter again and, when Cynthia announced her intention of going to the Keans' on the chance of being allowed to see Sybil, he walked with her to the door, but he did not offer to go in. Instead, he mounted a bus and went out to Richmond. Arrived there, he made for the Park and walked until he was tired out. It was late when he entered the station and took the train back to London and he was worn out with hard exercise and lack of food, but he had at last come to a part solution of his difficulties. He had some supper at the club and then literally fell into bed. And this time he slept.

Next morning he rang up Cynthia, whom he found just starting for her dentist's. He picked her up there after her appointment and carried her oil to Kensington Gardens.

He waited until they had found chairs under the trees and then went straight to the point.

"You're an unusual person, Cynthia," he said appreciatively. "I've kidnapped you in the middle of a busy morning and you've not asked a single question."

"I've been worrying, though," she answered. "Do you realize that you've been looking as if you'd lost a shilling and found sixpence, as old Mrs. Doggett would say, ever since I've been in town? I nearly asked you before what was the matter, but I thought I'd wait till you came out with it yourself. There is something wrong, isn't there?"

"Nothing that affects you or Leslie," he hastened to assure her. "But you are right, I have been worried about something. The trouble is not my own, or I'd put the whole thing before you, and I don't mind admitting that I should be glad of an outside opinion on it. But that's out of the question. I'm sorry to be so mysterious."

Cynthia nodded. Her face showed complete understanding.

"Poor Uncle Fayre!" she said. "I know how you feel. One bothers and bothers over a thing until one can't see it straight at all and then one loses faith in one's own judgment. It's quite true, an outsider *is* a help sometimes."

"It's a help I shall have to do without in this instance," he admitted reluctantly. "Let's forget it and talk of something pleasant."

They chatted desultorily for a while, laughing and joking and taking a genuine pleasure in each other's company, as people with a keen sense of humour will, even though tragedy be close upon their heels, but Cynthia never ceased to be aware that there was an object in their meeting and knew that he was only waiting for an opportunity to broach the subject that was really on his mind.

He did so at last, so casually that, if she had not been on the alert, she might have missed the significance of his question. He had brought the conversation round to Sybil Kean and her illness.

"If only she doesn't have a relapse now," he said thoughtfully. "If would be a bit of bad luck for us if Edward were to throw up the case."

Cynthia turned to him with something like panic in her eyes.

"I hadn't thought of that," she exclaimed. "Of course if she were really ill he wouldn't be able to go to Carlisle. He'd never leave her."

"I'm afraid he wouldn't. He's utterly wrapped up in her. Sybil is a fascinating person, but I must admit that Edward's devotion was a revelation to me. I did not know he had it in him to care so much for any one."

"I don't believe anybody else would ever have understood him as Sybil does," said Cynthia slowly. "He's not an easy person to know."

Fayre gazed reflectively at the tips of his well-polished boots.

"You've seen a lot of Sybil in the last few years, haven't you?" he asked suddenly.

Cynthia knew that the question for which she had been waiting had come at last, but she could not see its point.

"Yes," she answered wonderingly. "I've stayed with her in London, you know, as well as seeing her often at Staveley. Why do you ask?"

"What do you really think of those two, Cynthia?" Then, seeing the genuine bewilderment in her face: "I'm curious about Sybil. Edward is, and always has been, absolutely devoted and there can be no question that, from his point of view, their marriage has been a very happy one. But what about Sybil?" Cynthia's face cleared.

"You mean, does she love him?" she said frankly. "It's funny you should ask that. I was puzzling over it last night. Eve Staveley told me a long time ago that Sybil had never got over her first husband's death and that she believed that it was only Edward's insistence that made her marry him. Well, I was wondering last night whether she was right."

"You think that Sybil's fonder of Edward than any of us realize?"

In spite of his efforts he could not subdue the urgency in his voice.

"Honestly, I believe she is fonder of him than she realizes herself," answered Cynthia slowly. "If you asked her, she'd probably tell you that she had never forgotten her first husband and could never care for any one else and she'd think she was speaking the truth, but I saw Sybil once when she was really anxious about Edward and I'm certain she cares far more than people think. You see, I'd just got engaged to John then and I suppose I was in the mood to notice that sort of thing," she finished, with a swift, shy glance at his intent face.

He nodded.

"I expect you're right. At any rate, I'm prepared to trust to your intuition."

He returned to the study of his boot-tips and, for a minute or two, they sat in silence. It was broken by Cynthia.

"Then it was Sybil you were worrying about," she remarked calmly.

Fayre jumped.

"I have been worrying about her ever since I got back to England," he began mendaciously; but she interrupted him ruthlessly.

"The thing that has been bothering you and that you said you wished you could consult some outside person about has something to do with Edward and Sybil Kean, hasn't it? I'm not going to ask indiscreet questions, Uncle Fayre, but Sybil's my friend as well as yours and it's only fair to tell me if she's in any real trouble."

Fayre hesitated for a moment and then he spoke frankly. "As I said before, I can't tell you what it is all about. But I can say this. There is something that, sooner or later, I shall have to tell Edward, something that affects him so nearly that, I honestly believe, were he to hear it now, would cause him to throw up the case. I would do anything to keep the knowledge from him altogether, but I cannot. My only problem is, whether I am justified in keeping this news back till after the trial. That's what I have been trying to decide and I've made up my mind at last. So far as I can see I shall be harming nobody if I hold the news over until after the trial is over, and I have definitely decided to do so. But I've got to a point at which I hardly dare trust my own judgment."

"Does Sybil know of this, Uncle Fayre?"

"Good Heavens, no! If she did I think it would kill her."

"And it will really make no difference to her if you keep this back till John's trial is over?" she persisted.

"None, that I can see. In fact, my instinct is to put off telling Edward as long as possible, but that's simply because I shrink from hurting either of them. He's got to be told in the end, but, what with the impending strain of the trial and all the worry he has gone through on Sybil's account lately, this seems the worst moment to spring bad news on him. Grey says that the case is one of the first on the list at the Carlisle Assizes and should come on early next month."

At the thought of the trial Cynthia's face blanched and she clenched her hands tightly on her lap to stop their trembling. Fayre realized that it was kinder to ignore her agitation.

"As I said," he went on quietly, "I made up my mind last night to hold this thing over. You can rest assured that, as far as I am concerned, nothing will happen to put a spoke in Edward's wheel and, if we can count on him, it will be half the battle."

He gave her a few minutes in which to recover herself and then saw her back to her aunt's house, after which he strolled slowly back to the club. On the way he pondered over Sybil Kean's words to the girl at Staveley. He could not reconcile them with her evident anxiety when she spoke to him about Leslie. No doubt she had seen that Cynthia was near to the breaking-point and had lied nobly in the hope of reassuring her. And yet that wasn't like Sybil, as he knew her.

She was the last person to kindle a false hope deliberately.

His mind was still dwelling on her as he picked up the little pile of letters that awaited him at the club and it was with a shock that he recognized her handwriting on one of them. He opened it eagerly. Inside was a closed envelope, unaddressed, with a covering letter from Sybil herself which ran:

"Hatter dear, the flowers were lovely. It was like you to think of them. In a day or two I shall have got rid of the doctor and be able to thank you in person, instead of in this silly note which looks so much more shaky than I really am. I am picking up wonderfully, but it was a close shave this time, Hatter, and it has made me think. Don't tell Edward, but I have a strong feeling that the next attack will be my last. I want you to do me a favour and put the enclosed among your most private papers. If I should die before John Leslie's trial is over and if he should be convicted I want you to open it and read it and then show it to Edward. If John Leslie is acquitted or if I am alive at the close of the trial I am trusting you to burn it unread. I expect you think I am mad, and sometimes, lately, I have wondered whether my brain is not going, but you are the only friend I have whose loyalty I know I can utterly depend on. I know I can trust you and that you will do what I ask unquestioningly. Good-by, my dear, till we meet. They won't let me write any more. Sybil."

Fayre stood staring blankly at the letter and the enclosure; then he crossed to a writing-table and wrote in his small, neat hand across the envelope: *"In the event of my death, to be destroyed unread."*

This done, he put it carefully away in his pocket-book with the snapshot Miss Allen had given him.

"She knows," he told himself heavily. "And she has kept the truth from Edward. No wonder the strain of it has almost killed her!"

CHAPTER XXI

SYBIL KEAN's amazing letter left Fayre in a condition of mingled bewilderment and relief. Out of all the tangle of events that he had been trying in vain to unravel one strand at least had inexplicably straightened itself. Lady Kean was not only already in possession of the information he had stumbled on so unexpectedly, information which he had hoped against hope might possibly be kept from her, but she had deliberately withheld it from her husband. That the truth was contained in the letter which she had asked him only to open in the event of her death he had no doubt, and that she was relying on him to break the news as mercifully as possible to Kean was equally evident. Little difference it would make to Edward, Fayre reflected grimly, once he had lost the one being in whom his whole life was centred.

His last action that night was to switch on the light over his bed and read her letter again for the tenth time, amazed at the strength and devotion of the woman he had thought he knew so well, but whom he had after all understood so little. He realized how great-ly he had underestimated her affection for Kean and how misled he had been in concluding that her heart was irretrievably buried in her first husband's grave, and he wondered by what feminine logic she had managed to reconcile her conscience with the deception she had practised on Kean. The one thing that puzzled him in her letter was her stipulation that he should not read the enclosure in the event of Leslie's acquittal. Try as he would, he could see no connection between the trial and the information he believed the enclosure to contain. One thing was obvious: at the earliest opportunity he must see Sybil Kean and tell her that he had surprised her secret. That she was, literally, worrying herself into the grave he had no doubt.

As it turned out, all his plans were frustrated. For the next three days Fayre called in vain at the house in Westminster, only to be told that Lady Kean was allowed to see no one and, on the fourth, that which the doctor had been dreading occurred, she had another heart attack even more violent than the last.

For a week she hovered between life and death and then, almost miraculously, took a turn for the better. Kean was invisible whenever Fayre called at the house and Grey, who was in hourly dread that Lady Kean would die, confessed to feeling more and more pessimistic as to Leslie's chances.

"It was an amazing piece of luck getting Sir Edward at all," he admitted to Fayre. "With such strong evidence against Leslie I never thought he would have acted. We've got Lady Kean to thank for that, I fancy, and perhaps, for her sake, even if the worst happens, he'll pull himself together and do his best for us. I know he's almost superhuman when it comes to work, but, unless she takes a turn for the better soon, I shall begin to regret that we didn't brief some one else."

"And we've got no further with the Page clue than when we first started," reflected Fayre ruefully.

The clerk Grey had sent to collect evidence as to the car which had been held up at York had reported a complete failure. Except for the first letter and number the car had entirely failed to answer to the description of the Page car. It was a two-seater, the number-plate had been intact and there was no sign of any damage to either of the guards, and they had had to face the fact that they had been following yet another blind alley.

In addition to his other anxieties, Fayre was troubled about Cynthia. The girl had faced things nobly, but already she was beginning to show signs of strain and Fayre dreaded the coming ordeal for her. Her mother had written to her peremptorily ordering her to go home. Cynthia, lost to everything but Leslie's danger, had taken no notice of her mother's letter. Fortunately, her father's sister, with whom she was staying, had proved more humane and had merely stipulated that the girl should stay in her house until the trial was over, realizing that she was not in a state to brook opposition. She welcomed Fayre's visits and, at her suggestion, he persuaded Cynthia to motor with him out into the country for a few hours every day.

A few days after Sybil Kean had been declared out of danger Grey rang him up suggesting that they should meet for lunch.

"I've heard from Sir Edward," he said as soon as he saw Fayre. "I'm to meet him this afternoon and he would like to see Lady Cynthia. Could you bring her round to his Chambers at about four o'clock? I gather Lady Kean really has turned the corner, so luck may be with us, after all."

Before sitting down to lunch Fayre rang up Cynthia and arranged to call for her. Grey followed him into the telephone-box.

"Tell her I've seen Mr. Leslie and he's in fine form. If he can keep his pluck up till next month he ought to make a good impression."

"How did you really find Leslie?" asked Fayre as they sat down.

"Just as I said. He's a plucky young beggar. I think he's more worried about her than about himself. Wanted to know how she was looking, and all that sort of thing. Said it wasn't only the war that came hardest on the women. They're a fine couple."

Fayre nodded absently. He was feeling horribly depressed and wished with all his heart that the whole wretched business were over.

"I don't suppose Sir Edward's in a laughing mood, but, if he were, he'd get a certain sardonic amusement out of the Page episode," went on Grey. "My man came back from the North yesterday. He's been kept up there on some other business till now. He told me a funny thing."

"About the car that was held up?" asked Fayre rather wearily.

He found it difficult to see anything amusing in connection with the Draycott murder.

"No; that belonged to a harmless little commercial traveller. But when he was looking over the back reports in search of a clue to our man he caught another fish altogether, Sir Edward Kean himself! He got hung up at York on March 14th for traveling without side-lights."

Fayre, who was blessed with a quick and accurate memory, stared at him in amazement.

"But Sir Edward came down to Cumberland by train!" he exclaimed. "He didn't have his car with him! I know, because I met him myself at the station. I'd gone down to see about a lost suitcase."

"His chauffeur must have been joy-riding. The licence was the chauffeur's. It's not the first time that's happened. Sir Edward, apparently, paid the fine without a murmur. What he said to the chauffeur is another matter!"

Fayre, knowing Kean, did not envy the delinquent.

Grey looked at his watch and rose.

"I must go," he said. "Now Leslie has been moved to Carlisle it will be more difficult for Lady Cynthia to see him. Tell her to let me know when she goes North again and I'll do my best for her. It'll buck him up more than anything if he can have a few minutes with her."

"And be uncommonly hard on Cynthia," remarked Fayre grimly.

He and Cynthia arrived punctually at Kean's Chambers. He had not returned, but had left a message asking them to wait for him. As Fayre sat chatting with Cynthia, his eye fell on a photograph of Sybil Kean that stood in a plain silver frame on the writing-table. He remembered suddenly that, owing to her illness, he had never answered her letter and it struck him that, if she were better and conscious, she might be worrying as to whether it had reached him. He decided to send a few noncommittal lines by Kean, saying that he had received it and would be delighted to do her commission. This would convey nothing to any one should she be too weak to read her own letters and would at least reassure her.

There were some sheets of writing-paper on the table and, with a word of explanation to Cynthia, he sat down and drew one towards him. Having written his note he looked about for an envelope, but could find none. Instinctively his hand went to the top drawer of the writing-table. It was unlocked and slid out easily and Fayre peered into it in search of the thing he wanted. He did not find it, but in the front of the drawer was lying an object he knew only too well, the "Red Dwarf" pen he had picked up near the gate of Leslie's farm. The cap the tramp had given him was now fitted neatly over the nib. He picked the pen out of the drawer and turned it thoughtfully in his fingers. The mud stain still clung to the side, half obliterating a long smear of black ink. Here, after all, he reflected, lay the real clue to the puzzle. Leslie, he knew, had never used a stylo and Mrs. Draycott was the last person to carry a cheap pen of that type in her gold bag. Everything pointed to its having been dropped by the murderer. As a last resort, Grey had inserted an advertisement in most of the daily papers asking Page to come forward and it had appeared for the first time that morning. If Page were the owner of the pen, Fayre concluded, he was hardly likely to make himself known.

With a sigh he replaced the "Red Dwarf" in the drawer. As he did so his sleeve caught in the edge of a large envelope that was lying near the back of the drawer and shifted it a few inches. Cynthia, who was standing near the window watching for Kean, did not hear the quick intake of his breath as he picked it up to replace it. For perhaps five minutes he sat motionless, the envelope in his hand, then he put it gently back in its place and closed the drawer. The letter to Lady Kean he slipped into his pocket, having apparently given up the idea of sending it.

When Cynthia looked round he was immersed in a copy of the *Times* he had found lying on Kean's table.

"Edward has just driven up in the car," she said, and almost as she spoke the door opened and he came in. He looked distressingly worn and tired, but was more cheerful than Fayre had dared to hope. The doctors had given a good report of Sybil that morning, he told them, and they considered that she was responding to treatment better than she had done after the former attack. Fayre wondered whether the letter she had sent him had not been at least partly responsible for her illness and whether, now that the effort of writing it was over, she was not benefiting by the relief to her mind.

"I was afraid we'd have to leave town without seeing you," he said. "It was too much to expect you to give your mind to anything while Sybil was laid up."

Kean looked up sharply.

"I should have carried on, in any case," he answered quickly. "If it's humanly possible to get Leslie off I'm going to do it."

Fayre was astonished at the depth of feeling in his voice, but he realized that Kean meant what he said and that he would fight for Leslie as he had never fought before. What would happen if he failed, Fayre did not dare contemplate. He was convinced now that, for some reason he could not fathom, the lines of Leslie's fate were inextricably intermingled with those of Sybil and Edward Kean and he had a grim conviction that more than Kean's professional reputation was at stake should he fail to get an acquittal.

He sat through the long interview between Kean and Cynthia like a man in a dream and his report of their conversation, had he been called upon to make one, would have been both vague and garbled. It was only at the close, when Kean offered to drive her back to her aunt's house, that he woke to a sense of his surroundings and managed to rouse himself to action.

"If you are going to steal Cynthia I'll be off," he said pleasantly. "I've one or two things I must do on the way home."

They were so absorbed that they hardly noticed his departure; but if Kean had happened to glance out of the window, he would no doubt have wondered why Fayre, instead of going directly about his business, had chosen to waste fifteen minutes or so in desultory chat with the chauffeur of Kean's car.

His talk finished, he hailed a taxi and drove to the club. Arrived there he went straight to his room and looked up the address Gregg had given him when he suggested that he should look up his chemist friend, Lloyd. Then, from the bottom of his portmanteau, he unearthed a pile of old photographs, adding to them the snapshot he had borrowed from Miss Allen. Thrusting them into his pocket he ran downstairs and got into the waiting taxi, giving the driver Lloyd's address.

He found him at home, an unkempt little man with a face not unlike that of an abnormally intelligent monkey, surmounted by a shock of untidy grey hair. Evidently he had been expecting to hear from Fayre and showed no surprise at his visit. His manner was business-like and a trifle brusque. He impressed Fayre as a man who had little time to give to the affairs of others, but who invariably bent his whole mind to the matter in hand, whatever it might be.

"I can't do much for you," he began frankly. "Never have known who the chap was that I saw with Mrs. Draycott in Paris and I don't suppose I ever shall, unless I run into him somewhere. And that's unlikely, as I never go anywhere if I can help it. Beastly waste of time. Hate society. Tepid tea and a lot of silly talk about nothing. Better ask me what you want to know. Quicker and more satisfactory." He ran his hand through his untidy hair and, sitting perched on the edge of his littered writing-table, blinked at Fayre expectantly through his strong glasses.

"If you'd give me an account of what happened in Paris I should be grateful," suggested Fayre. "I'm a bit vague as to dates, for instance."

"One gift I have got," went on Lloyd abstractedly. "That's a memory for faces. Never forget a face. Beastly bore sometimes it is, too. I should know that man if I saw him again. As regards dates, it was in the spring of 1920 that I saw him. Went over to Paris to consult a man at the Sorbonne and ran into this chap and Mrs. Draycott in a little restaurant in Montmartre. Sort of place I go to because it suits me, but this fellow wasn't the sort to go there at all. Wrong place for Mrs. Draycott, too. They were there because they didn't want to be seen and, of course, they were seen. That's how things happen. I'd met Draycott once and I knew this man wasn't he. Mrs. Draycott being what she was, I put the worst interpretation on it. May have been mistaken, of course. Don't quite know to this day why I followed them. Gregg was a pal of mine and I knew he was jumpy for fear she would make a grab at the boy and I'd just finished a big job and was at a loose end for the moment with a blank evening in front of me. Anyway, it was the third night I'd seen them and I happened to leave just behind them. She never even looked my way and, if she had, she probably wouldn't have recognized me. They were walking and I just went too. It was a dark night and I tagged along behind till they got to their hotel and watched them go in. A little place bang in the middle of the Latin Quarter. By that time I'd had about enough of it and I didn't wait to see if either of them came out, but a couple of days later I was in that part of the world and I dropped in and asked to see the visitors' book. Drew a complete blank. The only English names registered for months were a Mrs. Grant, whom I took to be Mrs. Draycott, and a George Collins. Apparently there was no other English man or woman staying in the hotel. I wrote to Gregg, telling him what I'd done and there the matter ended. I found out afterwards that Draycott was in Egypt at the time. I'm afraid that's the best I can do for you."

"You say you'd recognize the man if you saw him?" asked Fayre eagerly.

"Could pick him out anywhere. I tell you, I've got an abnormally good memory for faces."

Fayre took half a dozen photographs from his pocket, the snapshot among them, and placed them on the table.

"Do any of these suggest him to you?" he asked.

Lloyd ran through them quickly, then stabbed one of them with a long, yellow-stained forefinger.

"That's the fellow," he pronounced unhesitatingly. "It's an unusual head and quite unmistakable."

Fayre picked it up with a hand that shook a little. He had had a vague notion that Lloyd might pitch on the snapshot, though, in his secret heart, he had prayed that he would recognize none of the photographs.

This, of all others, was the last he had expected him to select.

CHAPTER XXII

THE NEXT SIX WEEKS dragged heavily enough for John Leslie within the four walls of his cell at Carlisle, but, to Cynthia, they were one long agony. She spent one short week-end with her people at Galston and then gratefully accepted Miss Allen's proposal that she should stay with her till the Assizes opened at Carlisle. Her mother's open antagonism to John Leslie made her home unbearable to the girl and she was thankful to get away.

Miss Allen's tactful sympathy and uncompromising common sense acted as a tonic to the girl and the older woman, who was never idle for long herself, managed to keep her guest employed with a variety of small occupations which gave her little chance to brood over the ordeal that lay before her.

"It's no earthly good meeting troubles half-way," Miss Allen assured her. "The more you think of things, the more likely you are to invent all sorts of horrors that will probably never happen. And, for heaven's sake, don't go off your food now or you'll be fit for nothing when the time comes."

In spite of her sharp tongue she watched over the girl like a mother, pampered her uncertain appetite with all sorts of unexpected and tempting dishes and developed an almost uncanny instinct for knowing when she was sleeping badly and would appear in her room with hot milk and biscuits in the small hours of the morning and sit and chat until she saw the girl's eyelids beginning to droop. Cynthia grew to love the sight of her bulky red-quilted dressing-gown and the grey plait that stuck out stiffly between her shoulders.

Fayre ran down to Staveley for a fortnight and spent most of his time over at Greycross. He and Miss Allen were fast becoming close friends and she had already promised to be the first of his guests when the cottage of his dreams materialized.

The rest of his time he spent in London, looking up old friends and haunting Grey's office, a disheartening pursuit, for the solicitor had little enough to report as time went on.

The middle of May found them all gathered at Carlisle. Dreading the publicity of a hotel Miss Allen had taken lodgings for herself and Cynthia. Grey and Fayre were at the station hotel, where they were joined by Kean on the night before the trial.

Fayre had tried in vain to persuade Cynthia not to go near the courthouse until she was actually called as witness for the Defence, but he received no support from either Kean or Grey, both of whom considered that her appearance would create a good impression and, in any case, he would not have succeeded in keeping her away. He could only feel thankful that she was in the keeping of so staunch a friend as Miss Allen and do all in his power to make things as easy for her as possible.

The trial seemed to drag on interminably and it was not till the afternoon of the sixth day that Kean rose to make his speech for the Defence. To Fayre, who had sat through the Counsel for the Crown's very able address to the Jury, Leslie's case seemed almost hopeless and he was beginning to feel that only a miracle could save him. He had watched Kean, on whom all their hopes rested, sitting motionless, his face utterly impassive, apparently entirely unmoved by his rival's eloquence, and had tried to read his mind in vain. And all the time he had thanked his stars that he had allowed Cynthia to influence him and had kept back until after the trial the secret that, even now, he dreaded to reveal to Kean. Indeed, it seemed to Fayre, during the long hours of suspense, as though his mind had become a sort of Bluebeard's chamber into which he no longer dared look. So much that he could not fathom and a little that he understood only too well he had locked away there until after Leslie's fate was decided. Even if Kean managed to secure an acquittal for him Fayre could only look forward with a kind of horror to the aftermath of the trial.

For one who wished nothing but happiness to his fellow men the world had indeed gone agley. The knowledge that lay at the back of all his thoughts and actions had come between him and Edward Kean and their friendship had lost its old ease and intimacy. In his distress he had lost all desire to see and consult with Sybil Kean and, in spite of the fact that her health was mending rapidly and that he had had a charming letter of invitation from her in answer to the note he had written in Kean's Chambers and had eventually posted from his club, he had felt unable to face her. Fortunately her health had given no further cause for anxiety and her improvement had been so steady that Kean had come north for the trial comparatively free from anxiety.

He was at his best now as he stood facing the Jury. Fayre, who had persuaded Cynthia to allow Miss Allen to take her home before lunch, fell so completely under the spell of his eloquence that, for a few brief moments, he forgot his personal interest in the case and was lost in admiration of the sheer genius that inspired it. It was not the first time he had heard Kean plead. One of his first actions on reaching England had been to go to the Old Bailey to see his old friend in harness. He had not been disappointed then, in spite of all he had heard of his ability, but to-day Kean spoke like a man inspired. One by one he took the very points which the Counsel for the Crown had used so effectively and turned them to his client's advantage. He possessed a beautiful voice and knew how to make the most of it. He had had Cynthia in the box the day before and had examined her with a skill that was so little apparent that it was all the more telling. And Cynthia, partly helped by her own quick wits and partly as the result of careful coaching, had backed him up nobly. He used her evidence now as the basis of his speech, turning even the quarrel between her and Leslie to advantage and playing on the emotions of his audience with a skill and audacity that was little short of amazing. Given a Latin jury, Fayre told himself, the result would have been a foregone conclusion by now and, not for the first time in his life, he cursed British stolidity as he gazed hopelessly at the inscrutable countenances of the twelve respectable citizens who composed the jury and tried in vain to follow the progress of their thoughts. To his excited fancy they seemed the only people in the packed courthouse who remained totally unmoved by Kean's eloquence.

Then, suddenly it was over and, like a douche of icy water, after the burning flow of Kean's impassioned appeal, came the calm, measured accents of the Judge as he summed up.

By the time he had finished Fayre was once more in the depths of depression and in bad shape to face the long wait while the Jury considered their verdict. He watched them file out feeling as near despair as he had ever been in his life and then settled down to endure a suspense that seemed interminable but which, in reality, lasted just over an hour and a half.

By the time the jury returned, the proceedings seemed to Fayre to have taken on all the unreality of a nightmare. As one in a dream he heard the Judge's voice break the tense silence of the crowded court.

"Are you all agreed?"

"We are all agreed, My Lord."

Then, as his numbed brain mechanically registered the fact that the foreman, surprisingly, spoke with a strong Cockney accent instead of the North-country burr he had expected, came the verdict.

"We find the prisoner guilty, My Lord."

CHAPTER XXIII

"To be hanged by the neck until you are dead." The sentence still rang in Fayre's ears as his taxi sped through the streets on its way to Miss Allen's lodgings. He could hear the thin, strained voice of the Judge, an old man nearing death himself, but still, after a long experience on the Bench, shaken and appalled at the awful magnitude of the words he was called upon to utter.

Fayre groaned aloud as the full sum of their meaning dawned upon him. Leslie, of whose innocence he was assured, cut off from life just when it was about to mean so much to him and Cynthia!

Fayre did not dare to think of Cynthia, waiting, torn between hope and fear, through the long hours in the grey old house where she and Miss Allen lodged. He wished with all his heart that it had not fallen to him to break the news to her.

He stopped his cab at the corner of the street and walked the last hundred yards to the house. At least he could save the girl the inevitable rush to the window at the sound of wheels and the moments of suspense while he entered the house and mounted the stairs. As it happened, he found the front door open and reached the sitting-room before she realized his presence in the house.

She sprang to her feet as he entered, and Miss Allen instinctively moved to her side.

His face must have given him away for, before he opened his lips, she knew.

"Guilty!" she gasped.

He threw out his hands in a gesture of utter helplessness.

"It went against him," he said, hardly recognizing his own voice.

With a little moan of anguish Cynthia turned blindly to the haven of Miss Allen's arms. She did not cry and, for a moment, he was afraid she had fainted, then, to his relief, Miss Allen led her gently from the room.

He stood by the window looking out into the grey, dingy street, waiting for her return. It was some time before Miss Allen rejoined him.

"How is she?" he asked eagerly.

Miss Allen's eyes were red and her voice was unsteady as she answered.

"As well as she is likely to be for some time," she said rather tartly. She was suffering from the aftermath of an unaccustomed emotion. "She's not going to die, if that's what you mean, but her last hope has just been taken from her. I must go back to her in a minute. If the child had a decent mother I'd send for her."

She crossed to the table and took a cigarette.

For a minute or two she smoked in silence. Then she turned to Fayre with a very pleasant smile on her homely face.

"I was a bear just now," she said. "I'm sorry, but I've had a bad quarter of an hour. Mr. Fayre, what are we going to do now?"

Fayre looked at her with utter misery in his eyes.

"I don't know," he said desperately. "I must see Grey. After that ... I don't know."

He buried his face in his hands.

"It's out of our hands," said Miss Allen softly. "How pitifully small we human beings feel when the big things happen. That child upstairs, with no experience of life to guide her, is dealing with something infinitely larger than anything I have ever known and I cannot help her. She must find her own way out, Mr. Fayre. On my word, I believe I would rather be John Leslie!"

"And I," answered Fayre, rising to his feet. "This is not the first time he has faced death gallantly and, as I grow older, I begin to wonder if it is as terrible a thing as we think. But to live on, with all the light taken from your life! I wish I knew what to do," he finished abruptly.

Miss Allen stared at him, puzzled.

"He'll appeal, of course?"

"I suppose so, but there's no hope there, I'm afraid. I can imagine no reason for upsetting the verdict. Kean was magnificent, but the facts were too strong for him. Don't let Cynthia count on it."

They talked for a few minutes and then he hurried back to his hotel, hoping to catch Grey.

The solicitor was waiting for him in their joint sitting-room.

"Sir Edward has gone back to town," he said. "He could not wait. He told me to say that he was sorry to have missed you. He's sick over this business. I've never seen a man so cut up at losing a case."

"You'll appeal, I suppose?"

"Of course, but I'm not sanguine; neither is Sir Edward."

Fayre looked him straight in the eyes.

"What's your honest opinion?" he asked.

Grey hesitated for a moment. Then:

"I think it's absolutely hopeless," he said frankly. "Nothing short of a miracle can save Leslie now."

"So that an appeal will simply mean the infliction of quite unnecessary anguish on two people who have already had more than their share of suffering?"

"I suppose you can put it that way," answered Grey soberly. "All the same, it's his last chance and we can't afford not to take it."

Fayre nodded thoughtfully.

"I'll travel up with you," he said. "Have I time to pack?"

"Plenty. I'm off to see Leslie. I'd hoped you might stay on and have a few words with him before he is moved. I think I can work it and it would mean a lot to him now."

The distress on Fayre's face deepened, but his lips were set in an obstinate line.

"I'm sorry," he said firmly, "but I must get up to town at once. I'd stay if I could, and anyhow I'll run down again later."

"Any message for him?"

"Tell him we're not beaten yet," said Fayre cryptically.

Grey raised his eyebrows.

"What's the idea?" he asked.

"I don't know. I wish to goodness I did!" was Fayre's rejoinder as he disappeared into his room to pack.

He and Grey reached London in the small hours of the morning. Fayre drove straight to his club and forced himself to take a couple of hours' rest, but he did not sleep and by nine o'clock he had bathed and breakfasted and was on his way to Kean's Chambers.

Early as he was, Kean was there before him and was already well started on a strenuous day's work. He pushed his papers aside when Fayre entered and came to meet him.

"I rather fancied you might turn up," he said sombrely. "We shall appeal, of course."

Fayre faced him as he had faced Grey.

"With what result?"

Kean did not mince matters.

"If I know anything of the law, none," he said. "I'm sorry, Hatter; I did my best."

Fayre's eyes did not move from his face.

"That's what I've come to ask you," he said slowly. "You made a very brilliant speech. It was a magnificent defence, and it failed. To any one but myself it would seem that you had done your utmost."

He paused and Kean turned on him sharply.

"I've worked harder over this case than I ever worked in my life," he cut in.

Fayre nodded.

"I admit it. That's not what I'm driving at. One or two things have come to my knowledge lately, facts that I have told no one, not even Grey."

He paused again. He was finding it very hard to choose words for what he had come to say and Kean made no effort to help him.

"Ever since I discovered certain things," Fayre went on, "I have been fighting against the conviction that you could have cleared Leslie if you had wished. Can you look me in the face now and say that you were not shielding some one from the beginning and that you undertook Leslie's defence because you hoped by sheer eloquence to get him off without being forced to give this person away?"

Kean had strolled over to the hearthrug and seemed absorbed in the selection of a cigarette from the box on the mantelpiece.

"I don't know how you managed to unearth all this," he said at last, "or what you think you have discovered, but you're right on one point. I *was* shielding some one."

"You've tried to save Leslie and failed," went on Fayre inflexibly. "What steps do you propose to take now?"

Kean hesitated.

"Before I answer that question," he said slowly, "suppose you put your cards on the table. How much do you know?"

"I know that, for some reason I have so far failed to discover, you allowed it to be supposed that you travelled by rail to Staveley Grange on March 14th, when, as a matter of fact, you motored from London to some station north of York and picked up the train there. You were held up at York for driving without side-lights."

Kean smiled.

"You've hit on a snag there," he said. "Blake, my chauffeur, was held up and nearly lost his job on the strength of it."

"I've seen Blake," was Fayre's quiet reply. "He was on his holiday in London and was with his wife that night. A summons was served on him which he brought to you and which you said you would deal with. He is under the impression that it was a mistake on the part of the police."

There was a pause during which Kean smoked thoughtfully. He seemed in no way disconcerted.

"Given that I was in York that night, what do you infer from that? March 14th was not the night of the murder, if that's what you are driving at," he said at last.

Fayre went on steadily.

"How long have you known Mrs. Draycott and what were you and she doing in Paris in the spring of 1920? You had been married to Sybil for less than a year and I know you too well to insult you by the suggestion that it was merely a vulgar intrigue."

Kean threw his cigarette into the fire.

"You're right there," he answered evenly; "it wasn't. You haven't entirely lost your sense of proportion yet, Hatter. I had my own reasons for wishing to see Mrs. Draycott, and, as she happened to be in Paris at the time, I went there. I stayed at the Bristol and she was in a small hotel on the other side of the river. Does that satisfy you?"

Fayre walked over to the writing-table and drew out the top drawer. From it he took two "Red Dwarf" pens and threw them on the table. With the exception of a brown earth stain down the side of one of them, they were identical, even to the black ink-stains that smeared the handles.

"One of these is the pen I picked up at the farm. Can you explain the other, or give any reason why you did not use this in your defence? We have proof that it did not belong to Leslie and that it was dropped some time before the murder. It would at least have proved the presence of a third person at the farm that night."

Once more Kean hesitated. Then he raised his head and spoke quite frankly.

"Because it was the property of the person I wished to shield. I give you fair warning, Hatter, that, however deeply you may have managed to implicate me, I do not intend to divulge the name of the owner of that pen. Any more exhibits?"

Fayre was stung by the contempt in his voice. He took his note-case out of his pocket and extracted a snapshot which he placed on the table beside the pens.

"Yes," he answered, and there was grief rather than anger in his voice. "This. I would have spared you this if I could, Edward."

Kean picked it up and examined it.

"So you've stumbled on that, too. You've been pretty thorough, Hatter."

"You knew, then?"

"That Sybil's first husband was alive? I've known it for the last six years. As a matter of fact, I fetched him from Germany myself and placed him in an asylum in Dorset. You know he's hopelessly in-sane, I suppose. Three specialists have pronounced him incurable."

"You've lived with Sybil for six years, knowing all the time that Gerald Lee was alive?"

Kean looked at him with frank speculation in his eyes.

"What would you have done in my place, I wonder," he said qui-etly. "Sybil's heart was in such a state that any shock might prove fatal. Lee was hopelessly insane, incapable even of recognizing her. I'm not exaggerating when I say that the mere sight of him would have killed her. Rather than take the chance of the knowledge of his existence reaching her now, I would kill you, here in this room, with my own hands, and take the consequences."

He spoke quite gently, but his voice carried conviction and Fay-re realized that he would shrink from nothing in the effort to spare his wife.

"Sybil knows," he said and, even as he spoke, he felt that he would have given anything to unsay the words.

For the first time Kean's composure deserted him. His face be-came suddenly grey and lined. "Impossible!"

Then, with sudden vehemence:

"Do you realize what you're saying? Good God, man, it can't be true!"

"It is true, unless I've made some ghastly mistake," answered Fayre steadily. "I thought she had discovered it and was keeping the secret from you."

"My God, if that woman told her!" muttered Kean. "It's the only explanation. What have you got to go on?"

"A letter Sybil wrote me, which reached me just after I had come on the photograph of Lee. I took it for granted that that was what she was alluding to."

"You didn't speak to her about it?"

"I haven't seen her since. I had meant to, but there's been no opportunity."

Kean sank into a chair and covered his face with his hands.

"Thank God!" he murmured. "There's some mistake. It's impossible that she should have found out. She would never ..."

He was interrupted by the insistent peal of the telephone-bell. With a half-frenzied exclamation he tore the receiver from its hook.

"Yes, Sir Edward Kean speaking," he said mechanically, his mind entirely occupied with the revelation Fayre had just made. Then, as he listened, the already ghastly pallor of his face increased.

"It's Sybil," he said, hardly above his breath as he dropped the receiver. "They've rung up from Westminster. It's another attack."

For a moment he sat staring blankly into space; then he turned to Fayre with a look of almost childish entreaty in his eyes.

"I must go to her, Hatter. For heaven's sake, don't keep me now!"

For answer Fayre picked up Kean's hat and coat and handed them to him.

"We must have this out soon, Edward," he said gravely. "No matter what happens."

Kean was already struggling himself into his coat.

"At the earliest opportunity I promise you a full explanation. Will that do, Hatter?"

Fayre nodded. A moment later he was alone with his troubled thoughts. He strolled over to the table and, picking up the snapshot, put it back into his notecase. As he did so the door opened and Farrer, the old head clerk, looked in.

"I thought I heard Sir Edward go out, sir," he said.

"He's been sent for. Lady Kean has been taken ill again. I doubt if he'll be back this morning. You'd better cancel any engagements he had for to-day."

The old man made a clucking sound with his tongue against his teeth.

"It's a pity she's so delicate, sir," he ventured.

And Fayre, overwrought to the verge of hysteria, almost laughed aloud at the utter inadequacy of the remark.

CHAPTER XXIV

THE REPORT of Sybil Kean when Fayre rang up at lunch-time was not reassuring. The heart attack had been less violent than either of those that had preceded it, but she had not rallied well. Fayre, remembering the letter she had sent him and the conviction she had expressed in it that the next attack would prove her last, wondered whether the wish to live had not forsaken her. In his heart he knew it would be better, both for her and for Edward, if she died. The connection between the unopened letter in his note-case and the Draycott trial was becoming clear to him at last. There was only one person for whom Kean cared enough to shield at the expense of his professional honour; that was Sybil, and Sybil, as was now evident from her letter to Fayre, had some secret knowledge of the case which she may or may not have been aware that she shared with her husband.

Fayre went over the events of the evening of March 23rd. So far as he could remember, he had parted from Sybil Kean in the drawing-room at Staveley shortly before six o'clock. From then onwards she had been invisible, presumably in her room, and had not appeared again until she joined the party in the drawing-room just before eight. He knew the country round Staveley well enough to realize that this would leave her ample time to reach Leslie's farm by six-thirty, or thereabouts. It seemed incredible that any one in her state of health should have been capable of such an effort and, in Sybil's case, doubly so, for, apart from her delicacy, she had always been indolent and easy-going to a fault, the last person to screw herself up to such a pitch of nervous tension as such an expedition would entail.

There was one other, and on the whole more probable, solution of the problem. Evidently Mrs. Draycott had become in some way possessed of a photograph of Gerald Lee. It was more than possible that she had had dealings with him in the past and that, in his distorted brain, he had harboured a grudge against her. Supposing

Kean had been aware of this obsession and had received news of his escape from the asylum in which he had placed him? If Lee had managed to waylay the unfortunate woman and had murdered her, Kean would have every reason to wish to keep his guilt secret. Once the affair got into the courts it would be impossible to hide the fact of his existence from Sybil. Where and how Lee and Kean had met on the fatal night, Fayre was unable to determine, but the complete lack of motive for the crime had pointed, from the first, to an act of almost insane malice, and that there was some connection between the events at the farm and the survival of Sybil Kean's first husband Fayre was becoming more convinced each moment.

He tried to picture the consequences of the inevitable disclosure which would follow should this second solution prove the correct one, and his heart sank. That it would mean the end of Edward Kean's career seemed certain. Not only was the part he had played in the grim drama bound to appear, but with the discovery of the identity of the murderer would come the disclosure of the damning fact that, during six years of his marriage to Sybil, he had been aware of the existence of Gerald Lee. And insanity is not recognized as a ground for divorce! If Sybil, knowing of Lee's existence, had concealed it from her husband it seemed hardly likely that she would leave him for Lee, who, according to Kean, was not even in a condition to recognize his wife should she return to him. And if she decided to stick to Kean? Fayre could picture them dragging out their existence, probably in Italy or the south of France, Kean bereft of the work that was as his life's blood to him and Sybil cut off forever from her friends and the world to which she belonged. He did not think she would long survive under such conditions and, Sybil once taken from him, what would become of Kean?

In a vain effort to get away from his own thoughts, Fayre went out and walked the busy streets until he was tired, but the exercise brought no relief and he was driven at last by sheer fatigue back to the club again.

He was dressing for dinner when he was called to the telephone. He was surprised to hear Kean's voice at the other end.

"Come round after dinner and we'll finish our conversation of this morning," he said.

Fayre's first feeling was one of relief. He knew that Kean would not have suggested an interview unless Sybil had definitely turned the corner. He gave a hasty assent, but before he could inquire after her, Kean had rung off.

As soon as he had finished his solitary dinner he set out for Westminster.

Kean met him in the hall and led the way into his study. He had been working and held a closely written manuscript in his hand. He pushed Fayre gently into an armchair and placed a box of cigars at his elbow, then he seated himself at the writing-table.

"I've got the whole story here," he said, pointing to the papers before him. "I suggest that you take it to Grey first thing to-morrow morning. He will know what to do with it. I might have sent it to you. In some ways it would have been easier for me, but I've got a feeling I'd rather you heard it from my own lips."

The amused contempt which had angered Fayre earlier in the day had gone from his voice and had given place to an utter weariness. His face was grey with fatigue, and Fayre, remembering all he had gone through that day, forgot his anxiety about Leslie and was conscious only of compassion. He rose impulsively to his feet.

"Look here, old man," he exclaimed, all the warmth of their long friendship back in his voice. "Let's leave the whole thing for to-night. You're not fit for it. I'll take that paper home with me and go through it there or, if you'd prefer it, we can have it out tomorrow. I don't know to what extent it will help Leslie but a few hours' delay can make little difference to him."

Kean shook his head.

"We'll go through with it now," he said, with a touch of his old vigour. "I shan't sleep till it's over and done with."

He sat for a moment in silence, his eyes fixed on the closely written sheets before him. When he spoke, his voice was as coldly dispassionate as though he were telling a story in which he was in no way concerned.

"As you have no doubt guessed," he began, "the whole thing dates from the year of my visit to Paris. How you got onto that, I don't know. You will remember that Gerald Lee and three other men were killed by a shell in the first year of the war. Identification was impossible, but his disk was found close to the spot and it was taken for granted that he was one of the victims.

"The first intimation I had that he was alive came from Mrs. Draycott, almost a year after my marriage to Sybil. She wrote from Paris, enclosing a copy of the snapshot you showed me this morning. It appeared that she had been staying with friends in Germany and, so far as I could make out, had had an affair with a doctor out there. It was like her, with her morbid love of sensation, to persuade him to take her over the local lunatic asylum. She had known Gerald Lee slightly in the days before the war and she recognized him at once and, with characteristic acumen, realized that she might make use of the discovery to her own advantage.

"I found out afterwards that he had been picked up unconscious by the Germans, badly wounded in the head, and that he had been passed from one hospital to another, never once recovering his sanity, until he eventually drifted to the municipal asylum at Schleefeldt. By that time he was in civilian clothes and all efforts to identify him had been in vain. All the authorities could find out about him was that he was an Englishman. They were much interested when Mrs. Draycott recognized him and did all they could to help her, one of the doctor's taking a snapshot of him for her to send to England.

"On receipt of her letter, I went at once to Paris and we had several interviews. I need hardly say that I had to offer to buy her silence, but I went to Schleefeldt myself and satisfied myself that she was speaking the truth before paying her the money she demanded. I also ascertained from the doctor in charge of the asylum that not only was Lee incapable of recognizing any one, but that he was considered absolutely incurable. Apparently there was some pressure on the brain which could not be removed. I may say that this diagnosis was confirmed after his arrival in England by three of our own brain specialists. So that, however much at fault I may have been, I have robbed Lee of nothing. There, at least, my conscience is clear. I confess that, taking into account Sybil's state of health, I do not see how I could have acted otherwise."

He unlocked a drawer at his elbow and, taking out a bundle of cancelled cheques, tossed them onto the table.

"That is what I found I had let myself in for," he went on bitterly. "For Sybil's sake, I did not dare appear in the matter, and, going on the principle that the fewer people involved, the better, I left the whole affair in Mrs. Draycott's hands, and I must say she proved both practical and efficient. Pretending to recognize him as a relation of her own, she had him brought to England and, in the capacity of her legal adviser, I was able to visit him and see to his installation in the best private asylum I could hear of. And then the game began. Mrs. Draycott had only to threaten to go with the story to Sybil and she had me absolutely at her mercy."

He picked up the packet of cheques and balanced it in his hand.

"Every one of these is made out to 'self,'" he said. "I was absolutely helpless and she was too clever to accept anything but cash. For six years I have been trying to trap her, in vain. And then, last January, I succeeded. Until then she had steadfastly refused to accept a cheque or give a receipt for anything I paid her. All the payments were in notes and I had no evidence that she had ever attempted to blackmail me.

"Then, last January, I caught her. She was at Nice and had been gambling heavily at Monte Carlo. When she wrote to me she was desperate and in such a hurry for the money that she accepted the cheque I sent her. As soon as I ascertained that she had cashed it I knew that I had a hold over her at last. On her return I went to see her and offered her a lump sum down, on condition that she did not molest me again, pointing out that, if she went to Sybil, I was prepared to take the matter into the courts and, on the evidence of the Nice cheque, she would not stand the ghost of a chance if she were sued for blackmail. She had begun to realize that Sybil might die and that I might then prefer exposure to the constant drain on my purse. Anyhow, she gave in, but for nearly a month she haggled over the terms and in the end agreed to accept seven thousand pounds down.

"Even then I did not trust her. She was a vindictive woman as well as a greedy one and, as you may imagine, our liking for each other had not progressed during our intercourse. I knew that, in a fit of malice or cupidity, she was capable of burning her boats and going to Sybil. Also, it was anything but convenient for me to realize so large a sum just then. At best, it would cripple me financially for some time to come, and retrenchment of any kind meant discomfort for Sybil. Just before my final interview with Mrs. Draycott I received the news that one of my investments had failed and I realized that I was going to have considerable difficulty in raising the seven thousand."

He paused and sat for a moment in thought, as though he were taking stock of his own past actions and appraising them.

Then his eyes drifted to where his wife's photograph, in its heavy silver frame, stood in the full glare of the reading-lamp.

"It was then," he went on, "that I made up my mind to kill Mrs. Draycott.

CHAPTER XXV

THERE WAS a tense silence, broken only by the sound of the distant traffic in Victoria Street. Fayre made an ineffectual effort to speak, but no words came. There was nothing he could say. His mind was a chaos of contending emotions, the strongest of which, even now, was pity: pity for the man who, in his blind arrogance, had wrecked the life of the one being he had hoped to save.

Something of what he felt must have reached Kean, for when he spoke again there was a gentler, almost apologetic note in his voice.

"I'm sorry, Hatter," he said. "Of all my friends you are the one I can least afford to lose. If it had not been for Farrer's appalling blunder in not letting me know in time that the case in which John Leslie was to appear had been postponed things would have turned out very differently. Luck was against me from the beginning.

"When Eve invited us to Staveley and told me that Mrs. Draycott was to be there I realized that my opportunity had come at last. I laid my plans carefully and thought I had covered any possible emergency; but I did not realize that I should have you to reckon with, Hatter. You were too intimately connected with us all to be a safe antagonist.

"On the plea that there had been a delay in the selling of certain securities I persuaded Mrs. Draycott to go on from Staveley's to her sister's, arranging to meet her while she was there and hand the money in cash over to her. We arranged to meet at the corner of the Greycross lane at six o'clock on the evening of March 23rd.

Meanwhile I had brought the car from London and garaged it at the garage at Whitbury. If you remember, Sybil was the first to arrive at Staveley and I followed her four days later, that is to say, on March 14th. I wired the time of my arrival and was met by the Staveley motor in the usual way and you all took it for granted that I had come by train. As a matter of fact, I drove the car myself from London to Whitbury, garaged it there and then went on by train to Staveley Grange. Unfortunately my sidelights gave out at York and I was held up. I had had the forethought to borrow my chauffeur's licence, on the plea that I had mislaid my own and might have occasion to use the car while he was on his holiday, and it was that licence that the policeman who stopped me saw. That was where you proved my undoing, Hatter. If it had not been for your long memory and the fact that you took the trouble to interrogate my chauffeur your suspicions would never have been aroused. Grey, who knew nothing of my supposed movements at that date, certainly wouldn't have jumped to it. As it was, that *Y.o.7.* number you were looking for was under your very nose and you never saw it!"

Fayre looked up suddenly.

"Then Page—?"

Kean nodded.

"Page was the name I gave when I garaged the car at Whitbury. It was there that the woman noticed my hands. I was startled when Grey told me that, I admit."

He spread out his hands on the blotter before him and regarded them thoughtfully. They were characteristic enough, with their long, clean-boned, sensitive fingers, and hard, muscular palms.

"Fortunately they are not marked in any way, or it might have been awkward. Apart from that, I had covered my tracks well. On the evening of the 23rd I was driven to the station from Staveley. There I took a ticket to London and got into the local train from Staveley Grange to Whitbury. At Whitbury, as you know, there is an hour's wait before the London express comes in. I had only a small suitcase with me and this I carried to the Whitbury garage, where I picked up the car. I drove to the corner of the Greycross lane, where I was joined by Mrs. Draycott. I had prepared a packet of notes, tied up in batches of one thousand pounds. The uppermost packet only was genuine, the rest were made up of sheets of paper, cut to the correct size."

He paused for a moment.

"Here I knew I was up against my one real difficulty, that of persuading Mrs. Draycott to go to the farm. Fortunately, the weather was on my side. She hated the country, at the best of times, and had suffered considerably during her short walk to the corner of the lane. So as not to arouse her sister's suspicions she had come out in the thin dress and slippers she had been wearing in the house, and it had been no joke struggling against a bitter wind in inadequate garments. I put it to her that she would have to count the notes in my presence before I could undertake to hand them over to her and that, in view of the size of the payment, I had no intention of making it without a receipt. I had some argument with her over the last point, but she had seen the notes in the light of my head-lamps and her cupidity had been aroused. Also, she knew that, since the affair of the cheque, I already had a hold over her. It was blowing a gale and bitterly cold and, while she was hesitating, a big branch came down with a crash in the field quite close to us. I think that decided her. I explained that, as we could not go to her sister's, I proposed to drive her to Leslie's farm, where we could complete our transaction under cover, telling her that he was away and that I had the run of the place. Leslie had let drop one day that he invariably left either the front or the back door open and I had taken stock of the place when Sybil and I had gone over to tea with him and Cynthia there. I knew that, if, by any chance, we found the door locked I could run the car into the barn and complete my plans there.

"As it turned out, the door was unlocked and I led the way into the sitting-room by the light of an electric torch I had brought with me. Mrs. Draycott sat down at the writing-table and I stood behind her, holding the torch in one hand so that its light fell on the table. I handed her the packet of notes and she began to count them. My revolver was in the right-hand pocket of my overcoat."

His eyes contracted as though, for a moment, the whole scene were vividly before him.

"The rest was easy. The thing was over in a moment. She fell forward without uttering a sound. I made sure that she was dead, then I picked up the bundle of notes and thrust the torch and the revolver into my pocket. Then I felt my way out in the dark. I must have left the front door open, but I only found that out after Leslie had been arrested. At the gate I undid my coat and placed the notes in an inside pocket. It must have been then that Sybil's 'Red Dwarf' pen rolled out onto the path where you found it."

Fayre drew in his breath sharply.

"Good God!" he muttered.

Kean's fixed gaze shifted for a moment to Fayre's face.

"You never guessed it was Sybil's. And yet she had used one for years. That wretched 'Red Dwarf' gave me more than one bad quarter of an hour. For one thing, I was terrified that you would mention it to her. She lent it to me on the morning of the 23rd, and I must have slipped it into my pocket; when I got back to Staveley on the 26th one of the first things she did was to ask me for it. I made the excuse that I had left it in London. If you had spoken to her about it after that she might possibly have put two and two together."

Fayre opened his lips to say that he had mentioned it, with ominous results, but Kean interrupted him. Afterwards he was thankful that he had not been given the chance to speak.

"I suppose you must have opened the drawer of the table at my Chambers and seen the two pens or you wouldn't have produced them as you did this morning. You probably also realized what I had been doing. I was afraid she would ask me for it again and, somehow, I could not bring myself to return her own to her, apart from the fact that I might have been called upon to produce it and did not dare let it out of my possession. So I bought another and stained it with ink, meaning to return it to her as her own. You guessed that?"

Fayre nodded.

"I knew, naturally, that you had been trying to fake a duplicate, but I was entirely at sea as to your object."

"I think, all along, Sybil was the person I feared most. She has more intuition than any one I have ever met and I was in terror that something in my manner or attitude towards the case would rouse her suspicions. Thank goodness she never dreamed that anything was wrong."

This time Fayre deliberately held his peace, but his heart turned sick within him, for, bit by bit, the patterns in the puzzle were beginning to slip into their places and, among them, Sybil's letter and the enclosure.

"There's not much more to tell," pursued Kean. "It was too late to pick up the London train at Whitbury, so I drove straight to Carlisle, counting on the fact that the express waited there for an hour. I just had time to garage the car and catch the train, arriving in London at the same hour and by the same train I should have arrived by had I taken it direct from Whitbury. I made a point of speaking to the three men who shared my table in the dining-car and went out of my way to give them a clue as to my profession, mentioning the fact that I had been staying at Staveley. I did not anticipate any trouble, but, had I been forced to prove an alibi, I have no doubt they would have come forward and it would have been taken for granted that I had travelled over the entire distance by train. But, from the time I left the farm, luck was against me. There was the collision with the farm-cart that put you onto the track of the mythical Page. You were right, by the way, about the number-plate. I broke it myself as a precaution. I had it replaced and the mudguard mended in Carlisle. You took it for granted that, when the car was removed from the first garage in Carlisle on March 26th it was driven to London. As a matter of fact, I simply moved it to one on the other side of the town, where I had the repairs executed and it stayed there till I picked it up on April 1st on my way to Staveley. The news that the case in which Leslie was to appear had been postponed and that he had already been notified was, I think, the greatest shock I have ever had. I had been so absolutely certain that he was in London. It was as though an abyss had opened under my feet. Until I actually saw the papers and read the first description of the case I hoped that he might not have received the notification in time. As soon as I saw them I knew that, unless I could manage to get him off, I was faced with disaster."

He raised his clasped hands and brought them down so heavily on the table that it shook.

"Everything was against me," he exclaimed with uncontrollable bitterness. "If the police had not found Leslie's revolver or if that wretched cat had not got caught in a trap, just at that particular moment in the whole of Leslie's career, I could have got him off without a stain on his character. As it was, I was helpless from the beginning."

He rose, picked up the sheets of manuscript from the table, and joined Fayre.

"The whole thing is here," he said, handing them to him. "It is signed and witnessed by two of the servants. I believe they thought it was my will," he added ironically. "I want you to take it to Grey first thing to-morrow."

Fayre sprang to his feet and laid his hand on the other man's arm.

"What are you going to do, Edward?" he asked.

Kean hesitated.

"Make a bolt for it, I suppose," he said grimly. "I may bring it off with luck."

"Where will you go?"

Kean looked at him curiously.

"I don't know," he said. "On my word, Hatter, I don't know."

"Edward," began Fayre impulsively; but Kean cut him off.

"There's one thing you can do for me, old chap," he said swiftly. "I want to see Cynthia. I've got something I must say to her, something that I cannot leave unsaid. It's early still and she won't have gone to bed. Will you go round there now and ask her if I can see her? What I've got to say won't take more than ten minutes."

Fayre stared at him in astonishment.

"Don't you realize that, if you are going, you must go now?" he expostulated. "Edward, there's no time to lose. For God's sake, don't take a chance like that!"

"There's time for that," said Kean dryly. "I will go straight from there. I can catch the night boat to Ostend. I don't suppose we shall meet again, Hatter, and it's the last thing I shall ask you to do for me. Will you do it?"

"I'll do it," answered Fayre reluctantly, "but I think it's sheer madness at this juncture."

"I want you to go to her now and ask her if I can come round. Don't tell her anything else. If she can see me, ring me up here and I'll start at once. After I am gone you can tell her the whole story, but get this through as quickly as you can first."

Fayre moved to the door. Half-way he stopped as though he had been shot.

"Good God, Edward!" he cried. "Sybil! You can't leave her without a word!"

Kean straightened his shoulders with a jerk, as though he were bracing himself to face something he was seeing clearly for the first time.

"Sybil died about an hour before I telephoned to you this evening," he said slowly.

CHAPTER XXVI

AFTERWARDS, in bitter anguish and remorse, Fayre cursed himself for his blindness. At first he had been deceived by Kean's attitude of cold detachment towards the whole gruesome business and the impression he had managed to convey that he had definitely decided on flight. Later, the news of Sybil Kean's death had stunned him and he had gone blindly on his errand to Cynthia, dazed with grief and consternation. But he could not forgive himself for not having insisted on staying by his friend in his extremity.

Instead, he had carried out Kean's instructions to the letter, had found Cynthia still up and had interviewed her in the rather dreary little room that had been her uncle's study.

He had sent a message by the servant, asking to see her alone, and she came to him, curiosity and apprehension in her eyes.

John Leslie was never out of her mind in these days and, though it would seem that the worst had happened, she lived in hourly dread of some further attack on her fortitude.

"Have you come from John?" she asked piteously. "When will they let me see him?"

He took both her hands in his and drew her to him.

"Listen," he said gently. "It's all right about John. He is cleared absolutely. In a short time you will be together and all this will seem like a bad dream. Steady, now," he added sharply, for the girl had swayed away from him and, for a second, he thought the news had been too much for her. But even as he spoke, a great rush of colour flooded her face and she drew herself erect.

"It can't be true!" she whispered. "Say it again, Uncle Fayre. John, free!"

Her hands were on his shoulders and she almost shook him in her eagerness.

"John's safe," he repeated. "Edward has cleared him. I have come from Westminster now. Edward wants to speak to you. Can I ring him up now and tell him you will see him?"

"Of course. Tell him to come quick. Does John know?"

"Not yet. Grey will see him to-morrow."

"Couldn't the news be got to him to-night? It's cruel to make him wait," she pleaded.

Fayre shook his head.

"I'm afraid not. But you can ask Edward when he comes. Where's your telephone?"

She led the way into the hall, and in another moment Fayre was ringing up the house in Westminster.

Kean's butler answered the call.

"Can I speak to Sir Edward Kean?" asked Fayre. "He is expecting a call from me. Mr. Fayre speaking."

"Mr. Fayre?" The man's voice was eager and hurried. "If you could come round, sir? We're in great trouble here and the responsibility ... There's no one ..."

The broken sentences tailed off oddly and Fayre was suddenly seized with an ominous sense of foreboding.

"What is it?" he asked sharply.

"Sir Edward, sir. He shot himself just after you left. ..."

"Is he dead? Quick, man!"

"Yes. He must have died at once. The doctor's here now. If you could come at once, sir ..."

"I'll come now."

Mechanically Fayre hung up the receiver and put the telephone down on the table. Then he collapsed completely, his face buried in his hands, his whole body shaking uncontrollably.

When he pulled himself together sufficiently to look up he found Cynthia standing by his side.

"What is it, Uncle Fayre? Not Sybil?"

In as few words as possible he explained the situation to her, omitting any mention of Kean's confession. He could not bring himself to speak of that yet to her.

She was terribly shaken, but she held back her tears until she had taken him into the dining-room and mixed him a stiff drink. While he was drinking it she telephoned for a taxi and within five minutes he was on his way back to Westminster.

It was late before he got back to the club, utterly worn out and shaken with remorse. If he had had the sense to stay with Kean he might have averted this final catastrophe.

Then, as he sat in his room, too tired and disheartened to face the task of undressing, his sanity reasserted itself and he knew that Kean had taken the only possible way out. Sybil was dead and nothing could hurt her now. If only he could be sure that she had not guessed!

With an exclamation he rose to his feet and picked up the note-case he had thrown on the table on first entering his bedroom. He drew out her letter and opened the enclosure. He had not read a dozen lines before his worse fears were confirmed.

"It is terribly difficult to write this," it ran, "and yet I must tell some one. I am so desperately afraid of what Edward may do. And the awful thing is that I may be wrong and yet I cannot ask him to explain. If what I think is true and he has kept this from me it is because it would break his heart for me to know. There is some extraordinary mystery behind it all. I can only tell you this, Hatter. I am almost certain that the pen you found after the murder was mine and, the day Edward motored me up to London in the car, I found some of the sequins from Mrs. Draycott's brown evening-dress between the cushions of the back seat of the car. The papers said she had it on when she was found and she wore it at Staveley the night before she left. And yet I know that the car was in London then! I can't understand it. But, Hatter, the night before Mrs. Draycott left Staveley I came out of my bedroom to go down to dinner and she and Edward were standing by the door of her room, talking. I must have opened my door very quietly, for they did not hear me, but I heard Mrs. Draycott say: 'This is the second time you've put it off. You know what to expect if you don't come up to the scratch this time.' I went back into my room and shut the door and they never saw me. I don't understand it, Hatter. Edward could not have been at the farm that night. He went up to town that afternoon. My reason tells me that I must be mistaken, and yet, all the time, I know that something is going on, something horrible that I cannot understand. Edward has never been like this over a case before. For once, his nerves are beginning to go back on him. I do not know what to do, but I am haunted by the fear that I may die before the trial is over and that Edward, in his desire to save me, may do something. ... I do not know what I am writing, Hatter; I am so stupidly weak still and my brain does not seem to work properly; but I want you to show this to Edward and tell him that, for my sake, he must not let John Leslie suffer. I am haunted by the thought that he may be led into doing something utterly unlike everything I know of him, something he may regret to his dying day, and I shall not be here to save him. I am so tired. I cannot write any more, but do your best for me, Hatter."

The letter dropped from Fayre's nerveless fingers and fluttered to the floor.

Shaken with pain and horror as he was, he could still give thanks for two things: Kean had never guessed that his wife knew and had gone to his grave believing that the crime he had committed for her sake had not been in vain, and Sybil had died in ignorance of her first husband's tragic survival.

CHAPTER XXVII

ON ONE of those perfect July days which are occasionally vouchsafed to the inhabitants of the British Isles Cynthia Bell and John Leslie were married.

They had chosen an old church, tucked away in an unfashionable corner of South London, as the scene of their wedding and had asked to the ceremony only those whose friendship they really valued.

Lady Galston had flatly refused to sanction the marriage or to be present at it, but Cynthia's father had, once more, asserted himself and had brought his daughter to London and insisted on giving her away himself.

"A good thing Lady Galston has taken that line," was the comment of that other woman who had mothered Cynthia so efficiently in her time of trouble, as she and Hatter Fayre drove together from the church to the Staveleys' house in Eaton Square which they had insisted on lending for the occasion.

"She's never been an atom of good to that child since the day she was born and, in her present mood, she'd cast a blight over a Bacchanalian orgy!"

They found Cynthia and Leslie in the hall on their arrival and it certainly did not seem as if Lady Galston's antagonism had served to dim the girl's radiance on this, the happiest day of her life.

She stood, her arm through Leslie's, talking to old Mrs. Doggett and surrounded by a shy, beaming crowd of Galston retainers who had come of their own accord all the way from Cumberland to see her married. Fayre, looking round, recognized the Gunnets and, with them, his own special protégé, Albert Small, late tramp, now boot-boy, dog-washer, bicycle-cleaner, etc., at Fayre's newly acquired cottage in Surrey. He was resplendent in an old suit of his master's and looked a very different being from the furtive and defiant tatterdemalion who had slept in John Leslie's barn on the fatal night of March 23rd.

At the sight of Fayre and his companion, Cynthia gave a little cry of pleasure and came forward eagerly to greet them.

"It's all much too wonderful to be true!" she said. "Even now, I feel as if I may wake up at any minute!"

"It's wonderful. But it's not my idea of a quiet wedding," gibed Fayre, looking round the crowded hall. "The whole village of Keys and all the tenants seem to have migrated from the North to wish you luck!"

"Aren't they pets? It never occurred to me that they would dream of coming so far, but Father received a sort of deputation, headed by Gunnet, to ask if they might be present. Gunnet said that, after what had happened, he'd take it as a kindness if he might be allowed to attend! They're all going back by the night train. There are some old friends waiting to see you upstairs. Even Dr. Gregg has turned up. I asked him, though I didn't think it was much in his line, and he said that, as he'd *be* in London anyhow on business, he'd be very pleased to look in. Do go and be kind to him; he looks so miserable and he's already been quite rude to Father, just to show that he isn't shy!"

"I'm glad you're not going too far away from them all," said Fayre. "Bill tells me that the farm is finished. It sounds charming."

Leslie had resigned his tenancy of the farm near Galston and built a comfortable, roomy house on some farm-land on the Staveley estate. After what had happened he had not cared to take Cynthia to the ill-fated house up the lane nor had he wished to settle down in the immediate vicinity of his mother-in-law. The Staveleys had been glad to have Cynthia as a neighbour and, Fayre suspected, had done a good deal towards giving Leslie a good start in his venture.

"It's lovely and the land's gorgeous. John's simply delighted. You're going to be our first guest, Uncle Fayre. Promise you'll come soon!"

Hatter Fayre's face grew a shade pinker than usual.

"I'll come with pleasure, on one condition," he said.

His voice seemed suddenly to have grown curiously hoarse and unmanageable.

"You can make any conditions you like, so long as you come," was Cynthia's cheerful rejoinder. "You don't want to bring that horrid old bicycle with you, do you?" she finished, struck by a sudden suspicion.

Fayre shook his head.

"I've finished with that old friend for the present. No, I want to bring something quite different. By the way, I've been busy with the stables."

"Hunters?"

"Yes, when I've finished my alterations. The stabling's too inadequate for my needs and there's a good deal to be done."

"Do you propose to travel with a couple of mounts? If so, John will have to put them up in the barn. After all, though, it's only July now and we expect you long before the winter—or do you take them about as pets in the off season? Is that your condition?"

"Oh, no. I'm not bringing any livestock—at least, not of that kind. ..."

"Well, I'm blessed!" ejaculated his companion suddenly and indignantly.

Then, as Fayre cast a helpless glance in her direction and began to flounder hopelessly, she took the matter firmly out of his hands.

"Livestock indeed!" she exclaimed. "The man's impossible! What he's trying to do, my dear, is to ask if he may bring his wife. And why he's behaving like a self-conscious schoolboy over it, heaven only knows!"

In spite of her brave words she was blushing vividly.

Cynthia fell on her neck.

"Oh, you darlings!" she exclaimed. "You haven't really done it! You and Miss Allen! Now I know I am going to wake up and find it's all a dream. It's too perfect to be true!"

"Not Miss Allen, but Mrs. Fayre!" he corrected, with immense satisfaction. "We stole off all by ourselves and did it yesterday. And we're not a bit ashamed of ourselves, either, thank you."

THE END